A cold chill told me something from the dark was close; it ran powerfully up and down my spine. Before I even opened my eyes, I heard the sound of a girl weeping, and footsteps pacing back and forth beside the bed.

I looked at her. The ghost was that of a young girl, probably no older than seventeen. She had long hair pulled tightly into a bun at the back of her head. Like many ghosts, she was very pale, all the color having been left behind with death.

All the colors but one.

The front of her long pale nightdress was soaked in red blood, from neck to hem.

A New Darkness

JOSEPH DELANEY

GREENWILLOW BOOKS

An Imprint of HarperCollinsPublishers

A New Darkness
Copyright © 2014 by Joseph Delaney

First published in 2014 in Great Britain by The Bodley Head,
an imprint of Random House Children's Books, under the title
The Starblade Chronicles: *A New Darkness*.
First published in 2014 in the United States in hardcover by Greenwillow Books.
First Greenwillow paperback edition, 2015

The right of Joseph Delaney to be identified as the author of this work has been asserted by him in accordance with the Copyright, Designs and Patents Act, 1988.

The text of this book is set in 12-point Venetian 301 BT.
Book design by Paul Zakris

Library of Congress Cataloging-in-Publication Data
Delaney, Joseph, (date.)
A new darkness / Joseph Delaney.
"Greenwillow Books."
pages cm
Summary: Although his apprenticeship was not done when John Gregory died, Tom Ward spent years learning to fight boggarts, witches, demons, and more and feels prepared to be the new county Spook, but while his youth causes many people to distrust him, Jenny is determined to be his apprentice.
ISBN 978-0-06-233453-4 (hardback) — ISBN 978-0-06-233454-1 (pbk)
[1. Supernatural—Fiction. 2. Apprentices—Fiction. 3. Monsters—Fiction.
4. Witches—Fiction. 5. Horror stories.] I. Title.
PZ7.D373183New 2014   [Fic]—dc23   2014011963
16 17 18 19 20 PC/RRDH 10 9 8 7 6 5 4 3 2 1

 Greenwillow Books

FOR MARIE

Thomas Ward

I
A Mysterious Death

THERE was a cold draft coming from somewhere; maybe *that* was making the candle flicker, casting strange shadows onto the wall at the foot of the bed. The creaky wooden floor was uneven; perhaps *that* was why the door kept opening by itself, as if something invisible was trying to get in.

But ordinary commonsense explanations didn't work here. As soon as I'd walked into the bedroom, I'd known that there was something badly wrong. That's what my instincts told me, and they've rarely let me down.

Without doubt this room was haunted by somebody or something. And that's why I was here, summoned by the landlord of the inn to sort out his problem.

My name is Tom Ward, and I'm the Chipenden Spook. I deal with ghosts, ghasts, boggarts, witches, and all manner of things that go bump in the night.

It's a dangerous job, but someone has to do it.

I walked over to the bedroom window and pulled on the sash cord to raise the lower half. It was about an hour after sunset and the moon was already visible above the distant hills. I looked down on a large graveyard shrouded by trees, mostly drooping willows and ancient elms. In the pale moonlight the tombstones seemed luminous, as if radiating a strange light of their own, and the elms, which cast sinister shadows, were like huge crouching beasts.

This was the village of Kirkby Lonsdale, just over the County border, and although it was less than twenty miles northeast of Caster, it was an isolated place, well off the beaten track.

I went downstairs, leaving the inn through the front room, where three locals drank ale by the fire. They stopped talking and turned to watch me, but not one called out a greeting. No doubt any stranger to the village would have received a similar response—silence, curiosity, and a drawing together against the outsider.

Of course, there was an additional factor at work here. I was a spook who dealt with threats from the dark, one of only a few scattered throughout the County, and although I was needed, I made people nervous. Folk often crossed over to the other side of the street to avoid me, just in case a ghost or a boggart was hovering close by, drawn by my presence.

And as was the way of things in the County, by now, all the inhabitants of this isolated village would know my business here.

A voice called to me as I walked through the front door and out onto the street.

"Master Ward, a quick word in your ear!"

I turned and watched the landlord approach. He was a big, hearty man with a florid face, full of forced good cheer—something that he had no doubt cultivated for the benefit of his customers. But although I was spending the night in one of his rooms, he didn't treat me like that. He showed the same impatience and superiority that I'd noted when he dealt with his staff and the man who'd delivered fresh casks of ale soon after I arrived.

I was the hired help, and he expected a lot for his money—which annoyed me. I had changed a great deal over the past few months; a lot had happened, and I was far less patient than I used to be . . . and quicker to anger.

"Well?" the landlord said, raising his eyebrows. "What have you found out?"

I shrugged. "The room's haunted, all right, but by what I don't know yet. Maybe you could speed things up a little by telling me everything you know. How long has this been going on?"

"Well, *young* man, isn't it up to you to find out the

situation for yourself? I'm paying you good money, so I don't expect to have to do your job for you. I'm sure your master, God rest his soul, would have had the job done by now."

With this last sentence, the innkeeper had gotten to the heart of the problem, and it *was* his problem, not mine. John Gregory, the Spook who had trained me, had died the previous year. He had been fighting to help destroy the Fiend, the devil himself and ruler of the dark, who'd threatened to bring an age of tyranny and fear to the world. As his apprentice, I had now inherited his role and was operating as the Chipenden Spook. But, in truth, I hadn't really completed my apprenticeship and was young to be plying my trade alone like this.

Over the months I'd spent working alone, I'd met quite a few people who shared the innkeeper's attitude. I'd learned that it was important to set them right from the outset. They had to understand that they were not dealing with a boy who was still wet behind the ears; young though I was, I had been well taught and was good at what I did.

"Mr. Gregory would have asked you the same question that I just did, make no mistake about it," I told the innkeeper. "And I'll tell you something else—if you'd failed to answer, he would have picked up his bag and gone straight home."

He glared at me, clearly unaccustomed to being spoken to like that. My dad had taught me to be polite and to display good manners, even if the person I was dealing with was rude. So while I stared back without blinking, I kept my expression mild and my tongue still. I waited for him to speak.

"A girl died in that room exactly a month ago tomorrow," he said at last. "I employed her in the kitchen, and sometimes, when it got busy, she helped out by serving ale in the bar. She was fit and strong, but one morning she didn't get up, and we found her dead in bed with a terrified expression on her face and blood all down the front of her nightgown. But there was no sign of any wound on her body. Since then her ghost walks, and I can't let the room—or any of the others, for that matter. Even down in the ale room, we can hear her pacing back and forth. There should have been a dozen people taking that room by now, with more to come. It's affecting my business badly."

"Have you seen her ghost?" I asked, wondering how strong the manifestation was. Some ghosts could only be heard.

"There's been no sign of her down here or in the kitchen. The sounds all come from the bedroom, but I've never been in there after dark when she walks, and I wouldn't ask my staff to do so, either."

I nodded and offered him my best sympathetic expression. "What about the cause of death?" I asked. "What did the doctor have to say?"

"He seemed as puzzled as everyone else but thought it might have been some sort of internal hemorrhage, possibly in her lungs; she'd coughed up blood."

I could tell that the man wasn't convinced by this explanation, and indeed he continued. "It was the look of horror on her face that made us all uneasy. The doctor said seeing all that blood coming out of her mouth might have terrified her and caused her heart to stop. Or she might have carried on bleeding inside. To my way of thinking, he didn't really have any idea why she died."

It was strange and horrifying. I had to get to the bottom of the mystery, and I knew the best way to go about it.

"Well, hopefully I'll be able to tell you more tomorrow," I replied, "after I've talked to her ghost. What's her name?"

"Her name was Miriam," the innkeeper replied.

With that, I gave a nod and walked off down the street. Before long I turned down a passageway that brought me round the back of the inn to the edge of the churchyard I'd seen through the bedroom window. I opened the ornate trellis gate and took the narrow path through the tombstones that brought me past the small church.

I needed a walk to stretch my legs and get some fresh air

to clear my head. I wanted a bit of time by myself to think about the situation, too.

In the County, it usually got chilly after dark, even in summer, but this was a warm night in late August—probably the last of the good weather before the autumn cooled the air, ready for winter.

I came to a slope that offered a spectacular view of a valley; the range of hills in the distance was bathed in moonlight. It was something that cried out to be painted, and it held my attention for a long time.

Since John Gregory's death, I'd changed a good deal. I still felt a sense of loss—I really missed him—but along with that, there was also anger. A friend had been taken from me, as well as a master. I now spent most of my days alone, with a lot of time to brood on things, but there was one source of solace. Increasingly, I'd come to appreciate the beauty of the countryside, with its varied landscape of meadows, woods, fells, and marshes. This view at Kirkby Lonsdale was as good as anything I'd seen, if not better.

My mind wandered back to the cause of Miriam's death, and I sat down on a tree stump to allow my mind to mull over the situation. The girl had been young and strong, so there was a possibility of foul play. It wasn't unknown for a murderer to hide his own involvement by blaming witchcraft or some other supernatural occurrence. But there had been no wound . . . maybe she'd been poisoned . . . or it could have been a natural death, and the horror of dying in pain was what had brought that expression to her face.

I hoped to find out the truth soon enough. It all depended on what the ghost remembered of her own death.

After a while I retraced my steps through the churchyard and went back up to the haunted room. I closed the curtains, then pulled off my hooded cloak, hanging it on a hook on the back of the door. Next I tugged off my boots and lay down on the bed, fully clothed and ready for action. I was slightly nervous, as I always am when dealing with spook's business, but I wasn't afraid. I'd dealt with lots of ghosts before.

I've always been good at seeing in near darkness, and once my eyes had adjusted to the faint moonlight filtering through the curtains, I studied the room carefully. There were shadows in the corners—a particularly dark one just below the window. I spent some time trying to work out whether it was natural or not. It wasn't. After a while, satisfied that it was nothing to be concerned about, I listened carefully. Sometimes you could hear ghosts before they wanted you to. Some rapped softly on doors or walls; others pattered across the floorboards, sometimes almost indistinguishable from mice.

This room was absolutely silent. I had a couple of hours,

so I relaxed, closed my eyes, and allowed myself to drift off to sleep.

I would sense the arrival of the ghost and wake up immediately.

Sometime later, I woke exactly as I'd predicted. All spooks are seventh sons of seventh sons, and this means that we possess certain gifts. One was operating here: a cold chill that told me something from the dark was close; it ran powerfully up and down my spine. Before I even opened my eyes, I heard the sound of a girl weeping, and footsteps pacing back and forth beside the bed.

I looked at her. The ghost was that of a young girl, probably no older than seventeen. She had long hair pulled tightly into a bun at the back of her head. Like many ghosts, she was very pale, all the color having been left behind with death.

All the colors but one.

The front of her long pale nightdress was soaked in red blood, from neck to hem.

2
The Girl with the Mousy Hair

I looked at Miriam's ghost and sat up in bed to face her. Then I gave her my warmest smile. I tried to be reassuring. "Stand still, Miriam," I said softly. "Stand still and look at me."

She turned toward me, gave a sob, and her eyes opened wide in astonishment.

"You can see me! Can you hear me?" she asked. Her voice had a slight echo to it and seemed to come from a distance.

"Yes, I can both see and hear you. I'm a spook, and I've come to help you."

"I've been asking for help for days, but nobody listens. Nobody even looks my way."

"You mean up here in the bedroom?"

"No—I went down to the kitchen where I used to work. Nobody comes up here after dark."

Ghosts could be seen lingering by their graveside, but usually they haunted the place where they had died. As a seventh son of a seventh son, I might have been able to see or hear her in places where other folk wouldn't.

"Do you know why that is?" I asked gently.

"It's because I'm dead," she said, beginning to cry again.

That was good—an important first step. Some ghosts didn't know that they were dead. The hardest part of my job was convincing them of that fact before persuading them to move on.

"Yes, you're dead, Miriam. It happens to us all eventually. But now you can move on to the light. You can go to a better place than this world. I'll help you to do that, I promise, but first I need to ask you a few questions. Can you tell me how and why you died?"

The girl stopped crying, and an expression of terror came onto her face. "Something evil killed me," she said.

I tried to keep my face calm, but my mind was whirring with thoughts. I was keen to find out what creature of the dark was responsible for this brutal murder.

"Something sat on my chest. It was heavy and I couldn't breathe. Then it sank its teeth into my throat and began to drain my blood. I could hear it sucking and snarling. Its eyes were red. It wore a long coat like a man's, but it was definitely some kind of animal, because its arms were hairy and it had a long tail."

I listened in astonishment to her description. This was completely outside my experience—I had never even heard of such a creature—but I tried not to reveal anything in my expression. I wanted Miriam to remain calm so that I could get as much information as possible from her.

The doctor had found no wounds on her body, including her throat . . . so could it be that what she was describing was really a nightmare she'd experienced alongside some sort of physical pain?

"It had happened before," she continued. "I'd felt that weight on my chest and woken up sweating and weak. And when I got out of bed, I felt dizzy. But this was far worse. I could see its red eyes. The creature seemed to be in a frenzy—it kept on drinking my blood until my heart faltered and stopped."

"Think carefully, Miriam. I want you to remember all you can about the creature. How big was it?"

"No! No!" She covered her face with her hands. Her whole outline began to shake as she sobbed.

"Try, please, Miriam," I persisted. "The information you give me might help to save other girls in the future."

"I'm sorry. I can't. I'm not strong enough. I can't bear to think about my death again. You said that you were going to help me. So please, please, help me now!"

I'd heard enough. It was time to give her peace from this torment.

"Listen carefully," I told her, coming slowly to my feet and smiling at her. "I want you to think of the happiest moment you ever experienced."

She fell silent, and a puzzled expression came onto her face.

"Think hard," I said. "Was it when you were a child?" Quite often the happiest memories the dead retained were moments in their childhood; a time when they felt safe, protected by their parents; when life hadn't yet had a chance to hurt them.

"No! No!" she cried out in some agitation. "My childhood was unhappy." She gave a shudder but didn't explain why this was so. Then, suddenly, the sides of her mouth curled up in a smile. "It was when I came here to work. I had a room all to myself, and on the very first morning I saw the sun rise, bathing the hills in its warm glow. The graveyard directly beneath the window had seemed creepy the previous night. But now I saw that it was a peaceful place, well tended, and flowers had been left by relatives who loved those they had lost. And beyond it was that wonderful view, with the valley rising up toward those hills in the distance. I felt lucky to be in such a nice place. I was really happy then."

"Go back to that moment," I told her. "Feel that happiness again. The sun is rising, bathing the hills in light. Can you see it?"

"Yes! *Yes!* It's so bright!"

"Then walk toward it. Go to the light. You can do it. Just a few steps and you'll be there!"

The ghost was smiling now. She took three paces toward the window and then faded away completely.

My task was over. She'd gone to the light, and that gave me great satisfaction. Often a spook fought the dark and found only fear and violence. It was satisfying to be able to help a lost soul like Miriam. This job had been far easier than most, but today that wasn't the end of the problem.

The girl had mentioned something heavy sitting on her chest. I would have dismissed it . . . but for one thing. This was the third County girl who'd died in similar circumstances in the same number of months. And each ghost had given the same account of feeling a heavy weight on her chest. But Miriam was the first to have woken up and seen a creature feeding from her.

I was dealing with something very unusual. There was work to be done.

I returned to the house at Chipenden. I'd inherited it from my master, and it was mine to live in as long as I worked as a spook. That suited me fine. As far as I was concerned, this was a job for life.

The following day I got up soon after dawn, picked up my staff, and went out into the garden. There was a tree stump there that my master and I had routinely used for practicing our fighting skills.

Soon I was driving the blade of my staff into the wood again and again until I was breathing hard and dripping with sweat. I was out of condition, a long way off my former peak of fitness.

The staff, with its retractable silver-alloy blade crafted to fight witches, was a spook's main weapon, and I needed to regain my former skill in using it as soon as possible.

I tried the move in which I flicked my staff from one hand to the other before driving it into the stump. I was clumsy, so I kept at it until I felt I'd improved.

Since my master had died, almost ten months ago now, I'd done my best to deal with the dark, but I hadn't kept up my fighting skills. Gradually I'd done less and less. I hadn't had the heart, because it reminded me too much of the days when John Gregory and I had trained together. But now I realized that this must become a daily routine again. I needed to be ready for any eventuality. The death of the third girl had brought home to me the fact that I needed to keep both my wits and my skills sharp and to continue to gather knowledge—there was still much I didn't know.

Before going back to the house, I also practiced for ten minutes with my silver chain, the spook's other main weapon, casting it again and again over the post in the garden. I was pleased to discover that my skill with this was undiminished. I didn't miss once. It had always been one of my strengths—I could cast it over a witch even when she was running directly toward me.

Pleased with myself, I headed back for breakfast. I'd built up a good appetite.

I sat alone at the table with a big portion of ham and eggs steaming on the plate before me. At one time I would have wolfed it all down and helped myself to more. But my appetite was poor these days, and I only picked at my food.

During breakfast, my master and I used to discuss previous events or our plans for the coming day. I missed all that, but of course I wasn't truly alone.

I could hear a faint purring.

It was the boggart, Kratch.

There were many different types of dark entities like this, and it was a spook's job to deal with them. For example, there were ripper boggarts that drank the blood of animals and people; stone chuckers that threw stones. Both of these could kill, so a spook had to bind or slay them. Other boggarts just played tricks on folk and scared them; they were just moved on to a different location—usually a deserted spot far from human habitation. However, Kratch was a cat boggart, and although it was dangerous and could kill, my master had dealt with it in a different way.

This boggart cooked the breakfast and guarded the house and garden. In exchange, after issuing three warnings to any intruders, it was permitted to kill them and drink their blood. My master had made this pact with Kratch, and I had renewed it.

The creature rarely made itself visible, but when it did so, it took the form of a ginger tomcat that varied in size depending on its mood. The purring faded now, and I sensed it moving away from me. Moments later it appeared on the hearth rug, curling up in front of the embers of the fire. I wondered if perhaps it was some type of boggart that had killed the girls. But almost immediately I dismissed that possibility. For one thing, the murderous creature had worn a long coat, and boggarts definitely didn't wear clothes of any type. Secondly, none of the places where the girls had been killed were on ley lines—the invisible paths along which boggarts moved from location to location.

After finishing what breakfast I could manage, I went down to the village to pick up the week's provisions, calling in at the shops in the usual order: the butcher's, the green-grocer's, and finally the baker's.

In recent months, the dark had been relatively quiet. Few had visited the withy trees crossroads outside the house to ring the bell that would summon me. However, I had spent much of my time thinking and trying to puzzle out what had killed the girls . . . so far, without success.

As I walked along the street, I received the usual furtive glances, and villagers would occasionally cross to the other side to avoid passing near me. That was to be expected, but today there was something new. I felt that people were whispering behind my back. It made me feel uncomfortable, but I ignored it and went about my business.

Carrying the full sack over my shoulder, I set off up the hill toward the house. As I neared the top of the lane, I saw someone waiting there.

A girl was sitting on the stile next to the gate. For a moment my heart leaped in my chest with a strange combination of anger and grief. It was Alice! Alice had been trained as a witch but had later become my friend and had stayed at the Chipenden house with us. She had been gone for a long time now, but I still missed her. However, almost immediately I realized that this was not Alice after all. Alice was about my own age—seventeen—while this girl was at least a couple of years younger. She had mousy hair, freckles, and a bright, cheerful face. She was wearing a neat dark blue dress that came down well below her knees, and a pair of sensible walking shoes. At first glance you'd have taken her for a healthy farmer's daughter, but there was something about her eyes that was very unusual.

The left eye was blue and the right eye was brown.

Not only that—their expression was strange in a way that I couldn't quite put my finger on. Whatever it was, I knew instantly that she was no ordinary girl. I had no sensation of cold, so I knew she wasn't a witch, but there was something about her I didn't quite trust.

"Hello," she said as I approached. "Are you Mr. Ward?"

"That I am," I replied. "Are you here to ask for help? You should have inquired down in the village what to do. You see, it's best to visit the withy trees crossroads and ring the bell. I'd have gone there right away, and you wouldn't have had to wait like this."

"I don't need help," she said, jumping down and coming toward me. "You're a new spook, aren't you? So you'll be looking for an apprentice. I'm applying for the job."

I put down the sack and smiled at her. "I'm sorry, but I'm not looking for an apprentice. Anyway, this is not a job that you can just apply for. You need certain innate abilities, even before you start—special talents that help you fight the dark. I'm new to the job myself. My own apprenticeship was cut short, and I'll still be learning for at least a few more years. I'm hardly in a position to train anyone else, am I?"

"That's not a problem," she said with a smile. "We should spend all our lives learning, and I know you already have lots to teach me. I can help by doing chores as well. I could have collected your food from the village and saved you the bother. I could make your breakfast, too. My mam says I'm a good cook."

"I don't need anyone to make my breakfast," I said, not bothering to explain that I had a boggart that did that already. "How did you know I'd been down in the village collecting provisions?"

"I watched you going into the shops. Then, when you went into the last one, I ran up here to wait for you."

"How did you know it was the last one? Have you been spying on me?" I asked.

"I wouldn't call it spying, but yes, I've watched you for a couple of weeks and I know your routine—you go to the butcher's, the greengrocer's, and finish at the baker's shop. I've seen enough to make me realize that you are the one who should train me."

"Listen, I'd better tell you what's what so that you won't get your hopes up. To become a spook's apprentice you have to be a seventh *son* of a seventh son. That gives you some immunity against witches and enables you to see the dead and talk to them. That's the basic requirement. I might as well be blunt. You're a girl, and you just don't qualify." I picked up my bag, nodded at her, and started to climb over the stile.

"I'm a seventh daughter of a seventh daughter," she said. "And I *can* see the dead. Sometimes they talk to me."

I turned and looked back at her—a seventh daughter of a seventh daughter with those powers . . . ? I'd never heard of such a thing.

"I'm sure you can," I replied, "but I just don't need an apprentice. Have I made myself clear?"

Then I headed for the house, putting her from my mind.

3
Bad Things Happen

I spent the afternoon and evening in the library. The house had been burned to the ground a couple of years ago, and John Gregory's original library, a vast collection of books—some of them written by generations of previous spooks—had been destroyed.

The house had been rebuilt, but the library was far more difficult to replace.

Now the new shelves were mostly empty. They housed a very small collection of books. These included a few notebooks of my own and my master's, including his Bestiary, the illustrated dictionary of the entities he'd encountered during his years as a spook defending the County against the dark.

I sat at the desk and began to write up the happenings of the previous day in my notebook. I'm sure John Gregory would have had much to say on the subject, but I was alone now, and it was up to me to find an explanation. The library couldn't help me. I was getting nowhere and needed a plan.

The following morning I woke up early, no nearer to finding an answer to the mystery. It was too soon to go down to breakfast. The boggart became very angry if you went into the kitchen before it was ready for you, and it was not wise to annoy such a dangerous creature.

So I went outside and strode toward the western garden. It was a good place to think. The weather had turned, and I was surprised to find a thin coating of hoarfrost on the grass. The air was unusually cold for late August, much colder than I'd expected. Even in the County, which was known for its long winters, we didn't usually get the first frosts until late September or early October. It could well be that winter would come early this year, more severe than ever.

I sat down on the bench and gazed toward the fells, listening to the birdsong and the hum of insects. This was where my master used to teach me. I would sit taking notes while he paced back and forth.

His grave lay near the bench, the mound of earth now covered with grass. I read the words on the gravestone. I'd chosen them myself.

HERE LIETH

JOHN GREGORY OF CHIPENDEN,

THE GREATEST OF THE COUNTY SPOOKS

The Spook had served the County well. He'd been a good master, and as I thought about him, tears came to my eyes.

I reflected on the years of training he had given me, and all his warnings against the dark; his instructions on how to deal with it. We'd faced many foes, but malevolent witches had been some of our most dangerous enemies. We had fought them, and captured them, and bound them in pits within his garden.

But a change had come. We weren't strong enough by ourselves, so we had been forced to compromise in order to have any hope of finally defeating the Fiend. So, even though it had made my master uncomfortable, we had formed an alliance with Grimalkin, the witch assassin of the Malkin clan.

I remembered how Grimalkin had helped us, on so many occasions. She had forged a sword especially for me, and I had carried it during our final struggles to destroy the Fiend—a sword that, while I wore or held it, would protect me from dark magic. Grimalkin had named it the Starblade because she had crafted it from the ore of a meteorite.

I had carried the sword into battle gratefully, but afterward, sickened by all the killing and the death of John Gregory, I had told her that I would never use it again—that I would become the Spook my master had trained me to be and use only the weapons of my trade.

Suddenly I was roused from my thoughts by the ringing of the bell down at the withy trees. I went back to the house, pulled on my cloak, grabbed my staff from where I'd left it leaning against the wall by the back door, and set off at a brisk pace to answer the summons.

As I moved out of the morning sunlight and into the gloom of the willow trees that shrouded the crossroads, the bell stopped ringing. That sometimes happened. People lost patience and returned home. Or sometimes they were nervous about meeting a spook, persuading themselves that there would be no response and escaping while they could.

At first I thought that this was what had happened here. The rope was still dancing and the bell swinging. Perhaps the sound of my approach through the trees had sent my visitor home. Well, no doubt whoever it was needed help, so I decided to set off in pursuit.

I walked up to the bell and examined the flattened grass, searching around to discover which way the tracks led.

"You took your time!" The voice came from behind me.

"I was starting to think that you'd left on a job."

I spun round angrily, recognizing the voice. The girl from yesterday was smiling at me, arms folded, legs slightly apart, head held high.

"I thought I made myself clear," I said. "You are wasting my time—and your own. I neither want nor need an apprentice."

"A man never knows what he wants until he's got it!" she replied, her smile widening into a grin. "Then he wonders how he ever managed without it."

Her grin was infectious, but I didn't allow it to work on me. "Look . . . " I attempted a different approach. "It's a very dangerous job. People die learning the spook's trade. I was my master's last apprentice, and there'd been twenty-nine before me. A third of them died violent deaths during their training. The one before me, Billy Bradley, got his hand trapped beneath a big stone that he was using to bind a ripper boggart. It bit off the fingers of his left hand at the second knuckle, and he died of shock and loss of blood."

"Bad things happen," she said, no longer smiling. "I had a cousin who was a laborer. He got crushed between a farm wagon and a gatepost. It took him almost a week to die. He kept the whole village awake with his screams."

"I'm sorry that your cousin died, but *that* was an accident. *My* job is a constant war against the creatures of the dark; they kill us if they get half a chance. John Gregory's own master, Henry Horrocks, was once tracking a boggart known as a bone breaker. As they crossed a field, it struck without warning, tearing off his apprentice's hand at the wrist. It was being controlled by a witch, and she wanted it to bring her his thumb bones. The poor lad died. There was nothing Horrocks could do to save him. If you became my apprentice, there's no guarantee that you'd even survive the first six months."

"Now you're talking," the girl said brightly, the smile returning to her face once more. "You're considering the possibility, aren't you?"

I shook my head, regretting my words. My patience was rapidly running out, but I tried to remember my dad's advice about being polite. I spoke to her calmly and firmly. "You're a girl, and so not suitable for the job, as I told you yesterday. You're too old as well. My master took me on for training when I was only twelve. How old are you?"

"As old as my tongue and a little bit older than my teeth," she replied.

I turned my back in exasperation, ready to return to the house.

"John Gregory trained for the priesthood first," she said to my back. "He was almost twenty when Henry Horrocks took him on, but he turned out to be an excellent spook.

I'm easily young enough to learn the trade."

"How do you know that? Who told you that about John Gregory?" I demanded, stopping and turning around.

She smiled mysteriously, answering my earlier question instead. "I'm fifteen," she said brightly. "I'm just two years younger than you. We have the same birthday—the third of August."

"You're making that up!" I snapped angrily.

It was late August now, and yes, she was right about the date of my birthday. How could she know that? She really *had* been spying and digging for information.

"Why should I make things up?" she asked. "I like strange things, and the truth is often stranger than fiction. That's what my mam once told me, anyway. Don't you agree?"

I turned again and headed for the house, and didn't look back this time. She was really starting to annoy me.

The boggart had cooked the bacon to perfection that morning, and my fried eggs were exactly the way I liked them—just slightly runny. I cut thick pieces of warm bread and buttered them before smearing them with yolk. I managed to eat about half the meal. My appetite was improving a little, though it was still nothing like it had been; previously I'd have polished off that breakfast and still been hungry.

"My compliments to the cook!" I announced, and in response I heard a purring from underneath the table. Kratch always liked to be thanked. For a couple of seconds it flickered into view; it was licking its ginger tail.

The movement suddenly reminded me of what the dead girl, Miriam, had told me about the creature that had killed her.

"It wore a long coat like a man's, but it was definitely some kind of animal, because its arms were hairy and it had a long tail."

Did it walk upright? It had clambered up onto her chest—so not necessarily. But it was unlike any creature I'd read about in my master's once-extensive library. I suddenly realized that it might well have left some unusual tracks. It was certainly worth taking a look.

So after breakfast I collected my bag and staff and set off over the fells toward Caster. I could have visited Broughton or Penwortham, where I'd managed to send the other two murdered girls to the light, but it seemed best to go where the trail would be freshest. My destination lay northeast of Caster. I was going back to Kirkby Lonsdale, where the spirit of the dead girl had actually seen and remembered her killer. Now I was going to have another look at the surrounding area.

I would hunt for the beast that wore clothes.

4
Where the Beastie Lives

It was pleasant walking high across the fells, looking down upon the County. To the west, in the far distance, the sea sparkled in the sunlight. The air was still chilly for the time of year, but the sun had some warmth, and it felt good to be alive.

I found a sheltered hollow about five miles south of Kirkby Lonsdale, trapped a couple of rabbits, and cooked them slowly. The walk had improved my appetite; it was the first food I'd had since breakfast, and I savored every mouthful before settling down for the night. I fell asleep quickly despite the temperature, which dropped quickly once the sun had set.

I awoke suddenly in the middle of the night and sat up, my heart racing. I had a strong feeling that I was being watched, that something was out there in the darkness, gazing at me.

I held my breath and listened carefully. I could hear nothing but the wind sighing through the grass. There was no coldness warning me that something from the dark was out there. It was probably nothing, I told myself—maybe just a fox hoping to scavenge something from the leftovers of my supper.

However, it left me feeling uneasy, and it was a long time before I got to sleep again.

In the morning, clouds had raced in from the west, threatening rain. I nibbled a piece of cheese for my breakfast. My master had taught me to eat sparingly when about to deal with the dark. You needed to maintain your physical strength, but the odd nibble of cheese sufficed for that. Not that my stomach agreed! It was rumbling with hunger, but I couldn't afford to listen to it. I might soon come face-to-face with the murderous creature.

Three girls had died. The first had been bad enough, but with each successive death my anger and sense of failure had increased. As a spook, I was supposed to protect the County. I was failing badly and was desperate to do something about it.

I headed northeast as fast as I could. I didn't go into the village of Kirby Lonsdale itself but circled it slowly, looking for tracks. My master had taught me to be patient when tracking and to pay attention to the slightest thing. I spent most of the day searching the main approaches to the village from the northwest and southwest. I was thorough and circled it twice.

Then, late in the afternoon, my perseverance was rewarded. I found tracks beside a path. Something had left the path to approach a nearby stream, and the small prints could be clearly seen in the mud. At first I dismissed them as being of no significance. The size told me that they belonged to a child no older than seven or eight, but there were no adult-sized prints nearby. Then I noticed that the prints were unusual—too long and thin for a human foot. And I saw something else that told me I had found the tracks I'd been looking for.

In places, the small prints had been partly obliterated. It was almost as if some kind of snake had slithered over them. It might well be a tail.

Soon afterward I found fresh tracks. This new set of prints was heading roughly in the direction of Caster. At first I was elated and began to walk faster. But within an hour, my optimism began to fade.

The tracks had disappeared. I'd lost the trail completely.

I have certain gifts, courtesy of being a seventh son of a seventh son. However, I have inherited abilities from my mam, too. She was a good wife and mother, and loved my dad and all her sons, but she was also a lamia—the first that ever existed—and she passed some of her powers on to me.

One was the ability to track someone without physical evidence of their movements. I just knew where the people I sought were to be found. That gift had helped me in the past, but it could not be relied on, and now, no matter how hard I tried, I could sense no trace of the creature I was pursuing.

Disappointed, I turned and headed for home.

I arrived back at Chipenden about an hour before sunset. I was hungry and exhausted. To my annoyance, I found the girl there again; this time she was waiting on the edge of the garden.

"You look exhausted!" she exclaimed. "Have you had a difficult day?"

I walked straight past her, not bothering to reply. I'd almost reached the edge of the trees when she shouted something at my back.

"I know what's been killing those girls! I know where the beastie lives!"

"How do you know about the dead girls? You're lying!" I shouted angrily, turning back to confront her.

She stared into my eyes. "I don't tell lies—and certainly not about spook's business, where innocent victims are involved.

"Everybody knows," she continued. "They're talking about it in every village for miles. They're scared for their families. Some think that John Gregory would have sorted the problem out by now."

Her words were like a slap in the face. I felt hurt and angry, but I took a deep breath and controlled my feelings. I knew that she was telling the truth, and I had to face it.

It made me realize how isolated I was. That was the problem with being a spook—you never heard the local gossip or knew what people were thinking. It was even worse now that I was working alone. I had nobody with whom to share the burden and talk through concerns and problems.

"So you know what's been doing the killing? Enlighten me!" I replied sarcastically.

"I don't know exactly *what* it is, but it's hairy and lives inside a tree. At night it wanders about and finds its way into people's houses. It can change its size. I know that in one of those houses, a girl died. I heard about the other deaths—I'm thinking they might be the same."

"So you've been spying on this hairy beastie as well as me. But we have a problem here. How come when you followed the supposed creature, it didn't see you?"

"For the same reason you weren't aware of me when I followed *you*. I was there close by, but you didn't see me."

"You can make yourself invisible?" I said skeptically. Then I scowled. "What are you, a witch? Perhaps you belong in a pit," I suggested. In truth, I knew she wasn't a witch. I was just trying to scare her, really—though I knew it was beneath me. I regretted the words the moment they had left my mouth.

"No. I'm a seventh daughter of a seventh daughter," she replied, "just as I told you. It's one of the gifts I was born with. I can't make myself truly invisible—I can't just disappear before your very eyes. But if you didn't know where to look and I stood very still, you wouldn't be able to see me."

When the girl had confronted me previously, I'd dismissed the idea of a seventh daughter of a seventh daughter. It was something I'd not considered before. The Spook had never referred to such a thing—there was certainly no record of one in his Bestiary—nor, for that matter, in any of the books I'd read before his library burned down.

"I've never heard of such a thing!" I exclaimed.

"So what?" the girl cried angrily. "Just because you've never heard of it doesn't mean it doesn't exist. Why shouldn't it apply to girls as well? Why can't a seventh daughter of a seventh daughter be born with powers to fight the dark?"

She seemed very determined and confident, and it suddenly struck me that my mind had been closed to the possibility. Traditionally, spooks had always been male. This was no doubt because it was men who usually held positions of power and decided how things should be done.

I took a deep breath and bit back my annoyance. If this girl knew the location of the beast, I had to use her knowledge. Other lives could be at stake. The beast would kill again if I didn't deal with it first.

"Could you show me the tree where this creature lives?" I forced myself to ask the question in a civil tone of voice.

"If I do that, will you take me on as your apprentice?" she asked immediately.

I certainly had no intention of doing any such thing, but if she really *did* have information on the mysterious deaths, it was my duty to take advantage of it.

"I'm making no promises," I told her, "but I'll think about it. We can't let this go on. Do you want another death on your conscience when you could have prevented it?"

For the first time her confidence seemed to falter, and she lowered her gaze. "The tree is to the east. I'll take you there now, if you like. It's less than an hour's walk. We could get there before dark if we move quickly."

I nodded. "I have to collect a few things. Wait here. I'll be back in ten minutes."

I went back to the house and collected my silver chain. I also filled my left pocket with salt and my right with iron. Then I took a small portion of cheese for the journey.

When I returned to the crossroads, to my fury, the girl was no longer there. I paced up and down for a while, but there was no sign of her. After five minutes I lost patience. Had she been telling me lies, playing some sort of joke? I wondered.

I glanced around, gave a snort of disgust, annoyed with myself for trusting her, and prepared to leave. I would go back to the house, grab some sleep, and search for the creature in the morning. Then, out of the corner of my eye, I saw a movement. I looked around, and suddenly the girl was there. She seemed to step right out of a tree trunk. So the ability to be "invisible" was one thing she hadn't been lying about. . . .

No doubt she hoped I'd comment on her sudden reappearance, but I didn't want to give her the satisfaction, so I simply gave her a curt nod.

"What do they call you?" I asked.

"My mam calls me Jennifer, but I prefer Jenny."

I was stunned; my heart pounded. I tried to keep the astonishment from my face as I remembered where I had heard that name before. I must have failed, because she gave me a curious glance.

"What's wrong?" she asked. "You look like somebody just walked over your grave!"

I ignored her and looked straight ahead. "Lead on!" I said. "But warn me before we come in sight of the tree."

As we walked, I remembered how a dark mage had once conjured up in my mind a vision of a possible future—one where the house at Chipenden stood abandoned and derelict, with no spook working from it. I'd walked up to my bedroom, and there on the wall, where all the apprentices, including me, had scrawled their names, was a new addition:

JENNY.

It suggested that a girl apprentice had once been based there. It seemed very odd—as far as I knew, there had never been any female spook's apprentices. Since then I'd thrust the image from my mind, assuming that it was just one of the mage's tricks. But now a girl of the same name was asking to become my apprentice.

Was this simply coincidence?

Jenny had used that old County saying, too—I looked as if someone had walked over my grave. It seemed sinister in view of what I knew. I would never have abandoned the Chipenden house like that . . . not unless I *was* dead.

The future is never totally fixed. It changes with every decision we make. I'd no intention of doing so, but if I were to take on this girl as my apprentice, would it hasten my death and result in the house being abandoned?

Realizing that we were approaching a wood, I brought my mind back to the present.

"That's where the beastie lives," Jenny whispered, indicating the largest tree ahead of us. It was an oak of tremendous girth that must have been at least five hundred years old.

The sun had gone down, and the light was beginning to fail. I experienced no sudden chill that warned me that something from the dark was close, but once again that feeling of being watched came over me—just as it had when I'd awakened suddenly in the night, south of Kirkby Lonsdale.

Could the creature be watching me from its lair? I wondered.

I was dealing with an unknown entity, and anything was possible. I needed to be on my guard. Instinct made me take hold of my chain, but would that even help me here?

According to the girl, this was about the time when the creature usually left its tree. I just hoped we weren't too late and it hadn't gone already. I wanted to see it for myself.

I gestured to Jenny, indicating that we should crouch, and we both sank down onto our knees, peering through a thicket of young ash trees. For at least five minutes, nothing happened. Somewhere in the distance an owl hooted, and I tensed every time some nocturnal creature stirred or rustled.

Then, suddenly, there was silence—that absolute quiet that falls when some dangerous predator approaches. Soon afterward I heard a peculiar noise. It was a sort of slithering sound, as if a snake was coiling itself about a branch. Then there was a harsh rasp, and something was falling fast from one of the topmost branches.

It was almost dark and it was hard to make it out, but then I saw it silhouetted against the sky. The creature reminded me of a very large squirrel with a long tail.

It dropped a long way to the ground, but hardly made a sound when it landed. Then it scampered off, heading north—toward the village.

What now? Should I follow it? By doing so, I might just save someone's life. But it had moved very fast, and I suspected that it would be hard to track.

"Wait here!" I hissed at Jenny. "If I'm not back within the hour, go home!"

Then, without waiting for a reply, I set off after the creature. It was risky. I might lose its trail; even worse, it might sense that it was being followed, and I'd lose the element of surprise. But I had no choice. My duty was to the people of the County, and I wanted to prevent it from killing again. Within ten minutes, as I feared, I'd lost its trail altogether. I spent another half hour trying in vain to pick it up again. Once more I drew on Mam's gift to locate the creature, but once more it failed to work.

So, angry and frustrated, I returned to where Jenny was still waiting, and I quickly decided on my next move.

5
Purrai Have No Rights

"I'm going to climb up into that tree and wait for the creature to come back," I told Jenny.

"Good idea!" she said enthusiastically. "We'll take it by surprise."

"I said *I*, not *we*! It's dangerous. I don't know what we're up against here."

"Does that matter?" Jenny asked. "You've already told me that an apprenticeship to a spook is dangerous. I might as well start as I mean to go on and get used to it."

The girl was very argumentative. I wondered how John Gregory would have dealt with her. But I had to make up my own mind now, and I decided that she could be of more use to me outside the tree.

"Listen," I told her. "Your job is to keep watch here and warn me when the creature returns. Otherwise it might take *me* by surprise. Can you imitate the hoot of an owl?"

Jenny smiled and gave me a perfect imitation of a barn owl—it was almost *too* good. I'd heard an owl just minutes earlier. Could I tell her call from the real thing?

"Can you do the cry of a corpse fowl?" I asked.

"No," she said, "but I can do a pretty good imitation of a nightjar."

Her cry split the darkness, raising the hairs on the back of my neck.

It was good, but not quite as perfect as her owl. It was just what we needed.

"You do know that a nightjar is just another name for a corpse fowl?" I said.

"Of course I do! Can't you tell when someone's joking?"

I sighed. This was going to be hard work. "When the creature comes back, just give two quick calls, then count to three and give another. Can you manage that?"

"Of course I can, but please be careful! I've met a couple of other spooks—one in particular was a pig, and the second had hairy ears and a foul temper. If anything were to happen to you, who would train me? They certainly wouldn't!"

I wondered how Jenny knew these other spooks. Had she been spying on them too? But this was no time to start questioning her further.

"Yes, I'll take care. You do the same. Stay in hiding

and don't get any closer to the oak than this. Understand? Look after this for me." I handed her my staff.

She nodded, inspected it, and gave me a grin in return.

I turned and very cautiously began to approach the huge tree.

I made a slow circuit of its trunk, wondering if there might be another way in. It was worth checking, but I knew that I would probably have to climb the tree and search for an entrance higher up. After all, that was where the creature had emerged from earlier.

That's why I'd left my staff with the girl—it would simply have been an encumbrance. But it left me with fewer weapons at my disposal: my pocketfuls of salt and iron, and my silver chain.

I began to climb.

It took me a long time to locate the entrance to the creature's lair. I circled the tree at several different levels until at last I found it.

It was well camouflaged. A human would have made such a door square, oblong, oval, or even round. This bark-covered door was difficult to see because of its irregular shape. Once I'd spotted it, I found I could ease the door open with my fingernails. It swung out easily, on hinges that had recently been oiled.

The next problem was its size. The creature was a lot

smaller than me. It would be hard for me to squeeze through that doorway, and I realized that once I was inside it would be difficult to get out again in a hurry. But I'd have to deal with whatever came my way. I wriggled through headfirst, pulling myself through the opening with my hands. I was now pretty much trapped. I had to bind this creature and must not miss with the chain. I felt confident that I could do so—that was one skill I was proud of.

Looking about me, I was surprised by what I found. I had not seen the creature up close in good light, but Jenny had called it a beastie, and from a distance it had resembled a squirrel. I had expected its lair to be that of a wild beast, a predator, the floor perhaps strewn with bones and straw or grass.

So it was a shock to see rows of shelves, a table, chairs, and lambskin rugs dyed a brilliant red. This was an unexpectedly sophisticated dwelling that made me even more confused about what I was dealing with. Many shelves were filled with books, others with glass jars containing what looked like herbs or strange objects floating in a clear liquid or suspended in yellow gel. Each jar was labeled in some foreign language.

Then I spotted something else of interest. There were two bottles of red wine on the table. I knew that they were of human origin because I recognized the labels.

I plucked one of the books from the lowest shelf and opened it. The text was strange and resembled no language I had ever encountered. This creature could read but was clearly from somewhere far from the County.

What was I dealing with here?

As I returned the book to its place on the shelf, something spoke behind me. I say "something," because although it spoke our language, its voice was guttural, harsh, and rasping; too alien to belong to a human being.

"It is nice of you to come to visit me, human. I am hungry, and your presence saves me the need to hunt!"

For a moment I froze and my heart began to pound with fear, my mouth becoming dry as I realized that I had been tricked. I had assumed that I would be in control, would take the creature by surprise, but it must have known all along that we were watching its tree. It had pretended to leave and then doubled back once I'd entered its lair. I had heard no warning cry from Jenny—she must have failed to see it returning.

I quickly turned to face it. At first I found it difficult to make sense of what I saw. It was dressed in a long black coat fastened with white buttons that could have been made from bone. Its hands were covered in dark fur and its face resembled that of a wolf, but it had been shaved so that, apart from the elongated jaw and sharp teeth, it had a human quality, and the eyes were intelligent. The expression was human too: it showed a mixture of amusement, scorn and arrogance.

But the most significant thing about the strange entity was its size. This was nothing like a squirrel. It was at least as tall as me. Then I remembered what Jenny had said about her "beastie"—something that I'd dismissed at the time.

It could alter its size.

And I was trapped in here with it.

I stared at the creature, my confidence ebbing. It opened its mouth a little, and saliva began to drip from its jaws as if it was anticipating the first taste of a tempting meal. I was now on the menu. It would drain my blood if I didn't stop it.

"I'm here to put an end to your murdering ways," I told the creature, trying to take the initiative. But my voice wobbled with fear as I spoke.

"*Murder*, little human? What do you mean? I have killed nobody here yet. You will be the first."

"You've killed three girls. Don't try to deny it."

"Ah, girls—you mean *purrai*! That is not murder. Such females exist simply to obey, and their lives may be taken at whim. I am surprised you do not agree. I had a great thirst, so I drank their blood. It is my right and the way of things. Purrai have *no* rights."

I was appalled by his words, so casually spoken. "What you do in your own land is abhorrent to me," I told him. "But you are in the County now, and what you have done is a crime here."

The creature gave a grotesque smile, opening its elongated jaws to show its teeth. "Your land will soon belong to my people! Then your women will abide by our laws. As for the men and boys, they will all be dead."

The words spun around inside my head. I'd been given a warning, but I could think about that later. Now it was time to act!

Swiftly I reached into my breeches pockets and grasped what I had stored there. In my left hand I clutched salt; in my right, iron. Salt burns entities from the dark; iron drains away their power.

I hurled both handfuls at the creature, and the two clouds, one light, the other dark in color, came together perfectly on its head. This was often enough to destroy a boggart; it could also temporarily disable a witch, making it easier to bind her with a silver chain. But my target reacted in a way I'd never seen before.

The creature sneezed once, then shook its head. Next it gave me a bestial smile as the cloud of salt and iron settled at its feet.

"That was interesting, human," it rasped. "I have never

before been attacked in such a strangely ineffectual fashion. It was a total waste of our valuable time, for we soon shall be very busy together. I will take and you will give. I will have pleasure and you will have pain, until not one drop of your blood remains."

At first I'd felt alarmed, but I was now getting my fear under control. I took a deep breath, steadied myself, and prepared to deal with this beast in a different way.

My silver chain was in the left pocket of my gown. I brought it out already coiled about my left wrist. Then, in one fluent gesture, I flicked it toward the creature.

My cast was perfectly executed. The chain formed a helix above its head, then dropped to bind it from head to knee, one part lying directly across its teeth. This would have been the perfect cast were I dealing with a witch. If this beast was capable of uttering dark magic spells, it would prevent it from doing so.

I thought it was over.

I truly thought that I had won; that the creature was tightly bound.

I smiled. Now I would carry it back to the Chipenden garden and bind it in a pit there.

But I had completely underestimated my adversary.

I had just made one of the biggest mistakes of my life.

It escaped from the silver chain in a similar way to a

skelt. Skelts are large predatory water creatures that can fold their long bony limbs into small crevices to hide while waiting for prey to come within range. A skelt would contract its body and easily shrug off any chain that bound it.

But I wasn't expecting that now. I was terrified when my opponent suddenly grew smaller, so that the chain dropped off its body and lay in a useless coil upon the floor. Then, within seconds, the creature had inflated itself so that it was far bigger than me—at least nine feet tall. Its eyes glowed red, blazing with fury, and its jaws opened wide.

Jenny's "beastie" had transformed into a monstrous beast.

I stepped back in alarm, but it quickly reached out to grab me by the shoulder, dragging me toward its huge mouth. I tried to resist, but it was tremendously strong. Saliva dripped from its jaws again. I thought that it intended to start taking my blood there and then, but instead it breathed hard into my face.

I was enveloped in a sweet, spicy smell. Instantly the world spun about me, and I fell into darkness.

My last thought as I lost consciousness was that if it knew about me, it probably also knew about Jenny. She too would be in danger.

6
Help Me, Please

I awoke in a very different room, although I guessed I was still inside the oak tree. I could see the curve of the nearest wall, and a smell of damp wood assailed my nostrils.

This was indeed the lair of a beast.

I saw no table, no shelves, and no lambskin rugs. Instead, there was a heap of bones in the corner and a faint smell of blood.

It looked like a dungeon. There were chains hanging from the ceiling. I was lying on my side and was aware of movement to my left, something strange that I couldn't identify. What was happening? I wondered.

I felt befuddled. My head was throbbing and my vision was blurred. Only very slowly did I start to make sense of what I was seeing.

Finally, with a jolt, I understood the true horror of the scene before my eyes.

Jenny was hanging from the ceiling by her legs; her head, which was about three feet from the floor, was facing me. Her legs were bound together, her hands tied behind her back. The creature was sitting with its back to me, slightly to one side of the girl, and in its mouth was a thin transparent tube. The other end of the tube had pierced the girl's neck.

That tube was bright red. It was using it to drink her blood.

I tried to move, but I found that I was totally paralyzed. I could only stare in horror as the beast drained her blood.

Then Jenny opened her eyes and stared at me, her face twisted with terror. She was conscious. She knew exactly what was happening to her.

She mouthed something to me. I didn't understand, but then she repeated it:

Help me. Help me.

Desperate to go to her aid, I struggled to rise. But my body didn't respond; it no longer obeyed my brain. Sweat began to pour off me as I tried desperately to overcome whatever rooted me to the spot. It was like a nightmare that went on and on without end. Jenny shuddered and groaned, and the beast continued to drink her blood. And all the while, I could do nothing.

But all nightmares come to an end—unless they end in death. Gradually, feeling began to return to my limbs. It began in my extremities, with pins and needles, which spread up my arms to my torso, followed by a burning sensation, as if my limbs were being consumed by fire.

After a while the pain subsided, and I tried moving my fingers. I didn't want to alert the creature, but it seemed that my whole body was now capable of movement.

What should I do? I couldn't allow the beast to continue draining Jenny's blood, but I had no weapon at hand and it was extremely strong, even without any magical abilities it possessed. It had breathed into my face and caused me to fall unconscious.

What else could it do? I wondered.

Had we been on a ley line, I would have summoned the boggart. The pact between us specified that it would answer my cry for help, and in return could take the blood of my enemies. I was sure that it would have made short work of this beast. But my knowledge of the area told me that we were far from the nearest line.

I looked about me. Next to the bones I noticed half a dozen empty wine bottles. They could be improvised as weapons, but I would have to move quickly. My joints might be stiff and slow to respond after my time lying unconscious on the floor. Moreover, I reflected, even blows directed at the creature's head might not be enough to incapacitate it.

Whatever the risks, I had to try. Surely Jenny could not endure what was being done to her for very much longer. Soon, as a result of the blood loss, her heart would weaken and cease beating altogether.

Just as I'd made up my mind to act, the decision was taken away from me. The creature slowly drew the transparent pipe out of Jenny's neck and rose to its feet.

Was she dead . . . ? I studied her anxiously and was relieved to see that she was still breathing. Once more her eyes opened wide, and she mouthed the words: *Help me, please.*

Without even a glance in my direction, the beast crossed the room, pushed open the door, and left. Presumably it thought I was still unconscious. I could hear the wind sighing through the trees. It must have left through an outer door in the trunk, one at ground level.

Now was my chance to free Jenny and make our escape before the monster returned. There was a possibility that it was playing some sort of game with me. Perhaps it had realized that I could move and was waiting to ambush me outside, ready to take pleasure in ending my hopes of escape.

But I had to take a chance. I started to get to my feet. I

would release Jenny and escape! I could do it.

However, I barely had time to move before that hope was dashed. The door opened again and the beast came in—leaving it slightly ajar. I could see a jagged vertical line of pale yellow light. The moon must have risen.

The beast went over to Jenny and sat down beside her, ready to insert the pipe into her neck once more.

I racked my brain, desperately considering every possible course of action, then rejecting them one by one. I realized that there was only one thing I could do now; I had just one chance to save Jenny. I didn't want to do it, but I had no choice. How could I let her die?

I scrambled to my feet and lurched toward the door. I pushed it open and ran out into the night air. I glanced back once and saw Jenny staring out at me with a pleading look on her face, thinking that I had abandoned her.

I steeled myself and ran on, glancing back once or twice. To my relief, the creature had not followed me.

This was fortunate: I staggered as I ran, and the breath rasped painfully in my throat. The beast's magic had sapped my strength, and I would have been easy to catch.

Two minutes later, I crossed a stream and bent down to slake my thirst with cold, clear water. After that I felt a bit better, and as I ran my strength gradually returned; I picked up the pace. By now the moon had disappeared behind a cloud, but I knew the way well, and the darkness hardly impeded me at all.

At last I crossed into the Chipenden garden and ran toward the house. I didn't bother to go inside. I needed only two things—a lantern and a spade. I snatched both from the lean-to where the tools were kept and headed for the western garden.

This was where my master was buried.

Despite my sorrow and revulsion at what I had to do, I had no choice.

I had to dig up his coffin.

7

The Starblade

AFTER my master's death at the Battle of the Wardstone, Grimalkin wanted me to keep the Starblade and accompany her to face an even greater threat that she had scryed—from a savage people to the north, the Kobalos. I'd had no stomach for any more fighting and had offered the sword to her, but she had refused. However, I had made sure that it would never fall into the wrong hands. While the protection against magic worked only for me, the ore was very valuable and rare and could be crafted into a different weapon for someone else. I had hidden the sword in a place where only someone strong enough to get past the boggart would have been able to reach it: under my master's coffin. At the time, I couldn't imagine ever desecrating the grave to retrieve it.

Now, however, I had urgent need of it. I lit the lantern and hung it from a low branch so that it cast its light over the area. Then, with tears running down my cheeks, I attacked the grave, throwing spadefuls of soil over my shoulder.

"I'm sorry! I'm sorry!" I called out as I worked, my words addressed to John Gregory, my dead master. "I'm so sorry!"

What a fool I had been. Could I not have foreseen such a situation when I would need protection against dark magic?

The Starblade should give me a chance against the beast, a chance to save Jenny. I was sure of it.

At last there was the thud of metal against wood. I'd dug down as far as the Spook's coffin. Now, despite my need for haste, my digging became less frantic and more careful. I didn't want to damage the casket in which his body lay.

I dug to one side and, once my pit was level with the bottom of the coffin, threw aside the spade and scooped soil away with my hands, trying to excavate underneath it. I was careful at first, because the blade of the sword was really sharp. But then, realizing that time was running out, I threw caution to the wind.

But I couldn't find the sword!

I broke out in a cold sweat. Had someone stolen it? I wondered. How could that have happened when the boggart guarded the garden?

I wondered if Grimalkin had taken it with her after all. That night, after burying my master, she had worked her magic to lessen the disfiguring scar where the mage Lukrasta had sliced open my face. Afterward we had both slept, and then, after saying a brief farewell, she had taken her leave. She'd had time to dig it out and put back the soil; after all, I had offered it back to her. It was her right to take it, but how dearly that might cost me now . . . without it, I would be vulnerable to this creature's powerful magic.

Hope fading, my fingers continued their desperate search beneath the coffin. At last, to my relief, they touched metal. But pulling the sword free wasn't easy. My fingers found the edge of the blade, and that was enough to cut them and draw blood. I struggled to free the hilt, aware that the threat to Jenny was growing with every passing second. At last I got a firm grip, and moments later I had pulled the blade out of the soil and was sprinting back in the direction of the beast's lair.

Would I be in time to save Jenny? I feared that she might already be dead.

Once again the moon was out, and by its light I saw the oak tree ahead, clearly visible from a distance, a colossus that towered over the rest of the wood. I stopped running a couple of hundred yards short of it and continued more cautiously.

Speed was important, but I didn't want to give the creature any warning of my arrival. Surprise might make all the difference here.

The wood was totally silent. Nothing moved in the undergrowth. I could hear nothing from the huge tree, either.

Gripping the sword in my right hand, I approached the massive trunk, searching for the ground-level door. I expected to find it closed and perhaps impossible to open. In that case, I would hammer on the trunk. I would lose the element of surprise, but I would at least draw him out, away from Jenny.

But, to my surprise, it was still ajar—just enough for me to insert the fingers of my left hand. I took a deep breath and eased the door open very slowly. The beast had its back to me, and Jenny was still hanging by her feet. But the creature was no longer using the pipe to draw blood from her neck. Its jaws were clamped about her shoulder, and it was snarling as it shook her body. Blood had soaked through her dress. It had bitten her all over her torso.

Filled with rage, I stepped inside and raised the sword, ready to strike.

Suddenly the creature let go of Jenny and, without bothering to turn and face me, addressed me in its rasping voice. It had known all along that I was entering its lair.

"What a fool you are to return here, little human! Do

you care so much for a mere purra that you are willing to sacrifice your own life in a futile attempt to save her? You are breathing hard—you have been running. Did you fear that she would die unless you hastened back? Her blood is sweet and I sip it sparingly, savoring every mouthful. She will live for many days before I finally drain her."

The creature rose to its feet and turned to face me. It had shrunk and was now barely taller than me. When it spoke, I saw that its teeth and lips were stained red with Jenny's blood.

"Once sated, I would have hunted you down and slain you anyway. In truth, by returning, all you have done is hasten your demise. Though I have to admit, I am puzzled. I used boska to render you unconscious—a magic that has never before failed me. When I breathed into your face, it seemed as effective as usual. But the spell should have lasted for many days, unless I administered an antidote. How can it be that after just one short hour you have returned to consciousness?"

Its words made me realize how close I had come to disaster. Somehow, against all the odds, I had survived; better still, my recovery had taken the beast by surprise. I wondered if it was something else that I had inherited from Mam. Had my lamia blood enabled me to resist the full effect of this magic . . . whatever it was?

Without replying to the question, I took a step forward and prepared to strike. The creature smiled, muttered a few words, and advanced on me. It seemed totally confident that its magic would render me powerless.

For a second I was certain of this too. Iron and salt had proved useless against the beast, as had my silver chain. What if Grimalkin's magic was ineffective here too? After all, this was not any sort of human mage I was facing. . . . One way or another, I was about to find out!

I swung the sword straight at the beast's head.

The creature quickly moved backward, but the tip of my blade caught it just above the left eye. There was an expression of surprise on its face as blood began to trickle down its cheek. It muttered again—no doubt some spell. So I gripped the Starblade more tightly, hoping that the sword and Grimalkin's magic would prove effective against this unknown power.

There was nothing special about the appearance of the weapon. The hilt was not ornate, and the blade was a dull brown, as if covered with rust. But the balance was perfect for me, and Grimalkin had told me that it would never need to be sharpened.

"Your sword, little human—I have never encountered its like!" exclaimed the creature.

Then it did the last thing I expected: it turned and ran.

There had to be some reason, I thought. Perhaps it had gone to get a weapon?

I hesitated for a moment before giving chase, wondering whether I should cut Jenny free and lower her to the ground. But I decided that it was better to finish off the beast first. I couldn't bind it, so I would kill it and end its threat. Who knew what it might conjure against me if I delayed? I followed it up a spiral staircase cut into the inner trunk of the tree.

I emerged into the large room I'd first seen, the one furnished with the chairs, table, and shelves of books and jars. I looked again at the red lambskin rugs. I wondered if they'd been dyed with blood. But surely blood wouldn't stay so red. . . .

The creature appeared through a doorway to my right. It now clutched weapons in both hands: in its left was a curved sword, which is sometimes called a saber; in its right, a long-bladed dagger.

I attacked immediately, driving the beast backward. But it was very skilful: the saber met each blow of my sword, filling the room with the clash of metal upon metal.

I was wary of the dagger, which the creature held close to its side, waiting for an opportunity to strike. I resolved not to step too close. My opponent might drag me in and use that short blade.

There are two effective modes of combat. One is to remain cold and calculating, observing every detail of an opponent's technique, assessing strengths and weaknesses, before delivering the death blow. The other is to surrender to what the mind and body already know and fight using instinct, the weapons and moves mere extensions of one's own body, which then acts faster than thought.

But there is also a third, more dangerous way of doing battle—to fight driven by rage. Those opponents who attack you filled with a berserker fury are the easiest to counter and kill.

This was how I fought now. My anger was fueled by the creature's behavior—by the way it had treated Jenny, biting her back and shoulders, tying her up and hanging her by her feet from the ceiling like an animal ready for the slaughter before drinking her blood. Moreover, it had murdered the other three girls. Its arrogance and presumption . . . to think that it could enter the County, which I guarded against the dark, and treat women like slaves, taking their lives as if they were of no value.

In a fury, I drove the beast backward until I had forced it right up against the heavy table. Then I did something I hadn't planned; I simply used what was at hand. I seized one of the bottles of red wine from the tabletop and smashed it into the beast's head.

The bottle broke, showering the creature with red wine. It staggered back, shaking that huge head as if momentarily stunned. Taking advantage of its predicament, I thrust my blade past its guard and deep into its chest.

"This cannot be!" the beast rasped, falling to its knees as I withdrew the blade. It looked up at me, eyes filled with pain and surprise. It tried to speak again, but when it opened its mouth, blood gushed out, soaking the front of its black coat. Then it slowly pitched forward onto its face, gave a shudder, and was still.

I shuddered too, at what I had to do next, but I had no choice. Who knew what regenerative powers such a being might have? I swung the sword down with all my strength and cut the beast's head from its body.

I rushed over to Jenny, lowering her gently to the floor. I feared that she was dead. She did not appear to be breathing, and I could find no sign of a heartbeat.

In desperation I carried her through the trees to the nearest stream and laid her down on the grass beside it. Then I removed my cloak, tugged off my shirt over my head, and wet it in the cold water. I used it to clean her face and wipe the blood from the bite marks on her shoulders, whispering her name as I did so.

"Jenny, Jenny, Jenny . . . it's all right. You're safe now. Open your eyes. Please open your eyes."

8
John Gregory's Apprentices

I repeated Jenny's name for some minutes, willing her to wake up—until I remembered something Dad had once told me: an old laborer who'd once worked on the farm had what Dad called "funny turns." The man would become breathless and say that his heart was "all a-flutter." But Dad had a remedy for it. He would plunge the old man's head into a barrel of ice-cold water, and that would sort him out immediately. The funny turn would be over, and he'd be as spry and fit as before.

Dad reckoned it was the shock of the water that did it.

No doubt if you weren't already dead, such a shock could as easily kill as cure. But I was desperate, and I couldn't think of anything else.

So I rolled Jenny into the freezing water of the fast-flowing stream so that she ended up on her back. Then I knelt beside her. Her head I supported with both hands, but her whole body was immersed.

Suddenly she gave a gasp, opened her eyes wide, and stared up at me.

"Take deep breaths," I told her. "Concentrate on your breathing."

She tried to say something, but this started a choking fit. When it subsided, I continued to support her head with my right hand while using my cupped left hand to dribble water into her mouth. After I'd done this six or seven times, Jenny spoke again, this time managing to utter two words.

"The beast . . . ?" Her eyes widened again, and she started shivering.

"The beast is dead," I reassured her. "Concentrate on getting well."

"I'm cold," she said. "So cold . . ."

So I lifted her out of the water and laid her down on the grassy bank again.

"Take off your clothes," I ordered. "You can wear my cloak until they dry."

I turned my back, intending to give her some privacy, but after a few moments she cried out, "My fingers are numb!"

I turned, watching as she fumbled with the buttons of

her blouse. She couldn't get them undone. I had to do it for her—and there was no time to feel any embarrassment. Finally I wrapped her in my cloak.

"I'm wearing a spook's cloak!" she said hoarsely, a hint of a smile on her face.

I lit a fire by the stream and set some traps for rabbits. As the sun came up, I fed her—mostly the gravy, with just a few small pieces of meat. I was glad to see that she already seemed much stronger.

"I thought you'd left me to die," she said after swallowing the last mouthful. "It was the most terrifying moment of my life. Until that point I thought you'd work out some way to save me. When you ran, I couldn't believe it. I was desperate. But you came back . . . I owe you my life."

"I'm sorry I had to leave you. I ran back to Chipenden to get this." I held up the sword before her. "It was crafted by Grimalkin, the witch assassin of the Malkin clan. Have you heard of her?"

Jenny shook her head.

"She forges her own weapons and made this specially for me. While I wield it, magic can't be used against me. Normal spook methods had no effect on the beast. This was the only way I could defeat it."

"It's not much to look at." She stared at the blade. "It's covered in rust."

I nodded, studying it closely. It didn't look like much, but it was perfectly balanced for me to wield; I also knew that it would never break or lose its edge.

While Jenny rested, I went back to the beast's lair. I entered the tree cautiously. I was sure that I had killed it, but it had shown such power that I was taking no chances.

Some Pendle witches could die and yet still move and hunt, taking small animals for their prey, but a few were very fast and hunted humans. One even stalked her prey carrying her head underneath her arm. I would take no unnecessary risks with this creature.

Would it be better to take the body back to the garden and bury it in a pit with bars over the top, as I would a witch? I wondered.

I needn't have worried. I was instantly greeted by the drone of flies and the faint stink of death. The creature lay in exactly the same position; it was quite dead.

I took my time searching both the room where we had fought and the dungeon below. I was intrigued by the jars. I picked up one and looked at it closely. It contained what looked like yellow jelly, and suspended within it were small objects. What could they be? They looked like seeds—or perhaps very small eggs.

There seemed to be other rooms higher in the tree, but

the entrances were too small for me. Unlike the beast, I could not change my size.

What *was* I dealing with here? What could the creature possibly be? And then, suddenly, a name exploded inside my head:

Kobalos!

When I'd first confronted it, the creature had said, "Your land will soon belong to my people! Then your women will abide by our laws. As for the men and boys, they will all be dead."

I hadn't been concentrating on its words at the time because I'd been scared, but now, all at once, it made sense. Grimalkin had encountered this race on her journeys north last year. Her description matched the beast I'd faced. She'd told me that the Kobalos planned to make war on the human race and asked that I accompany her to face the threat. Perhaps the creature I had killed was a spy sent here to discover our strengths and weaknesses before the bigger attack came. But if so, why had he killed those three girls, drawing attention to himself?

There was only one way to find out for sure. I had to summon the witch assassin. During my research I'd come across a brief mention of these creatures in my master's Bestiary, but I hadn't made the link, and I knew I would only be able to find out so much from books. Grimalkin had been to their land. She would know much about them that could be useful.

I returned to Jenny, my mind full of what my next move should be.

By the evening she felt strong enough to walk, so we set off back toward Chipenden, taking our time. We arrived just before dusk, and I halted on the edge of the garden, calling out in a loud voice, "Hear me! This girl is protected. Harm not a hair of her head!"

After I had explained about the boggart to Jenny, we entered the garden and made our way toward the house. I gave the bench a wide berth—I didn't want her to see my master's disturbed grave. I was in no mood for explanations, and I was embarrassed. How foolish I had been to think of burying the Starblade there at all! Tomorrow I would have to fill in the Spook's grave for the second time.

Once in the house, I grabbed a clean sheet and a blanket. Then I lit a candle and gave it to the girl to carry. Upstairs, I pushed open the door of my room and beckoned her inside.

"You'll sleep here. This is to change the bed," I said, thrusting the bedclothes toward her. "In the morning, you'll hear a bell ring. That's the signal to go down to breakfast. But whatever you do, don't come down before.

The boggart cooks breakfast, and it doesn't like being disturbed in the kitchen. Understand?"

Jenny merely nodded.

"Look, you must be exhausted. I'll make up the bed for you," I said, reaching for the sheet.

But she smiled and shook her head. "You're tired too," she said. "I can manage, but thanks all the same."

Then she spotted the words carved into the wall at the foot of the bed—the list of names.

"Who are they?" she asked.

"They were John Gregory's apprentices. My name's on that wall somewhere."

I turned to go but had one more thing to say to her.

"You can write your own name there at the end of the month. . . . That's if you pass the test and seem capable of doing the job."

9

A Nettle Patch

I'D been reluctant to move into my late master's bedroom; it seemed somehow disrespectful. However, now that Jenny was in my old room, I judged that it was time to start using it. To my surprise, I slept well, but I was up before dawn. I went to the library, placing a small mirror on the table where I usually worked.

I tapped three times upon the mirror and uttered a single word:

"Grimalkin!"

At first the witch assassin didn't respond, and I suddenly wondered if she'd ignore my attempts to contact her.

Almost ten months earlier, soon after the death of my master, we'd parted on reasonably good terms. But I knew that I'd disappointed her. I'd refused to travel north with her to find out about the Kobalos, settling for the life of a spook and choosing my master's weapons—staff, chain, and salt and iron—rather than the blade she'd given me. I'd not seen her since, and a lot could have happened by now. She might even be overseas and out of reach.

I was about to give up when at last the mirror started to glow and Grimalkin's face appeared before me. She smiled, showing her teeth, which she kept filed to points and sometimes used as a weapon.

"There is something here that I would like you to see." I spoke slowly, mouthing the words carefully at the mirror. She could not hear me but would read my lips. Over time I too had become skilled at this.

Grimalkin shook her head. "I cannot come to Chipenden. I am busy with other things," she replied.

"I think you might want to change your mind," I persisted. "A strange creature has been murdering local women. I've killed it, but I think it's one of the Kobalos— probably one of their mages. It walked upright and had a hairy body but a shaved face. It wore a long coat too, just as it was described in the Spook's Bestiary. You really do need to see it."

For a moment or two the witch's face stared at me out of the mirror without blinking. Then she nodded.

"The fact that it has come so far south into the County is very worrying. I will be there within three days," she mouthed.

Then the mirror grew dark.

I wondered where she was. If she was traveling on horseback, three days was quite some distance away. But it could have been worse. The Kobalos lands lay across the Northern Sea, and many weeks' ride beyond its shores.

Next I went out to the western garden and filled in my master's grave, making it as tidy as possible. Then I went down on my knees and told him that I was sorry. I said it over and over again.

I knew he couldn't hear me, of course. By now he would have passed through limbo and gone to the light, but it made me feel better.

I was already seated at the table when Jenny came into the kitchen. There were two place settings, and a large plate in the center held generous portions of bacon and eggs. A further side plate was heaped with thick slices of buttered bread.

"You're late," I told her. "The bell rang five minutes ago."

"I'm sorry," she said with a cheeky smile. "I'll try to do better tomorrow."

"I suppose it's better than coming down to breakfast too early. I did that my very first morning in this house and got my ears boxed by the boggart!"

She nodded, sat down, and helped herself to bacon and eggs. Then, before she took her first mouthful, she looked me in the eye, a serious expression on her face.

"I *will* still be here tomorrow, won't I? You really did mean it about taking me on as your apprentice?"

"Yes, I meant it, but I'm giving you a month's trial. You have to pass a test first to convince me that you're up to the job."

I had decided to treat her as my master had treated me—and the apprentices before me. We'd had a month to prove ourselves. The test was to see if we were brave enough to face the dark.

"So we're going to the haunted house?"

"You know about that?" I asked, gazing at her in astonishment. "How did you find that out?"

"Easy!" she said mischievously. "Lots of boys failed the test. I talked to one of them—of course he's a man now, with sons of his own. He couldn't remember the name of the town where the house was, though. Somewhere south of here, isn't it?"

"It's in a place called Horshaw—but first we should go and see your parents."

"Do we *have* to visit my mam and dad?" Jenny asked, her face downcast.

"We do. We must do things properly. I have to explain

to them what it means to become my apprentice."

Jenny gave a big sigh of exasperation, but said no more. I wondered why visiting her parents bothered her, but I let it go for now.

"What's your second name?" I asked.

"Calder," she replied.

"And where is your home?"

"Just north of Grimsargh."

Grimsargh was about five miles south of the Long Ridge, so we could get there and back long before nightfall. It would make for a pleasant stroll, and I wanted to get this done before starting Jenny's training.

As we walked, I thought over what I might have gotten myself into. Taking Jenny on as my apprentice would change my life significantly. It would end my loneliness, true, but on the other hand, it would mean a lot of extra work and responsibility.

It was late morning when we arrived. Jenny's parents' home was a typical gray stone farm laborer's cottage, with small windows and a front door that led straight into the narrow front room.

I was going to knock, but Jenny walked straight in, and so I followed. It was gloomy inside, with a small fire flickering in the grate and a man and a woman sitting very close to it. The man was warming his hands. He was bald but for tufts of white hair over each ear. The woman wore a bonnet that looked none too clean, and her hands were wrinkled and covered with bulging blue veins. Both were getting on in years.

"Mam! Dad!" Jenny said without any preamble. "This is Master Ward, the Chipenden Spook. He's going to take me on as his apprentice."

Jenny's dad didn't even turn to acknowledge me. He just carried on warming his hands and staring into the fire. The mother didn't get up to greet me either, but at least she swiveled her head and met my eye.

"She's a wild one, that!" She nodded toward Jenny. "Nearly been the death of me, she has. Goes gallivanting all over the County and never thinks to help her poor old mam and dad. What a worry she's been. I wish we had a lad, not a mad girl like that."

"That's enough, Mother!" Jenny's dad rebuked her angrily. He turned in his chair and looked at me for the first time. "Well, Master Ward, let's get down to business. If you're going to put her to work, how much will you be paying us for her services?"

I smiled. "It's usually the other way round, Mr. Calder," I explained. "When my own master took me on as his apprentice, my dad paid him two guineas to start with, and another ten after the trial period was over. You see, I'm offering to teach her a trade that will eventually provide her with a good steady livelihood. Not only that . . . her food and accommodation are free. The guineas are just part of the contract and go nowhere near covering the full cost that I'll be put to."

"But she'll be working hard and making your life easier. There should be some payment for that, or it doesn't seem right."

"It's the way it's always been done," I explained calmly. "At first apprentices can do little to help. Even after several years' training, they rarely go out on jobs alone."

Of course, all I actually knew was John Gregory's way of doing things, but I wasn't going to admit as much to this man.

"Why's that, then?"

"Because it's dangerous work, Mr. Calder," I replied. "Some creatures from the dark can kill you—especially boggarts."

"Boggarts!" he scoffed. "It's a load o' rubbish! Ghosts and boggarts—they're just superstitious stories to frighten fools who'll pay good money for what you pretend to do. Still, don't get me wrong, if it makes you a living, I don't blame you one bit. Folks are gullible, but what you do at least gives 'em peace of mind, I'll say that for you."

I didn't see any point in arguing with him. Most folk

were nervous about spooks, but you met the odd one who didn't believe in the dark at all. It might be that they lacked sensitivity to the supernatural, but whatever caused them to adopt that attitude, they were sure they were right, and there was no point in trying to convince them otherwise.

"Your own pa must've been rich to afford twelve guineas," Jenny's dad grumbled.

I shook my head. "He wasn't rich," I explained. "He was just a hardworking farmer who had to support seven sons."

'Well, I'm not even a farmer. I just work for farmers, and a poor pittance they pay me. I can tell you that for nought!"

There was a silence then, and Jenny looked like she wished the floor would open and swallow her up.

There was a long silence, which I broke with another question.

"Do your other daughters no longer live at home?" I asked.

"They were good girls!" piped up Jenny's mam. "We'd no trouble marrying them off—no trouble at all. Now they both have children of their own."

I nodded and forced a smile onto my face, but my heart sank. This contradicted Jenny's claim to be a seventh daughter of a seventh daughter. Had she lied to me, assuming that I wouldn't pay a visit to her family?

"Both?" I asked. "What about your other daughters, Mrs. Calder?"

"We don't have any other daughters. We would have liked more children, but two was all we could manage," the woman told me. "That's why we adopted Jenny."

I was annoyed. I felt like walking out and heading straight back to Chipenden. But part of me *did* want to believe Jenny, and if she was adopted, then there was still a chance that she was telling the truth.

"Who were her parents?"

"If the Lord knows, he ain't telling!" she replied. "I found Jenny abandoned in a nettle patch behind the big barn out there. She was screaming fit to wake the dead. Had stings all over her little bum! Even though we were getting on in years, being good-hearted folk and wanting another child, we took her in."

I glanced at Jenny, who had blushed a bright red.

"Of course, she hasn't turned out quite the way we expected," the woman continued. "The nettle patch was right at the center of a big pixie circle made of the tallest and brightest yellow buttercups I'd ever seen. That's supposed to bring good fortune to any who dare enter it. But we've seen precious little of that!"

Pixies and pixie circles *were* just superstitious nonsense, but I didn't waste my breath explaining this to her. I'd had enough of the company of this couple. I knew that I was going to have to whistle for my guineas. In any case, they were probably too poor to make more than a token contribution to the cost of training Jenny.

"Well, I'll have to consider the situation," I said. "Jenny has to take a test first, to see if she's fit to become my apprentice. If she passes, I might call back to see you again."

That was the end of the conversation, and after bidding them farewell, I began to walk slowly away from the cottage, Jenny following behind.

"You lied to me," I said accusingly. "Are you actually a seventh daughter of a seventh daughter?"

"Of course I am!" she protested.

"How can you make such a claim?" I snapped. "You don't even know who your real parents were."

"My real dad and mam are both dead. But I know who my mam was," Jenny said, hanging her head. "And I know that I've six sisters."

"Are you trying to tell me that *you* know who your mam is, but your foster parents don't?"

"Yes. My real mother came to see me about three years ago. She explained why she'd abandoned me."

I stared hard at Jenny. Was she telling the truth?

"So why did she?"

"Because my dad had died suddenly and she was living in poverty with too many mouths to feed and no hope of things getting better. She was too proud to ask anyone to adopt me. So she left me somewhere I'd be found."

"Why did she seek you out after all that time?"

"Because she was dying. The doctor had given her only weeks to live. She came to tell me that I was a seventh daughter of a seventh daughter. She did it so I'd be ready when I started to see the dead. She was a seventh daughter of a seventh daughter too, and she hadn't been prepared for what had happened. It almost drove her insane, so she came to tell me what to expect."

"I saw the dead from a very early age," I told her. "You're fifteen now, so you must have been twelve when your mother came to see you. All those years, and nothing unusual had happened?"

"I heard a few whispers in the dark, and once something touched me with a cold finger, but I just put it down to my imagination. My real mam said things don't start to happen until you're at least thirteen. Perhaps it's different for a seventh son."

I nodded. That was a possibility . . . but I still needed to be sure. If Jenny's mother had died, maybe I could talk to her other daughters, to check that Jenny was telling the truth. I was finding this hard. I had nobody I could ask for advice. "So what was your mother's name, and where did she live?"

"She wouldn't tell me her name or where she lived."

I sighed in exasperation. If the girl *was* telling the truth, then discovering the whereabouts of her blood sisters would be like trying to find a needle in a haystack. The family home would now be occupied by someone else, and Jenny's older sisters would no doubt have families of their own.

Could I trust her? I wondered.

I shrugged. I was about to find out. We'd go and do the test now. If Jenny truly was a seventh daughter of a seventh daughter, she would pass the haunted-house test. While some who entered that house might just feel uneasy, thinking they were being watched or hearing a few raps, a seventh son of a seventh son would be receptive to the full ghast experience there. If she really *did* have similar powers, it would be the same for her.

"We'll head for Horshaw," I told her. "I'm going to give you the same test that my master gave me and all his other apprentices."

"I can't say I'm looking forward to it," Jenny said, "but I'll do my best. Whatever I face can't be as bad as being in the tree hanging by my feet with that beast drinking my blood and biting me."

She was certainly correct there, but in the tree she had been tied up and in no position to run. First of all, I needed to know if she could hear the ghasts. And second, if she would simply run. It was no good taking on an apprentice who fled at the first sign of danger.

10
The Haunted House

I handed Jenny my bag. "You'll be carrying this from now on," I told her. "It's one of the jobs apprentices have to do."

I was quite capable of carrying my own bag, but I was following in my master's footsteps, upholding the traditions that he'd learned from his own master, Henry Horrocks.

She smiled, but then pulled a face when she felt its weight. "What's inside this—the kitchen sink?" she asked. "When do I get my own bag and a staff?"

"Pass the test, and I'll give you a temporary staff until we get a chance to have one made for you. . . . By the way," I said mischievously, "a spook reserves the right to give his apprentice a new name. So which one would you prefer? I have three: Pixie, Buttercup, or Nettle?"

She didn't reply. Obviously she didn't appreciate my sense of humor.

So I made my expression stern. "Now come on—follow me and don't dawdle. We've quite a few miles to cover before sunset."

Jenny gave me a hard stare, and a look of annoyance flickered across her face. She was proud, and no doubt didn't like being spoken to like that. But she didn't say anything. I realized I'd told her not to dawdle—and that made me smile to myself. It was one of the expressions that John Gregory had always used.

Of course Jenny didn't see my smile. I'd set off at a furious pace, leaving her stumbling along several steps behind. That was another thing my master always used to do. Maybe he did it to set an example when he was in a hurry, but it certainly made it hard to keep up when carrying a heavy bag. I knew that only too well.

I had done these things almost without thinking, following my master's lead. But I knew that I would have to find my own way of working. I suspected that it was always hardest with the first apprentice. After that, it would become progressively easier.

Or at least I hoped so!

We reached the pit village of Horshaw just as it was getting dark. I had adjusted my pace from time to time to ensure that we arrived at dusk. I'm sure that's what John Gregory used to do with each of the apprentices he tested.

I could see a slag heap on the hill overlooking the town—that, and a big wooden wheel hooped with metal. The latter was used to control the descent of a wooden platform down a vertical shaft. This took miners down to the coal face to begin their work. When my master had brought me here, we'd passed a line of miners heading up the hill for the night shift. They'd stopped their singing on seeing a spook and his apprentice and had even crossed to the other side to avoid us.

Tonight, though, the narrow, cobbled streets were deserted, and soon we reached the bottom of the hill, turning in to a deserted lane with broken and boarded windows. It was a place I remembered well, but the last time I'd seen it, a sign hanging by a single rusty rivet proclaimed it to be Watery Lane. Now the sign was gone.

The terraced house on the corner, the nearest to an abandoned corn merchant's warehouse, was our destination. Its number, 13, was nailed to the door.

"This is the place," I told Jenny as I inserted the key into the lock.

Once inside, I lit a candle and handed it to the girl. Nothing within the small living room had changed. It was empty—there was only a pile of dirty straw on the flagged floor near the window. The curtains were yellow and tattered, the whole room full of cobwebs.

Jenny put my bag down on the floor and stared about her with wide eyes.

Suddenly a chill ran down my spine—the warning that a seventh son of a seventh son receives when something from the dark is close. Soon the ghasts would be active. Would Jenny be able to see and hear them? Would she be brave enough to face those terrible entities?

I pointed to the inner door, which was partly open. "That's the kitchen, and to the right there are stone steps leading down to the cellar."

I remembered descending those steps, struggling to be brave, readying myself for what might be waiting in the darkness of the cellar below.

"You can tell the time by the bell you'll hear chiming from the church tower," I continued. "What you have to do is simple. Go down to the cellar at midnight and face what's lurking there. Do that, Jenny, and I'll take you on as my apprentice for at least a month. This is a test of your courage when faced with the dark. Understand?"

She nodded, but she didn't look happy. She was shivering, all her earlier cockiness gone. It was chilly in the room, but was she trembling with cold or with fear? I couldn't tell, but I remembered all too well the terror I'd felt at being left alone in that house. It was only natural.

Then I recalled what else the Spook had told me. I gave Jenny the same advice now.

"Don't open the front door to anyone," I continued. "You may hear a loud knocking, but resist the temptation to answer it. That's one thing you mustn't do."

I knew what lay out there—the ghast that walked the street was even more dangerous than the two in the house. The Spook had told me about it the day after our visit here. There had been an old woman, a "rouser" paid by mine workers to wake them for their shift by rapping on their doors. But she used to creep into the houses and steal things. One day one of the householders caught her at it. She stabbed him to death and was hanged for the crime. Now, after dark, the ghast haunted the street, still trying to trick its way into the houses.

It fed on fear, but of course it couldn't actually kill you. Though if you gave in to your terror, it could drive you to the edge of insanity.

Jenny was strong-minded. I felt confident that she would survive such an encounter. I hoped she wouldn't open the door anyway.

"Whatever you do, don't let the candle go out," I continued.

My candle *had* gone out, but luckily I'd had a tinderbox in my pocket, a parting gift from Dad when I left home to become the Spook's new apprentice. Jenny wouldn't be able to light her candle again. So, in a sudden impulse of generosity, I pulled my tinderbox from my bag and held it out to her.

"Here. You can borrow this," I said. "Take care of it; it was a present from my dad and has sentimental value." Then, without another word, I went out through the front door, leaving her alone in the haunted house.

I knew what to do next. Long after my test, my master had told me what he routinely did with each apprentice: went round to the back door, slipped into the kitchen, and crept down the steps to the cellar.

So that's what I did. A couple of minutes later I was crouching down there in the dark with my back against a barrel. All I had to do was wait for Jenny. She had to come down to the cellar at midnight. Once she'd done that, I would stand up and tell her she'd passed the test. But first she would have to withstand a few very unpleasant experiences.

The house was haunted by ghasts, not ghosts, so the manifestations weren't aware of their surroundings. They were dark fragments of suffering spirits left behind when their larger selves had escaped to the light. They played over and over again the part of their lives that had resulted in trauma—as the girl would soon find out.

I waited. I hoped again that Jenny would have the sense to obey me and wouldn't open the front door to the more dangerous ghast. It had tried to trick me into doing so by using Mam's voice, plucking it from my mind and imitating it perfectly. I'd managed to resist the impulse to respond to it, but I wondered what voice the ghast would use to lure Jenny. No doubt someone from her past whom she liked and trusted. I suspected that if the girl *did* open the door, she'd be faced by something horrible—an old lady wielding a blade, with murder in her eyes.

Soon the ghasts of the main house began to make themselves known.

It started in the far corner of the cellar. I heard a rhythmic digging: the sound of heavy, damp earth being turned with a spade. There was a soft squelching as the spade lifted the soil from the cellar floor. The chill that came from being close to something from the dark intensified, and though I knew it would be far worse for the girl, I reflected that I'd be heartily glad when this was all over. I wasn't scared, but it was unpleasant.

The ghast was digging a grave, and it had a terrible story. It belonged to a miner who'd grown jealous, thinking that his wife was secretly seeing another man. One night, in a fit of rage, he killed her, striking her on the head with a big cob of coal, and had dug her grave down here in this cellar. But, even worse, she wasn't actually dead when he'd put her in the grave. He'd buried her alive. And then he'd killed himself.

So that's what I could hear now—the ghast of the miner digging his wife's early grave. If Jenny truly had the abilities she claimed, she would be able to hear it too. It was truly terrifying.

John Gregory had come up with this effective means of testing his apprentices. After all, what was the point of training someone for weeks, only to have them flee from the first really scary thing they encountered? There was no doubt: it was a hard job. You had to be tough to do it.

Suddenly the sound of digging stopped and the cellar grew quiet, a stillness that seemed to fill the whole house. Then there was a sequence of thumps. Heavy invisible boots were climbing up the cellar steps toward the kitchen. The ghast was moving away from me.

It was approaching Jenny.

A ghast feeds on fear and draws strength from it. The more scared Jenny was, the scarier the encounter would be for her.

After a while the invisible boots descended the steps again and crossed the earth floor of the cellar, passing very close to where I was sitting.

Next, the expected knocking on the front door began.

It went on for a long time, but Jenny had listened to me, and I didn't hear her respond.

When the distant chimes of the clock chimed half eleven, the ghost's digging started up once more. But to my surprise, it didn't climb the stairs this time. Jenny must have shown a brave face, which meant that the ghost had nothing to feed on and wouldn't bother her again.

There was no doubt about it: courage made spook's business much easier, and Jenny clearly possessed it in abundance. Of course, that was if she really was sensitive enough to experience the full horror of the ghosts. The next half hour passed slowly. Then at last I heard the clock chime twelve to mark midnight.

I waited expectantly for the sound of Jenny coming down the cellar steps.

But the whole house was silent.

Perhaps she had fallen asleep and hadn't heard the chimes? I thought. Her terrible experience at the hands of the Kobalos had taken a lot out of her, after all. So I was patient. I waited for the next chime to mark the half hour. Then I climbed the steps.

The front room was empty. The door was wide open.

Jenny had fled into the night.

11
A Rare and Special Type

I started searching around for her. Perhaps she hadn't gone far. . . . I walked up the hill, keeping to the main lane but checking each cobbled street to my right and left as I passed by.

Had she been lured into opening the door to the street ghast?

I didn't think so. I'd warned Jenny about that. She was sensible and would have resisted, just as I had during my test.

It seemed likely that she had simply given in to her fear and run, meaning that she had failed the test.

After about an hour, I stood on the steep grassy slope that led up to the slag heaps and mine workings and looked down at the village. Nothing was moving below. But for the wind sighing across the hill, all was silent. Everybody who wasn't down the mine working the night shift was safely tucked up in bed.

I gave up and walked through the night toward Chipenden. And as I did so, my doubts came rushing back. The truth is, I wasn't ready to take on a trainee. Although a practicing spook, with a good number of successes under my belt, I was hardly more than an apprentice myself. I reckoned I needed at least five more years before I had the knowledge and experience to train someone properly.

Not only that. She was a girl, and as far as I knew there were no precedents for a female apprentice spook. It might cause all sorts of problems. And who knew what powers a seventh daughter of a seventh daughter possessed? I had been hasty in taking her on—perhaps I'd done so to make up for almost getting her killed by the Kobalos. I knew that she could hide and make herself difficult to detect, but did she have any immunity to witchcraft? Could she really hear the dead and talk to them, as she'd claimed?

To tell the truth, my feelings were mixed. Although I had no evidence that she really *was* a seventh daughter of a seventh daughter, I had expected her to pass the test. In my mind I had gotten used to the idea of her being my apprentice. I was lonely—that came with the job, of course, but since my master died I'd been completely alone. Alice had left us and gone to the dark for good. I would have liked to have someone else living in the house again; someone to work with. I remembered something Alice had once said to me, back in the first year of my apprenticeship: "One day this house will belong to us, Tom. Don't you feel it?"

A lump came into my throat as I heard her utter those words again. Loneliness was a terrible thing, I reflected.

When Jenny first told me her name, I had been stunned, taken back to the vision of the future I'd been given by the mage . . . of the new name added to the list on my bedroom wall in the Chipenden house.

Jenny.

I shrugged in annoyance. Scrying did not always foretell the future accurately. The future could be changed with each decision we made, with every step we took or failed to take.

Jenny's steps had been in the wrong direction—away from the cellar. She had failed the test, and now her name would never be written on that wall.

Whatever the future might bring, I remembered with a curse that Jenny still had the tinderbox that Dad had given me. I wanted it back. If she didn't return it, at some point I would have to return to Grimsargh to collect it.

The next two days were quiet. Nobody rang the bell at the withy trees crossroads. So while waiting for Grimalkin to return, I spent my time on routine business. I put in some hours of practice with my chain and staff, determined to get my skills back up to their former level, and taking out my annoyance with Jenny on the tree stump.

I also started to read the Spook's notebooks again, in case I'd missed any mention of the Kobalos. There was only the short section in the Bestiary, but it comforted me to read my master's words and to hear his voice in my head.

John Gregory had written and illustrated the Bestiary himself, and now I read his final words about the loss by fire of his beloved library and the books it contained; books that were a bequest from past spooks to those yet to ply their trade.

Now I have had time to reflect, and I am filled with renewed strength and determination. My fight against the dark will continue. One day I will rebuild the library, and this book, my personal Bestiary, will be the first to be placed upon its shelves.

John Gregory of Chipenden

Before he had died in battle, my master had made good that promise. He had rebuilt the house and library. Unfortunately, as yet, there were precious few books restored to those new wooden shelves. That would be my task. During my lifetime as a spook, in addition to fighting the dark, I would endeavor to restock the Chipenden library.

It was early in the morning of the third day after Jenny had fled that Grimalkin arrived. I heard her call through the trees and went to the edge of the garden to escort her to the house and tell the boggart that she was here with my permission.

She'd arrived on horseback, and after taking a large envelope from her saddlebag, she left the animal grazing in the western garden. She greeted me curtly, and we walked toward the house in silence.

The witch assassin looked much as she had when I first met her. As usual, leather straps crisscrossed her body, holding a large number of blades. There were a few blood-stains on her clothes, but I doubted very much that they were her own.

"Is the leg giving you any problems?" I asked her.

Her left leg had been badly broken when she was attacked by the servants of the Fiend. It had been fixed with a silver pin that, although it restored that limb to its previous strength, gave her continual pain.

"Why do you ask?"

"The horse," I said. "At one time you used to walk or run everywhere."

She shook her head. "The leg gives me pain but functions as well as it ever did. I need the horse because recently it has been necessary to cover long distances faster than is possible on foot."

I nodded, wondering where her latest journeys had taken her, but she didn't elaborate. What she did as a witch assassin was her business.

I led her into the kitchen. "Are you hungry?" I asked.

"Water will suffice for now."

I poured her a large cup of water and she drank it down quickly.

"Did you bury the creature?" she asked.

"No, because I thought you'd want to see it. I left it inside its lair."

"It will be stinking by now—but yes, you were right not to do so. I want to examine it. Is it far from here?"

"About forty-five minutes by foot."

"Then let's waste no further time. How did you kill it?"

"With the sword you gave me. The beast had powerful dark magic. It shrank in size and slipped out of my silver chain. I was helpless against it. It paralyzed me for a while, but I managed to escape and ran back to get the sword."

"You dug it up out of John Gregory's grave?"

I bowed my head. "I had no choice. The creature held a

girl captive. It was drinking her blood and would eventually have killed her."

"You needed the sword just to survive, then. . . . It sounds as though you were dealing with a very rare type of Kobalos. You were a fool to bury the sword in the first place," Grimalkin said bluntly. "I expected better of you."

I did not reply. I knew that she was right.

"If it is who I think it is," she continued, "you were lucky to prevail, even using the sword."

"You know the creature?"

"Perhaps. I will find out soon enough. Here." She placed the envelope on the table. "This is a copy of a document that your master once had in his possession. It is a glossary of information about the Kobalos, collated by an ancient spook called Nicholas Browne. I suggest you study it closely."

I knew the name. Browne was mentioned by John Gregory in an annotation marked in his Bestiary; Nicholas was his source of information on the Kobalos.

"Where did you find this document?" I asked.

"I came across it when searching for information in the northern lands that border the Kobalos territories. They make a study of their ancient enemy and keep their own archives. This is the most succinct and useful description of the Kobalos and their practices that I have ever encountered. It is a good place to start; we can add to it as we learn more."

I noted that she had said "we" rather than "I." It seemed that she took for granted that I would be joining her in her enterprise.

I picked up the envelope, but Grimalkin shook her head. "There will be time enough to study that later. Let us go and see this creature's lair."

I didn't bother to take my staff. With Grimalkin by my side, I knew I wouldn't need it. Instead I collected a spade from the lean-to and carried it resting against my shoulder.

As we walked, I told her in more detail what had happened: how three County girls had died, how Jenny had told me of the beast's whereabouts. Then how, after we had been taken prisoner, I'd run back to get the sword and returned in time to save her. But I didn't mention taking Jenny on as my apprentice or that she'd fled from the haunted house at Horshaw. It wasn't relevant to the business at hand.

At last we reached the huge oak tree. We heard the flies before we saw them. And there were even more inside the trunk—big buzzing bluebottles, most of them crawling upon the dead body of the beast; the face was already writhing with maggots. The stench was so appalling we had to cover our noses with our hands.

Grimalkin muttered something under her breath, and

the buzzing ceased. I heard the *ping* of flies falling to the floor, slain by her magic. Then she brushed the dead flies and maggots off the creature's face and stared at it for a long time.

"What do you think I should do if I encounter another of these creatures?" I said, interrupting the silence. "If I captured one alive, could it be contained within a pit like a witch?"

"It would be safe enough if you cut out its tongue and stitched its lips together for good measure," said the witch assassin, "but my advice to you is never to take such a chance. Kill it at the first opportunity. These creatures have powerful magic—some, such as shifting size, are innate and do not even require a dark spell. They can breathe into your face and render you unconscious or take away your will."

"As I know, to my cost," I said ruefully.

"This is a rare and special type of Kobalos mage—a haizda," Grimalkin continued. "I met one when I traveled north. I suspect this creature is only young, hardly past its novitiate, the early stage of its training. But never underestimate them. They are very dangerous. The one I met called itself Slither and was a formidable warrior. You would not have slain it so easily. In fact, I doubt you would have survived such an encounter."

I felt a flicker of annoyance at that.

With one hand, Grimalkin seized the dead Kobalos mage by the left foot, her other holding its head by the hair; she dragged it out of its lair and into the open, and I followed behind.

"This is as good a place as any," she decided, letting go of the beast about eighty feet away from the tree, clear of most of the roots.

"You dig the grave and I'll start my search," she said. "Drag the beast into the pit, but don't cover it with soil yet."

"Are you looking for anything special?"

"I'm seeking to learn all I can about our enemies."

12
Nicholas Browne's Glossary

WHEN I'd dug the grave and dragged the mage into it, I leaned my spade against the tree trunk and went inside. Grimalkin had pried the lid from one of the jars and was sniffing the contents. It contained a light green slime flecked with small gray particles.

"Find anything interesting?" I asked.

"There is much here that is outside my knowledge. For example, I suspect that this green gel is some kind of preservative. Within it are small pieces of living tissue, but from a creature I have never encountered. What its purpose is, I have no idea. . . . I'd planned to travel north again tomorrow, but this is a treasure trove. I will stay here until I have learned all I can—days, or even weeks, if necessary."

I nodded. "After I've filled in the grave, I'll get back to the house and leave you to it. If you ever want to eat a meal at my table, you're more than welcome. In any case, please call in before you go. I'd like to know something of what you learn."

"Leave the grave to me," answered Grimalkin. "I want a closer look at the body before it's buried. As for what I discover, I will tell you all you need to know. You may be reluctant to combine forces to meet an anticipated Kobalos attack, but by presenting this to me you have advanced our cause significantly."

"Who are your allies?" I asked.

"Witches from Pendle will eventually join with me to face the threat that I have scryed. The people far to the north across the sea have faced the Kobalos in battle before; they will be our allies. We have now reached a crisis. The birth of the Kobalos god, Talkus, has already taken place, increasing the power of their mages threefold and triggering war. Soon they will burst out of their city, Valkarky, and make war on all humans, starting with those who border the Kobalos lands."

"Do you think this mage was a spy?" I asked, nodding down at the body.

"It is more than likely," Grimalkin said. "The haizda mages usually live alone, far from other Kobalos, but I wouldn't have expected to find one this far south."

With that, we parted company, and I headed back

toward Chipenden. But one of Grimalkin's remarks had been interesting, to say the least.

"All you need to know . . ."

It implied that she might well withhold other information. Why? Because it was knowledge of dark magic that she would use to add to her own strength? We had been close allies once, but by failing to join her quest to destroy the Kobalos last year, I had created a gulf between us. I had to remind myself that, after all, she was a witch; in spite of our past, we were not natural allies.

I had another disquieting thought. Grimalkin had visited the Kobalos city, Valkarky, and knew a good deal about the enemy. . . . Had I perhaps withdrawn from the coming confrontation a little too easily? I was the Chipenden Spook, after all.

Would my master have left it all to Grimalkin? I wondered.

Back at the house, I pulled the document written by Nicholas Browne out of the envelope. It was a glossary of Kobalos words that revealed much about their magic and culture.

I skimmed through it with interest. My master had once read a copy of this, but he had dismissed it, thinking it was unlikely to be accurate. He had made a brief reference to it in his Bestiary.

I decided to make another copy. It wasn't a particularly

lengthy document—it would only take a couple of hours. I could then keep one in the library and use the new one for study.

I left spaces in my new version to enable me to insert extra entries as we learned more about the Kobalos, and to add comments to Browne's entries in case they needed augmenting or refuting.

Once that was done, I read it carefully from beginning to end. I then went straight back to the entry on mages.

Mages: There are many types of human mage; the same is also true of the Kobalos. But for an outsider, they are difficult to describe and categorize. However, the highest rank is nominally that of a high mage. There is also one type, the haizda mage, that does not fit within that hierarchy, for these are outsiders who dwell in their own individual territories far from Valkarky. Their powers are hard to quantify.

It was obvious that Browne had known little about haizda mages. I could only hope that Grimalkin increased our knowledge in case I ever encountered another. It certainly wouldn't do to face one without the Starblade. And it was scary to think that there were many other types with magical power. The Kobalos were beginning to sound more and more dangerous.

I read the entry on boska, too:

Boska: This is the breath of a Kobalos haizda mage, which can be used to induce sudden unconsciousness, paralysis, or terror in a human victim. The mage varies the effects of boska by adjusting the chemical composition of his breath. It is also sometimes used to change the mood of animals.

I decided to begin my updates here, adding my own observations and possible countermeasures.

Note: This was used on me; it leached the strength from my body. But I was taken by surprise. It is wise to be on our guard against such a threat and not allow a haizda mage to get close. Perhaps a scarf worn across the mouth and nose would provide an effective defense. Or perhaps plugs of wax fitted into the nostrils.—Tom Ward

The following day I tried to settle back into my routine, but I soon became restless. Apart from the three hauntings that I'd investigated, each a direct result of the incursion by the haizda mage, things had been quiet for months.

The Battle of the Wardstone had resulted in the destruction of the Fiend, and the dark had now become unusually quiet in the County. But the god Talkus had been born, and the Kobalos would eventually wage a war to exterminate us.

That was what had obsessed Grimalkin. I doubted that she had been performing the routine work that was demanded of the Malkin witch assassin: dealing with the enemies of her clan. She was traveling and gathering information about our future Kobalos enemies. And now she could study this dead mage's lair. It was good to have made a useful contribution—though I still wondered if I should have insisted on staying involved.

I was the Chipenden Spook, but I now had no clear task ahead of me. I was at a loose end, so I decided to visit Grimsargh and reclaim my tinderbox from the girl. It was a precious link between me and Dad, something that kept him in my mind. It had helped me out of difficult situations more than once.

I had been hoping for a bit more sun and warmth before the winter set in. The air was still cold for the time of year, but it was dry, so I set off southeast toward Grimsargh, striding out at a good pace.

As I approached the Calders' cottage, Jenny opened the door, stepped outside, and closed it behind her. It was almost as if she knew I was coming. Had she been watching from behind the curtains? I wondered.

She met me about twenty paces from the door; she was

carrying my tinderbox and held it out toward me.

"No doubt you've come for this," she said sheepishly, avoiding my eyes.

"Of course I have," I said brusquely. "It's of great sentimental value. It belonged to my dad—it was the last thing he gave me before he died. . . . There's one thing I want to ask you," I went on, putting the tinderbox carefully into my bag. "Why did you run from the haunted house?"

"Does it matter?" she asked me, her voice bitter.

"Yes, it does. You were brave when dealing with the beast in the tree. I thought you'd have been brave when facing ghasts."

"In the tree I was the creature's prisoner. I had no choice in the matter."

"No! I mean before that. You risked following it. You found out where its lair was."

Jenny shrugged. "I didn't know how dangerous it was at the time."

"No? You knew that it had killed three girls. You could have been next, but you persisted despite the danger."

"I *was* scared—absolutely terrified at times. . . . I knew that it was a killer, and I suspected that it was very powerful. But I forced myself to do it because I knew that I could use the knowledge to persuade you to let me become your apprentice."

"And yet when you finally got that chance, you fled from the haunted house? Were you that scared that you'd give up your dream? I remember my own experience in that house when I was an apprentice. I was terrified too, but there was no way I would have run. That would have meant letting down my mam, who had faith in me and wanted me to learn from John Gregory. I faced my fear and stuck it out. You could have done the same. Did you run when the ghast came up the stairs from the cellar?"

Jenny nodded, and a single tear trickled down her cheek.

"Why didn't you face your fear?" I demanded harshly.

She turned away, but she wasn't fast enough. I'd already seen the tears streaming down her face.

"Why did you run? There must have been some other reason. Come on, Jenny, tell me." Suddenly I felt sorry for the girl. She'd dreamed of becoming a spook, and I knew that it had hurt her to fall at the first hurdle.

"I was scared," she said, without turning round, "but it wasn't the fear that made me run. It was the anguish of the miner and his wife. I knew exactly how they felt. I knew what it was like to be them and experience what they went through. He was jealous beyond all reason and murdered his wife, but then instantly regretted it. He was in torment as he buried her because he'd loved her so much; now he'd lost her forever. And she was lying there paralyzed, waiting to be buried, but she was still alive, aware of everything that was happening to her. She was in terror of being buried alive. And the terrible thing was that she loved him with all her heart. She loved him every bit as much as he loved her. And she hadn't been unfaithful. I lived through every moment of her terror, every moment of his fear and anguish. And yes, she went alive into that grave and had to watch as her own husband threw earth over her until it grew dark and she couldn't breathe. . . .

"You see, that's one of my gifts as a seventh daughter of a seventh daughter. I have a strong empathy with others. I can't read their minds, but sometimes I can sense their emotions so strongly that they become my own. So that's why I ran. I couldn't stand being so close to the miner and his wife any longer. When he came up the stairs, I just had to get away."

She seemed to speak from the heart, and my instincts told me that she wasn't lying. I was impressed. Empathy could be very useful for a spook's apprentice. She had been able to attune her mind to the anguish of ghasts, something I certainly couldn't do.

"Right," I told her. "Turn round!"

She turned to face me, her eyes swollen, her face wet with tears.

I held out my bag to her. "Carry this!" I said. "It's one

of the advantages of being a spook that you don't have to carry your own bag. That's what an apprentice is for."

"You're giving me another chance?" she asked, her eyes widening in astonishment.

"Yes, one more chance!" I told her. "The very last."

However, I still needed to find out how strong she really was.

The Spook had used his haunted house test on all of his apprentices.

I'd just thought up one of my own.

13
Tom Ward's Test

JENNY had been aware of the ghasts in Watery Lane, but it was supposedly her feelings of empathy with them that had caused her to flee. Could she get *really* close to one and stand her ground? If not, there was no way I could take her on as my apprentice. To deal with the dead, you had to be able to do exactly that. It was a necessary part of the job.

Many years ago, there'd been a bitter civil war, and the victorious army had hanged some soldiers in a place that became known as Hangman's Hill. It was on the northern boundary of Dad's farm, the place where I'd been brought up.

When the ghasts of the dead soldiers were particularly active, I'd been able to hear them twisting and groaning on the ends of their ropes. It had even kept some of my older brothers awake and made them uneasy—though my eldest brother, Jack, had slept through it all like a log!

Jack was one of the least sensitive people I'd ever encountered, but even he wouldn't go into the north pasture when the ghasts were at their most active. So you see, everybody has *some* sensitivity to the dark.

The fact that Jenny had been so aware of the ghasts in the haunted house didn't mean that she had what was necessary to become my apprentice. She had to demonstrate courage too. For all I knew, all that talk about empathy was just an excuse, and she'd fled in fear. I had to be sure.

My test would be to take her to confront these ghasts on Hangman's Hill.

We approached it from the north, heading up into the gloom beneath the trees. It got colder as we climbed—that special kind of cold that sometimes warns a seventh son of a seventh son that something from the dark is close by.

I wondered if Jenny could sense it too.

"How do you feel?" I asked.

"A bit chilly," she replied.

I made no further comment.

I heard the branches creaking and groaning before I saw them. The dead soldiers were in among the trees just below the summit, hanging from the branches, still in their uniforms and boots. Some dangled, inert, with bulging eyes and twisted necks; others danced and kicked or spun; all had their hands bound behind their backs. They were young too, mostly about my age. It was a pitiful sight.

As we drew closer, even nature seemed to change. The leaves vanished from the trees—the branches were stark and bare. I was seeing something from the past.

On the morning I'd begun my apprenticeship all those years ago, my master and I had left Dad's farm and come straight up this hill. We could have taken a different route, but the Spook had brought me this way deliberately. He wanted our first confrontation with the dark to be close to home, close to something that had scared me as I'd grown up.

He'd taken me up to one of the dead soldiers. Now, suddenly, I heard my master's voice inside my head, as clear as if he was standing next to me. I remembered his advice.

"There's nothing to be afraid of. Nothing that can hurt you. Think about what it must have been like for him. Concentrate on him rather than yourself. How must he have felt? What would be the worst thing?"

And it had worked. I'd become sad rather than afraid. Soon the ghosts had faded away.

I came to a halt. "What can you see?" I asked Jenny.

"Dead soldiers hanging from the trees." Her voice was hardly more than a whisper. "They're just young boys. It's not right. They were too young to fight in a war."

"Are you afraid?" I asked.

"Yes, it's scary. But I'm more sad than afraid. They didn't deserve to die like this."

"Do you see that one?" I pointed to a boy who couldn't have been more than fifteen. His mouth was opening and closing as he struggled for air, and his eyes bulged in his head. "Let's go and stand in front of him. I want you to walk right up to him—so close that if you reached out, you could touch his shoulder."

Jenny nodded. I could tell that she had to force herself to take each step. We walked forward, side by side, until we were as close as I'd instructed.

"His name is George, and he's only fourteen," Jenny said suddenly. "He lied about his age so that he could join the army. Now he's terrified and in awful pain. But there's something wrong with his mind. It's as if he isn't all there. Maybe the terror of being hanged has done that to him. . . . Send him to the light, please! Don't let this go on any longer."

I was stunned. My master had simply asked me to *imagine* what it was like to be in a dead soldier's place. That way I identified with his plight and overcame my fear. Jenny seemed to *know* what it was like, as if she could read his mind in some way. It was something that was beyond me.

"He's not a ghost, Jenny, he's a ghast," I explained gently. "The largest part of him has already gone to the light. This is just the fragment that's broken away from his spirit and stayed behind to haunt this hill with the others. That's what ghasts are—the parts of a spirit that suffered terrible pain or committed acts they couldn't bear to remember, like the miner who killed his wife. They couldn't go to the light with that part of them, so it broke away and became a ghast. Do you understand?"

She nodded, and the ghasts began to fade away. Within moments, the leaves were back on the trees. Jenny had faced up to the ghasts bravely. She hadn't run.

I smiled at her.

"Have I passed the test, then?" she asked.

"Yes, you passed, without a shadow of a doubt. As far as I know, John Gregory never kept anybody on after they'd failed the test in the haunted house. But I have the right to do it my way. For him, it was just a routine procedure to see how brave a lad was. But I believe that you *are* telling the truth, that you didn't run because of fear. So I'll keep you on—at least for a little while. The worst that can happen is that I'm wrong and you'll run away again."

"I won't. But next time, if I feel the same about something and it's getting too much to bear, I'll warn you."

I nodded and smiled.

"So I'm your apprentice now? It's official?" Jenny asked. "Even though I'm a girl?"

"It's official. As far as I know, you're the first girl ever to become a spook's apprentice. That makes you special," I added.

The image of my dead master came into my mind. I could imagine him shaking his head in disapproval. I felt sure that he would never have taken on a girl apprentice.

"My mam and dad, they'll never pay you," Jenny said.

I shrugged.

"Don't you mind?"

The truth was, I wasn't sure whether I minded or not. Being a spook was never going to make me rich. Getting money out of some people was harder than getting blood from a stone. But it was a steady job and you didn't go hungry, so it didn't really matter that much whether Jenny's foster parents paid up or not.

But the trouble was, I kept comparing myself with my master. John Gregory would never have stood for that. I felt somehow lessened by letting the Calders get away with it. It made me feel weak, as if I was a soft touch. For now I shrugged away the worry; there were more important things to be concerned about.

"I don't mind," I told her. "Money isn't everything. All that matters is that you try to be a good spook. I'd like you to meet some of my family now. They live in the farm just the other side of this hill."

"I'll bet your mam and dad are nicer than mine," Jenny said.

"They're both dead now. My eldest brother runs the farm. He has a wife, Ellie, and a little girl called Mary, and a baby son too. Another of my brothers lives there as well. He's called James, and he's the local blacksmith. He has his forge on the farm."

"What knocked down all those?" Jenny asked, pointing to the huge swathe of felled trees as we began the descent. "Was it a storm?"

"It was far worse than a storm," I told her. "One day I'll tell you all about it. It'll be part of your training."

The trees had been knocked down by the Fiend; he'd chased after me, and I'd taken refuge in the farmhouse. There were lots of things to tell Jenny, but most of them could wait for another time.

My own apprenticeship had been cut short. I hoped that she would get her full seven years. And I hoped that I would be good enough to train her.

Mam's rosebush was still growing up the farmhouse wall, but instead of the usual brilliant display of County red, the blooms and buds were blackened by the early frost. Usually it didn't strike until October.

Ellie came to the door, drying her hands on her apron.

Her face lit up, and she gave me a hug. "Oh, Tom, it's good to see you!"

"It's good to see you too, Ellie. This is Jenny," I said, by way of introduction. "She's my first apprentice."

I saw Ellie's eyes widen in surprise at that, but she smiled warmly and gave Jenny a hug too.

Little Mary came running up to me. "Uncle Tom! Uncle Tom!" she cried. "Have you come to kill another bog?"

"Not this time, Mary," I laughed. By a "bog," the child meant a boggart. On my last visit, she had been very interested in the local boggart I'd dealt with; it had been a dangerous stone-chucker.

"Come in and see the baby," Ellie said, beckoning us inside. So we went into the farmhouse kitchen and then up the stairs.

"This is Matthew," Ellie said, lifting the baby out of its bed. "It's made Jack so happy to have a son."

I knew that my brother would love both his children equally, but for a farmer it was something special to have a son who could help with the tough physical work, which only became harder as you grew older. The first son inherited the farm, too. The others were found trades. My dad would have found it difficult to find someone to take on his seventh son, but Mam had intervened. It had been her idea all along for me to become a spook's apprentice.

"Would you like to hold him, Tom?" Ellie could see the reluctance on my face; she shook her head and sighed. "He won't break, Tom. Babies aren't that delicate!"

She was right. I was nervous about holding babies because they were so small and their heads were floppy. Of course, little Matthew was a few months old now, so he was much stronger than Mary had been when I first saw her—she'd been only six days old. So I held the child for a few moments, and Matthew stared up at me with his wide-open blue eyes and made little gurgling sounds.

"Could *I* hold him, please?" Jenny asked.

"Of course you can, love." Ellie took the baby from me and handed him over.

"Where's Jack?" I asked.

"It's Friday morning. He's gone to the market at Topley with James," she replied.

Of course. Friday was market day. I'd been away from the farm for so long that I'd forgotten its routines. The Friday visit to the local market, straight after morning milking, had been part of my life. Still, they'd be back before noon, and I was looking forward to seeing them.

We gathered around the big wooden table for the mid-day meal. Jack was at its head, Ellie on his left. Mary was seated on a high stool next to her mother. I was opposite

Jenny, while James, my brawny blacksmith brother, sat at the foot of the table, head down, tucking into a massive plate of hotpot.

"What puzzles me," said Jack, resting his knife and fork on his plate to give Jenny a stare from beneath his bushy eyebrows, "is why a young girl like you would want to do such a dangerous and terrifying job. Wouldn't it be better to find a kind man and raise a family together?"

"Oh, Jack!" cried Ellie. "Leave Jenny alone! A woman can do most jobs that a man does. She's even better at certain tasks! What you've got to remember is that Tom's job often involves helping people and making it possible for them to live their lives without fear—something to which a woman's well suited."

"*I* want to be a spook!" Mary cried out. "Want to talk to a bog!"

We all laughed, and I smiled at Ellie. More than once my job had brought danger into their lives. It had scared Ellie, and I knew that she preferred it if I wasn't around the farm after dark. But it was nice to hear her talk about my job like that. It made me feel that she appreciated what I did.

"Why don't we let the girl speak for herself?" Jack wiped up the last of his gravy with a big slice of bread.

"A woman has to make her way in the world as well as

a man. There aren't that many jobs she can do to keep the wolf from the door," Jenny said, meeting Jack's eyes. "Like Tom, I have special abilities that make me fit for this line of work. Of course, one day I would like to have children, but having a family doesn't stop you from working. Your mother was a healer and a midwife, perhaps the best in the County. She raised seven sons and yet found time for other work. I hope to do something similar."

Once again, I was stunned by all that Jenny knew. She must have asked around to find out about Mam. Or maybe Mam had visited her village . . . she'd been well known and respected throughout the County.

The table became quiet at that. What Jenny had said was quite true, but it made us think of Mam and her absence from the family table. She was sorely missed.

"Is this just a family visit, Tom?" James said, breaking the silence. "Or have you got spook's business in the area?"

"No, things are fairly quiet at the moment. I was just passing nearby and took the opportunity to visit you, that's all. But have you heard about any problems around here? Has anyone gone missing . . . ?" I didn't want to alarm my family, but I was worried that other Kobalos mages might be loose in the County; I had to ask.

"There's been nothing untoward in these parts," Jack said, frowning at me. I knew he would probably be annoyed at me saying that in front of Ellie. He didn't want her scared.

"Nobody's said anything to me," James agreed. "They travel to my forge from miles around and always give me the latest gossip while I work. The thing that seems to be bothering everybody is nothing to do with the dark. It's the weather. We've never known it so cold at this time of year, especially at night. It looks like winter's on its way early, and my fear is that it'll be a bad one. But of course that's just Mother Nature—it doesn't concern you in your line of work."

I smiled at James and nodded, but his words filled me with foreboding. Until now I hadn't given much thought to the unseasonably cold weather, but I suddenly remembered that the Kobalos came from a land of ice and snow far to the north. They thrived in cold conditions. Their god, Talkus, had been born and would now be growing in power, strengthening their mages. Could their magic even be changing the climate? I wondered.

We set off back to Chipenden in the afternoon. Ellie said good-bye to us at the gate.

"Lovely to see you again, Tom—and wonderful to meet you, Jenny!" she exclaimed. "I wish you all the best in your new job. Taking you on as his apprentice is one of the wisest decisions Tom's ever made!"

Jenny grinned so widely I thought that her face was going to split in half.

With that, I headed off up the hill again. Jenny followed at my heels, carrying my bag.

On the way home, I thought through all I would now need to do. I must begin Jenny's training in earnest. I needed to supply her with a temporary staff and a note-book. She could have my old spook's bag—I had started using John Gregory's, as it had a certain sentimental value and, being of good-quality leather, had many years of use left in it. She would also need a cloak; I would order one for her from the village tailor.

I realized that with Jenny to do some of the chores, such as collecting groceries, I was likely to have more free time. Perhaps I should write something to add to the library—a book that would advance our knowledge; part of my legacy to future spooks. . . .

It was something to think about.

Jenny Calder

14
Mother and Daughter

WHAT I have dreamed of for more than a year has finally happened.

At last I am a spook's apprentice!

My master has given me a notebook, in which I write up the theory that he teaches me, and also the practical work that we do in dealing with the dark.

But he has also given me another little book, in which to tell the story of my development during my training and the dangers we encounter. He did the same while being trained by John Gregory. So much is lost from our memories as the years pass, and he says that it helps to record such events and review them later. We learn from the past, and so avoid repeating our mistakes.

So here is my first account. It will tell the story of how I came to become involved in what Tom Ward calls "spook's business."

I chose my future job after the day that changed my life forever—the day I met my true mother.

I'll never forget that afternoon. I was hurrying away from the market with my groceries when an old woman approached me. She wore a shawl over her head even though the day was sunny and warm, and walked with slow, shuffling steps.

"Good day to you, daughter," she wheezed, looking up into my eyes. "Would you be willing to listen to me for a while?"

I smiled at her, wondering how best to get away without offending her. I was in a rush to get back and make the evening meal. I'd stayed at the market too long, and my father got very angry when his tea was late. Although it was more than a year since he'd last taken his belt to me, I was still scared of him. The previous week he'd trembled with rage when I simply dropped a spoon, clenching his fists so that the veins on his arms bulged in purple knots.

"You're not too old to feel my belt, girl!" he'd roared.

I had decided that if he hit me again, I'd leave home. But to think it was easier than to do it. Where could I run to? I'd no relatives to offer me shelter. How could I pay my own way in the world?

"I'm afraid I have to get home," I said to the woman apologetically. "Perhaps we could talk next market day?"

"I may not be here next market day, daughter," she said, a little breathlessly. "I think it best that we speak now. This may be our only chance."

It was then that our eyes met for the first time and I noted with a shock that her eyes were like mine—the left one blue; the right one brown. I wondered if people sometimes stared at her as they did me and made cruel remarks or whispered behind their hands. Most folk didn't like it if you were a little different.

The woman's face was lined and yellow, and suddenly I saw that she was not old at all. She was just very ill.

"Shall we go and sit over there in the shade?" She pointed to a bench against the church wall in the shade of an old elm tree.

Despite my fear of the consequences of getting home late, I nodded and followed her. There was something strange and compelling about this woman, I thought. I just knew that it was the right thing to do.

We sat together on the bench and turned to face each other. Our eyes locked again, and I shivered. Suddenly, in the shade of the tree, I felt cold.

"Twice I have named you 'daughter,'" said the woman. "It was not merely a manner of address that might be used in friendliness from an older woman to a younger one. You are indeed my daughter. I am truly your mother. You are the flesh of my flesh. My blood runs through your arteries and veins."

I stared at her and saw the truth in her eyes, and anger flared within me. "*You* are my mother!" I hissed. "*You* are the mother who abandoned me, who left a defenseless baby exposed to the elements!"

The woman nodded, and two tears trickled down her cheeks. "I had no choice, child. Your father was dead, and I already had six daughters whom I could barely feed. I knew of the couple who adopted you. They wanted another child, so I placed you where they would find you. I knew they would put a roof over your head and fill your belly. I loved you, child. I loved you with all my heart, and it tore me apart to leave you like that. But it had to be done, for all our sakes."

I could understand why she'd done it, but it still hurt. Of course, she couldn't have known that the man she chose to be my foster father would turn out to be violent.

She buried her face in her hands; her whole body was trembling with emotion.

There were tears running down my own cheeks. "So why seek me out now? Why, after all these years?"

"Because I am dying, child." She looked straight at me again. "Something is eating me from within. It is a disease that twists my stomach and withers my skin. Within weeks

I will be dead. So, while I can still walk, I have come to tell you what you are."

"What do you mean?" I cried, frightened by her words. Was she really my mother, or some madwoman?

"The blood of the Samhadre runs through the veins of our family. In most it is weak or nonexistent, but in a seventh daughter of a seventh daughter it first flares up around the time of her thirteenth birthday. I am such a daughter—and so, my daughter, are you. Your foster mother named you Jennifer, but that is not the name I gave you, which you must not reveal to anyone."

"Who are the Samhadre, and what name did you give me?" I demanded. I'd never heard of such a people.

"They are the Old Ones, daughter—those beings who walked the earth while humans were no better than dumb animals who sat in their own excrement. The Old Ones were powerful, wise, swift, and compassionate, but deadly. You will inherit some small part of what they were. Soon gifts will come to you. I want you to prepare your mind to receive them. Nobody told me what to expect; I thought I was going mad. I want you to accept that the gifts are real. That is the first step that will enable you to survive."

This seemed to me like an old wives' tale, something told before a winter fire to wide-eyed children while the shadows of the night deepened. But I was certainly intrigued; I couldn't tear my gaze away from the face of the woman who claimed me as her daughter.

"There are many possible gifts, but it is different with a seventh daughter of a seventh daughter," she continued. "One is empathy—the ability to feel what others feel, to share both their sorrow and their joy, and thus to respond and counsel them if necessary. That is one of the basic talents, but sometimes it can be more than that. . . ."

I'd certainly never experienced anything like this—but I was still only twelve. Could such a big change suddenly take place in me when I turned thirteen? "You told me that these gifts came to you as a surprise and made you believe you were going insane," I said to her. "Why didn't your own mother explain what would happen?"

"She was just a seventh daughter, and had neither the power nor the knowledge. She didn't know what was wrong with me. Finally, after years of torment, another found me—using one of her gifts, she sensed my anguish—and told me what I was."

"What name did you give me?" I asked.

The woman—my mother—leaned forward and whispered my true name into my left ear but warned again that I must never reveal it to others: some who served the dark could gain power over a seventh daughter of a seventh daughter by knowing her true name.

So I will keep it to myself. Tom Ward told me that my notebooks should eventually go into the library. They are a legacy of experience and knowledge that we leave to future spooks. I'll not write anything down here that I am not prepared for others to read.

We talked for almost an hour that day, my mother and I, and she told me of the other possible gifts that I might inherit. After this, we agreed that, if she was well enough, we would meet at the market the following week.

As we parted, we embraced, tears trickling down our cheeks.

Then I ran home with my basket—but I ran in vain.

My false father took off his belt and, for the first time in more than a year, thrashed me.

The pain was excruciating, but I did not allow myself to cry. I think that angered him even more.

15
A Girl Like You

My mother did not come to the market the following week.

I never saw her again.

No doubt her illness had become worse, preventing her from returning. I imagined her slowly dying but still able to speak. I was desperate to talk to her and find out more about what I would become. I knew now that she was indeed my true mother, and all my bitterness at having been abandoned melted away. I understood why she had acted as she did. I needed to see her just one more time before we were parted forever.

That was the beginning of my wanderings. I searched for her in the surrounding villages, starting with the Long Ridge. After that I tried the towns, and ventured as far south as Priestown and as far north as Caster. Sometimes I was away for days; each time I returned to receive a fresh beating.

Gradually I was forced to accept that I would never see my mother again, but still I wandered. Even in winter, it was better to be abroad in the cold than home in that hateful cottage with a violent foster father and a foster mother who was terrified of her husband.

I didn't fully understand why he was doing it. As I spent more time away, he reacted ever more fiercely, trying to beat me into submission. Did he beat me because he felt I was disobedient and beyond his control? I wondered. If so, the beatings just made me worse. He didn't know what he was doing; he was like a dumb animal, acting without thinking. It frightened me but didn't change the way I behaved. And still I would not cry.

Then, on the eve of my thirteenth birthday, everything changed. I woke up suddenly in the middle of the night and saw my first ghost. It was the night of the full moon, and a bright shaft of yellow light illuminated the foot of my bed. There was a fat old lady sitting across my legs, squashing me. She was so heavy that I felt as if the bed might collapse at any moment. She looked at me, opened her mouth, and gave a cackle. She had no teeth, just slobbery gums, and she was blind in one eye—it was all milky white.

As I screamed in shock and fear, the weight left my legs. The ghost floated upward and disappeared through the ceiling, drool dibbling from her open mouth.

My frantic scream woke up my father, and I received another beating.

That was the last time he ever hit me.

Before the week was out, another gift had emerged— the first one my true mother had spoken of: that of empathy. I will never forget the moment when it came to me.

I'd been walking through the center of the village when I saw a youth slouched on a bench opposite the greengrocer's. He was staring at the shop doorway. His face was blank and expressionless, but I had to stop, suddenly deeply aware of the sadness that filled him. He was fighting to hold back tears.

What radiated from him was overpowering; it brought a lump to my throat and tears to my own eyes. It was much more than just a feeling: I knew what he was *thinking*. He was remembering how, as a young child, he'd once sat on that very bench waiting for his mother to come out of that shop. She'd come out and smiled at him, put down her shopping bag, and opened her arms wide. He'd run straight into them.

But now he was almost fully grown; his mother had died the previous winter. He was concentrating hard, trying to see that moment of happiness again, seeking to re-create the past.

I could almost read his thoughts—and it was painful to share them, so I moved on quickly.

This gift wasn't something I'd be telling other people about. Nobody would like the idea of someone probing inside their head.

Once the new gift was known to me, I could read my father's moods—and my mother's, too. As newlyweds they had been happy; had remained happy while raising their own children. But when my two sisters had married and gone off to have families of their own, there'd been nothing left between them: no love, just boredom and emptiness. Finding and adopting me had made them feel better for a while, but it hadn't lasted.

Now at last I knew why my father beat me. I felt his pain. He'd been beaten by his own father and was scarred by that experience, and angry because he himself had never become a man of any consequence. He had dreamed of owning some land, but he worked for farmers who paid him a pittance. He felt bitter knowing that he would never be able to realize that dream.

He felt sorry for himself. He was a selfish pig, wallowing in self-pity, and he hurt others to lessen his own pain. But I saw too that he was a coward at heart. He would never strike a man. I was his easiest victim—along with my adoptive mother, whom he also slapped occasionally.

Sometimes I heard raised voices from their bedroom, and in the morning she'd sob while making the breakfast, head bowed to hide her bruises.

Then I discovered my third gift.

I suppose I'd had it quite a while before I became aware of it. I had noticed for years that, on the way to market, when I smiled at people who seemed down in the dumps, they would cheer up. Hours later, on my way home, they still looked far brighter.

After meeting my real mother, I began to wonder. Could it be that I was having some effect on them?

Then I got proof that it was indeed so. At the market there was a stallholder who always looked so sad that I longed to cheer him up—especially as I knew exactly what was wrong with him.

His wife had died suddenly the previous year, and his children had all left home; he had nothing to brighten his life or give him hope. He'd once been a keen gardener, growing both produce and flowers to please his wife. On warm summer evenings, they used to sit in the garden together and watch the sun go down. It had been one of their greatest pleasures.

So I planted a seed of happiness in his mind.

Within days, he was planting his own seeds. By late summer his garden was in bloom, and in the autumn he was selling his own produce at market. He was smiling at everybody.

What I'd achieved with the stallholder had given me an idea. Instead of continuing to meet anger with anger, I would strive to help my false father. I would try to make him feel better inside. Then his attitude toward me might change . . . at least he might leave me alone.

Some weeks later, at dusk, I found him leaning on the wall at the foot of the garden. "It's a nice evening, Dad," I said pleasantly.

"What's nice about it?" he muttered angrily.

I worked away inside his head, trying to improve his mood. As I did so, I put my idea to him.

"This is quite a big garden," I pointed out. "You could grow vegetables, and Mam could sell them at the market."

He shook his head dismissively. "There's not enough land to make it worth the while."

"Then why don't you take one of those allotments the village council is offering?" I persisted. "The rents are low. After a few years, you might even have grown and sold enough stuff to buy a small field of your own."

Recently a farmer had died and bequeathed to the council a large gift of land. They'd decided to parcel it up and make it available to the villagers for a nominal rent.

"That's pie in the sky." He snorted. "Do you think I've

strength left in my body to do that after working my fingers to the bone for others all day long?"

"Mam could help you. I could help you a bit too. There are times when things are slack and there's no farmwork. That would give you the chance to till your own bit of land, wouldn't it?"

He snorted again and went inside without a word. But I could sense the change in him. My idea had gotten him thinking. Within the week, he'd taken on an allotment.

As I'd promised, I did help out from time to time. Having the allotment made him a lot happier. He was still a grumpy old devil, but he now had something to work for. He had a dream. He had hope.

That's all most people need.

He never beat me again.

As my powers developed, I began to wonder what other uses I could put them to. Would it be possible for them to provide me with a living in some way?

Above all, I longed for independence; I wanted to make my own way in the world—not just be married off to some man my adoptive parents deemed suitable.

But I feared that if I used my skills to help people, I might be seen as a witch. They hanged witches at Caster. Even worse, witch finders sometimes visited the County and tortured the witches they found. They swam them in ponds: if the women sank, they were declared innocent; those who floated were considered guilty and were burned at a stake. They died either way. It was too dangerous to sell my skills, I realized.

Then one afternoon, about eighteen months after I met my true mother, I witnessed something that pointed to the answer to my problem.

I had a wanderlust that by now took me all over the County, much farther afield than my first journeys. Sometimes I stayed away from home for over a week at a time. Far to the south of Priestown, I was exploring a small town called Salford when I saw a big man dragging a small skinny woman through the market by her hair. She was shrieking and screaming and it was terrible to watch, but not one person from the busy market interfered.

I asked one of the stallholders why the man was doing that.

"She's a witch," the trader replied with a scowl, polishing an apple on his dirty apron. "That's Spook Johnson. He has at least fifteen witches in pits. He's got a big garden, but he's going to run out of space soon. He does a good job keeping us all safe from the evil eye."

I'd heard of spooks before, but Johnson was the first I'd ever seen. I knew that these men fought the dark and dealt with witches, boggarts, and ghosts, keeping farms and villages safe. My know-it-all foster dad thought they were frauds; he didn't believe in creatures from the dark. I did. By now I'd seen at least three ghosts and often sensed unseen things in dark, quiet places.

It was horrible to watch Johnson at work, but it also fascinated me, and the seed of an idea started to germinate within my head. I hung around Salford for a few days and managed to find out where he lived. I learned that he had a big house on the edge of town, and I studied it from a distance. It was built of ugly brown stone with rusty iron railings around the garden and a thick hawthorn hedge so that you couldn't see inside. But I could hear noises—faint groans and the occasional scream.

Then I made a mistake. A big one.

Spook Johnson caught me spying on him.

He ran at me through the trees, roaring like a bull, and grabbed me by the shoulder, spinning me around to face him.

"What you want, girl?" he demanded in a big booming voice. "Been spying on me, have you? Don't try to deny it. I've seen you watching me!"

I was really scared. He looked hard and cruel, and I don't think he knew how to smile. To make it worse, he had really big ears with tufts of brown hair sprouting from within them. Some people shudder at spiders. For me, it's hairy ears. They're revolting.

"I was just curious," I told him, trembling with fear.

"Curious? *Curious!* Don't you know what curiosity did? It killed the cat. Well, little kitten, I'll give you two minutes to explain yourself. And if you can't, you're going into a pit. My guess is that you're either a witch or the relative of one of those I've got bound in my garden. Thinking of a way to help her escape, were you? So which is it, eh? Come on, speak up!"

I was already slipping into his mind, trying to change his mood. Not everybody was susceptible to my gifts, and he was harder to affect than most folk, but suddenly I felt his anger soften, and he began to relent.

"I want to be a spook!" I blurted out, putting into words what had been spinning around in my head for days. "I want you to train me!"

My words sent him into fits of laughter. "You're just a slip of a girl and still wet behind the ears!" he roared. "You have to be a seventh son of a seventh son to be taken on as a spook's apprentice. Be off with you! Get back to your mother. Learn how to be a seamstress or, even better, a good obedient wife—that's what a girl like you should aspire to. Be off with you, I say, before I change my mind about that pit!"

I ran away while I could and went back to Grimsargh, raging at the way Spook Johnson had treated me. Some men were pigs! But the idea of becoming a spook's apprentice was growing inside my head. I was becoming more set on it.

It would be the ideal job for me. I could see the dead, and no doubt with training I could talk to them as well. I felt sure that my gifts fitted me to become a spook, especially when I learned that the basic qualification to become a spook's apprentice was to be a seventh son of a seventh son.

My dream suddenly seemed possible. I was the seventh of a seventh too. No doubt spooks had similar gifts to mine. I already knew that they could talk to the dead. So boy or girl, what difference did it make? I knew now that, being a girl, I'd find it hard to get a spook to take me on. But I'd never been one to give up easily; I hated the way men seemed to make up all the rules and decide how the world was run. Things could change, couldn't they? I would *make* them change! Then I would have a job that gave me real independence; I could make my own way in the world without having to rely on marriage.

Soon after encountering Spook Johnson, on the night of the full moon, I became aware of a new ability—my fourth gift. I could make myself almost invisible. My success at this depended on conditions. It was much easier in low light, when I cast no sharp shadows. I also had to keep very still; some folk had sharper eyes than others.

Yes, a spook's apprentice was the trade for me. Johnson hadn't been right for me, but that didn't mean all spooks were the same. To my delight, I found out that the best spook in the whole County was based in Chipenden, not more than eight miles or so from where I lived.

His name was John Gregory.

So I went to Chipenden and asked around. His master before him had been called Henry Horrocks, and since his death, John Gregory had been doing the job for more than sixty years. He had lots of experience. He would be a good master, an ideal person to train me.

Then I received a big disappointment, another setback.

He already had an apprentice—a boy called Tom Ward.

For a while my dream faded. I traveled farther in search of the right master and found out that spooks were in short supply. I heard there was one working north of Caster, so I tried him. His name was Judd Brinscall, and I talked to him a couple of times, but he wasn't much better than Spook Johnson; he got so sick of my pestering that he set his fierce dogs on me.

I'd almost given up when, a few months later, I learned that John Gregory had been killed fighting some witches.

It was the talk of the villages. Witches had arrived in the County in large numbers, scaring folk, threatening them and thieving. Eventually there'd been some sort of big battle east of Caster that had put an end to the invasion, but John Gregory had been killed. They said that, although only just turned seventeen, his apprentice, Tom Ward, was now the Chipenden Spook.

I heard people talking about him. Some thought he was still wet behind the ears—far too young for the job. Others had kinder words. They said he was polite, hard-working, and brave. In Chipenden it was said that, as a new apprentice, still well short of his thirteenth birthday, he'd saved a young child from the clutches of a dangerous witch.

Whatever his gifts, it didn't sound very promising. Surely he wasn't much more than an apprentice himself, too young to train someone else. . . . But I went to Chipenden anyway to have a look at him.

I liked him at first sight.

He was young but really good-looking, apart from a faint scar that ran down his cheek. He seemed nice, but my gift of empathy told me that he was in torment. He was full of sadness at the death of his master; there was anger there too. He had been very fond of a girl who had eventually betrayed him.

Before I approached him, I found out as much information as I could. I was delighted to learn that we shared a birthday—the third of August. It was a sign, and he was exactly two years older than I was. This time I was much more careful than when I'd spied on Spook Johnson; I used my gift of invisibility.

Finally he agreed to train me.

What I have dreamed of has finally happened.

At last I am a spook's apprentice!

16
The Bones of Little Children

Two days ago, the bell rang at the crossroads. I perked up at that. At last there might be some local spook's business to deal with, the traditional County sort that many generations of apprentices had cut their teeth on. Tom had begun my training, and it was interesting, but this was the real thing!

So, carrying my staff and Tom Ward's bag, and wearing my new cloak, I followed him toward the withy trees, excited at the prospect of some sort of adventure. Little did I know how it would turn out and how differently I would feel afterward.

I could feel the sadness emanating from the woman's mind even before we moved into the gloom beneath the willows and saw her properly. She was in torment. She'd stopped ringing the bell and was standing with her back against a tree trunk, with tears streaming down her face.

She was young, no more than twenty-five, but her face was haggard with grief.

"My little girl's missing!" she cried out as we approached. "A witch has her!"

"Where are you from?" Tom asked calmly, with a sympathetic smile.

"Ribchester," she sobbed.

It was a village southeast of the Long Ridge, less than half a day's walk away. I'd visited it more than once on my travels.

"And when did your child go missing?" Tom asked. "It might just be that she wandered off. . . . Why are you so sure that a witch is involved?"

My initial excitement faded a little. Tom was right. The child might just have wandered off and gotten lost. Things like that happened all the time. There'd been an old woman in our village who some people thought was a witch. But it was just a lot of nonsense. She was lonely and talked to her cat, that was all. This might not be spook's business after all.

"I look after my daughter well!" the woman snapped angrily. "I wouldn't allow her to wander off and get into danger. Yesterday, just after dusk, I went into the garden through the back door to peg out some washing. I'd left her sitting on her little stool by the kitchen hearth, eating a biscuit. I wasn't away more than a couple of minutes. When I got back, she was gone. The witch had come in through the front door and taken her. The door was blowing in the wind, slamming back against the bricks. That door had been locked."

Tom stared at her silently. I could sense his concern growing.

"What's your daughter's name?" I asked.

"Katie, her name's Katie, and she's only three."

I began to wonder if this might be the work of another Kobalos beast, but the woman's reply to Tom Ward's next question confirmed that it was indeed a witch.

"You've searched the whole area thoroughly, no doubt?" he asked.

The woman nodded, tears streaming down her face. "We know where she is, but nobody dares go there. Even the men are scared. Five of them, led by my husband, set off with dogs to track Katie. They found the witch's cottage, all right, but could do nothing. Ahead of them, they heard the dogs howling in the darkness, as if they were being skinned alive. Then they fell quiet, and before the men knew what was happening, something truly monstrous attacked them. When they returned to the village, my husband had to be carried. He's maimed for life—his kneecap's shattered and his leg's broken in three places.

They spoke of a huge invisible creature that came through the trees and smashed his leg. It's made a cripple of him. He won't be able to do farmwork anymore. How will we live?"

I'd been looking forward to going out on a job with Tom, but this was beginning to sound really scary.

"Who is this witch?" Tom asked, frowning. "What does she call herself?"

"She calls herself Bibby Longtooth and she's an incomer. She's only been in the area for about a month. She talks funny. Somebody said she was from down south, somewhere in Essex."

Without delay, we set off for Ribchester with the woman, whose name we learned was Margaret. We didn't talk much, but Margaret continued to sob all the way. She was so upset that I found it difficult to be near her. Her anguish seeped into my mind. I experienced her sorrow and torment as if it was my own; I couldn't keep it at bay.

When we reached the village, we talked to Margaret's husband. He kept breaking down and crying too. I don't like watching men cry. They try to be strong most of the time, so when they go to pieces like this, you know it's really bad. Mostly, I knew, he was crying for his missing child, who he didn't expect to see again, but he also cried for himself and for his hopeless future.

This was the first time I'd seen Tom in action since he'd rescued me from the beast. He seemed very businesslike. A little cold, maybe, but you probably need to remain slightly aloof to function as a spook. You had to keep your anger and fear locked inside in order to do what had to be done.

The sun was going down as we left the village and the weeping parents behind. I was feeling really nervous about confronting this witch. And what was the creature that had crippled the father? I asked Tom about it.

"It's called a thumper," he explained as we walked. "It probably killed the dogs, too. It's part spirit—an elemental born in a dark place—and part spell. The witch will have used dark magic to bind it to her will and strengthen its malevolent power. No doubt it patrols the area around her cottage to drive people away. It should be easy enough to deal with, using salt and iron . . . providing I don't miss!" He gave a grim smile. "But it's dangerous, make no mistake about it. A thumper can kill. If anything happens to me, turn and run away as fast as you can."

"What about the witch?" I asked.

"My silver chain should do the trick!" he said. "It never fails!"

"Providing you don't miss!" My joke fell flat, even to my own ears, though Tom managed the ghost of a smile. "Will she try to use dark magic against us?" I went on.

"That's more than likely. But a seventh son of a seventh son has some immunity to witchcraft. Let's hope that's also the case for a seventh daughter. We're about to find out, I suppose. Don't worry too much. You're just here as an observer, to watch me and learn. It'll be over before you can blink."

By the time we reached the cottage, it was quite dark. A cold wind sighed through the trees, and the sky was patchy with fast-moving clouds. The moon was up there somewhere, but at the moment it was hidden from view.

Tom pointed up through the trees. They were mainly sycamore and ash and covered a small hill, with the cottage at its summit. I could see a faint flickering light in the distance.

"That's a candle in one of the cottage windows," he said, "so I'm pretty sure she's at home. It would be better to wait until daybreak, but there's a slim chance that the child's still alive. It's dangerous, but we have to take the risk. It's our duty, and we always put that before our own lives. Do you understand?"

"Yes," I said, beginning to tremble with fear. I sensed that Tom was nervous as well, but you wouldn't have guessed it by looking at him. And there were other things emanating from him, too: determination, fear for the child, and a sense of duty.

"Whatever you do, Jenny, stay close behind me," he instructed. "First I'll deal with the thumper, and then the witch."

He entered the trees, and I followed, carrying his bag and both our staffs. Tom needed his hands free. He had salt and iron in his pockets, and the silver chain was tied loosely around his waist.

It was cold, and I shivered, but I knew that it was mainly fear that made me shake so badly. I wanted to pull the hood of my cloak over my ears to warm them, but that would restrict my view, and I didn't want anything sneaking up behind me.

Then, suddenly, I heard the thumper. It was well named, because that was exactly what it sounded like—a sequence of heavy hollow *thump*s that met the ground with great force. They were getting nearer and louder with every second, and I could feel the rhythmic vibrations in the earth beneath my feet. Tom came to a halt and put both hands into the pockets of his breeches.

For some reason I'd thought that the thumper would be invisible or semitransparent and that Tom would have to direct his throws by sound alone.

I was wrong. There was a great dark shape looming over

us, blotting out the light from the cottage window; a shape that threatened to tread us into the earth and pulverize our flesh and bones.

Tom pulled his hands out of his pockets. There was salt in his left hand, iron filings in his right, and he threw them perfectly so they came together in a cloud against the center of the dark shape.

Suddenly there was a thin wail, and the thumping ceased.

It was gone.

I couldn't believe it had been so easy.

"Now for the witch," Tom said as he headed toward the cottage.

Surely it wouldn't be so easy to deal with the witch herself, I thought. What if he missed with the chain?

The witch came out to meet us, shrieking her hatred to the sky. She was tall and thin, with a great mass of long, tangled hair. Her eyes were wild and angry, her face like something from a nightmare—thin, bony, and warty; the flesh looked as if it had laid rotting underground for a long time. She radiated malevolence; it was a pain inside my head.

But suddenly things got a lot worse. She began to change into something truly grotesque and terrifying. Her hair became a nest of snakes writhing toward us with forked tongues spitting deadly poison. Her eyes bulged and turned red; her forehead distorted and erupted with yellow-headed boils. Now she had the face of a demon, and I was overcome by waves of terror and dread of the creature that was striding toward us.

How could anyone face that horror? It just wasn't possible. I was indeed afraid of the witch—though my greater fear was that I might turn and run. Tom wouldn't give me another chance after that. It would mean the end of my apprenticeship. It was at this moment that a strange calm came over me.

I took a deep breath and looked more closely at the witch.

As I stared, she changed back, returning to her previous shape: the snakes became hair; her eyes no longer bulged; the boils melted back into the flesh. It had all just been some sort of magical illusion . . . and for a moment I breathed a sigh of relief.

But then she was running at Tom, shrieking at the top of her voice, "I'll take your bones! I'll gouge out your eyes! I'll drink your blood! I'll flay you slowly until you scream and writhe. I'll strip the meat from your skinny ribs and boil up your brains to make a broth! You're mine, young spook! I've a use for every tasty inch of you, and the soft flesh of the girl will be my sweet dessert!"

The witch clutched a long blade in each hand and looked like she knew how to use them. Suddenly I was scared again. Those blades could slice me to pieces. Once she'd dealt with Tom, I would be next. My breath caught in my throat, and my heart began to hammer.

At first Tom didn't react. He just stood there, waiting for her to get closer. I wondered what his plan was. His mind seemed blank . . . either that, or my gift wasn't working properly. Was it because I was scared and couldn't concentrate?

At that moment, the moon came out from behind a cloud.

Despite my fear, in those seconds I saw something really strange.

I saw Tom's shadow cast by the moon. It was impossibly big, stretching over the witch and right up the wall of the cottage behind her.

Distracted, I missed seeing Tom cast his chain, but it now formed a helix, hovering in the air and gleaming in the moonlight. Then it fell perfectly over the witch and tightened around her body and across her mouth so that she collapsed to her knees.

"That's why you need to practice," Tom said, turning to smile at me. "It comes in very useful at moments like this."

We left the witch there and went into the cottage to see what had happened to the child.

As we had feared, little Katie was dead. And we found the bones of other children, too. The sight made me so sick that I almost wrenched my stomach inside out.

I could have killed that witch. I could have stabbed her with her own blades. That's what I really wanted to do.

And I knew then that, in the right circumstances, I was capable of killing someone.

How could she have done this to little children? I wondered. She didn't deserve to live another second longer.

Tom dragged Bibby Longtooth back to Chipenden, still wrapped from head to toe in his silver chain, and together we dug a pit for her in the eastern garden. This time he did most of the work, sending me down to the village to engage the services of a blacksmith and a stonemason. It was probably for the best; I was so filled with rage that I couldn't bear to look at the witch.

The men carved a stone to go over the pit and fitted it with iron bars. Once Tom had rolled the witch into the pit, they set to work, lowering it into place while she glared up at them with wild eyes, spitting and cursing.

At last the witch was safe in the pit, but I still felt nauseous. I thought I would enjoy being a spook's apprentice, but now I have real doubts about the job.

It's dark, terrible work. Nobody should have to see the sights we do and face witches like Bibby Longtooth—and, what's worse, see what they've done.

I'm not sure about being a spook now. I'm not sure at all.

Never until my dying day will I forget those little bones . . . the bones of all those children.

Thomas Ward

17
Practical Lessons

Two days ago we captured a malevolent bone witch called Bibby Longtooth and brought her back to Chipenden. Now she's safely bound within a pit. But we were unable to save the child she'd snatched, and Jenny took it badly. She told me that she was thinking of ending her apprenticeship. It was hard to talk her out of it, but I remembered my early days of doubt; I'd once gone back to the farm and begged my mam to let me give up the job. I told Jenny how my mam had been right to refuse, that I'd achieved a lot—and she would too.

The only way I could snap her out of her despondency was to work her hard. So her training began in earnest. Each morning now, we visited the six-foot post in the western garden and I let Jenny practice with my silver chain, something she really enjoyed. From a distance of eight feet, she was able to cast the chain over the stump successfully two out of every three times she tried. It had taken me a long time before I managed a sequence of one hundred perfect casts. She was making good progress.

I demonstrated the casting technique for her again. "Look . . . you must coil it over your left hand like this, and then flick your wrist so that it falls in a left-handed spiral. Ideally it should cover a good part of the witch's body, from her head to her knees. Get it across her mouth, and she can't mutter spells at you." I cast the chain, and lit by the morning sun, its shining spiral seemed to pause in midair before falling perfectly and tightening against the post.

"Of course, you have to keep practicing," I told Jenny as I collected the chain and handed it back to her. "It's a skill that should be honed, not just for your apprenticeship but during the whole of your subsequent life as a spook. And don't forget—this is just a post. As you saw the other night, a witch won't stand still for you! Later, when you improve, you can practice casting the chain from different distances, and then while on the run. You can use me as a target."

I watched her for another five minutes or so. She was left-handed like me—maybe it was something that all seventh daughters had in common with seventh sons.

"Right, that's enough!" I said after a while; Jenny

was panting with the exertion. "Let's go and have some breakfast."

Even though the sun was shining, there was the chill to the air and our breath steamed. It was still a lot colder than was usual in early September—a fact that was really beginning to worry me.

"Why don't you teach me about witches rather than boggarts?" Jenny asked as we walked back through the trees. I'd told her that boggarts was the best topic with which to start her training—and I'd noticed a momentary tightening of her mouth. She hadn't said anything at the time, but now she'd obviously had time to reflect.

"In the first year, an apprentice always learns about boggarts," I told her sternly.

"Some of the practical work, such as casting the chain, applies to witches. So why can't I learn some theory too? Witches are scary, but they're more interesting."

"Are they now?" I said, an edge of sarcasm in my voice. "Well, soon you might get to meet another witch face-to-face. Grimalkin, the witch assassin of the Malkin clan, is studying the lair of the Kobalos mage that captured you. When she's finished, she'll no doubt call in here to tell me what she's learned."

Jenny's face showed a flicker of fear.

"Don't be scared," I said gently. "She's an ally."

"I wasn't thinking about the witch," Jenny retorted. "I was remembering how it felt to be helpless in the jaws of that beast."

"It'll take time to get over a terrible experience like that, but the memory will pass."

Jenny nodded and looked thoughtful. "She's a witch who kills people—is that right?" she asked.

"Yes, but she usually kills clan enemies."

"You're a spook and she's a witch, so why aren't you dealing with her? Shouldn't you put her in a pit? It's almost as if you're on the same side."

"A few years ago we formed an alliance with her," I explained. "My master, John Gregory, didn't like it, but in the end even he accepted it as a necessity. The beast that nearly killed you is just the advance guard of thousands of dangerous Kobalos warriors. They are Grimalkin's enemies, and also ours. That's why a spook is in alliance with a witch."

Jenny fell silent, and we headed for the kitchen and had our breakfast. Immediately afterward, I collected the measuring rod and a spade and led the way to the southern garden. Holding the spade brought back the sad memory of burying my master, but I forced it from my mind and concentrated on the lesson.

I halted under the branch of a tree and pointed upward.

"You're going to dig a pit suitable to bind a boggart in," I told Jenny. "First of all, you have to choose the right location. This must always be under a branch. It has to be a strong branch, too, because a block and tackle—a system of chains and a pulley—will be hung from it to support the stone lid that is eventually lowered to bind the boggart in the pit."

Jenny nodded doubtfully. "So I'm going to dig a pit here, even though we have no boggart to bind?"

"Yes, you got it first time. It's good to know that you're listening to what I say," I told her, failing to keep the sarcasm from my voice. My dad always used to say, "Sarcasm is the lowest form of wit!" He'd had no time for it, and I was suddenly disappointed in myself. I resolved to do my best to avoid it in the future. It wasn't a good idea when you were trying to teach someone.

"This is a practical lesson, and you are going to dig a practice pit," I explained more kindly. "Ours is a craft that involves certain skills, and this is one of them. You have to dig the pit to meet precise measurements, because the stone lid has to fit perfectly. It's got to be exactly six feet long, six feet deep, and three feet wide."

"Why does the depth have to be so precise? Surely that can vary a little?"

I forced myself to control my anger. I'd certainly not

questioned my master in this way. I had asked him questions—he'd encouraged me to do so on many occasions. I could hear his voice now saying those very words: "Come on, spit it out! Don't be afraid to ask questions, lad!" But it seemed to me that there was something disrespectful in Jenny's tone.

"The width and length have to be precise so that the stone will fit. Six feet has been proven to be the best depth for containing a boggart. Generations of spooks agree that it should measure exactly that!" I said firmly.

I showed Jenny how to use the measuring rod to mark the pit's outline, and then I told her to start digging. After a while I could see that she was finding it hard; she was breathing heavily, and sweat was dripping from her forehead. But it was part of a spook's trade. She had to learn how to do it.

After about an hour I took pity on her. I told her to take a break, and I leaned against the tree while she sat on the edge of the pit, red in the face from her exertions. Digging practice pits hadn't been one of my favorite lessons, either.

"Did you hear those strange noises last night?" Jenny asked once she'd gotten her breath back.

I shook my head. I'd slept like a log, only waking when the dawn light came through the window. What strange noises did she mean? She was new to Chipenden, and what

I accepted as normal might be startling to her. The boggart sometimes made noises as it moved through the garden.

"I like to sleep with my window open, and I could hear them clearly."

"You've been sleeping with your window open on these cold nights?" I asked in astonishment.

"Yes," she said. "It's good for you. The air in a bedroom can get stale."

My window had been firmly closed. I preferred stale air to cold air. "What were the noises like?" I asked.

"Something between a scream and a roar," she said.

"It might have been the boggart warning somebody off. You've never heard the boggart before, have you?"

"I did wonder about that at first, but it seemed too far away to have come from the boggart. It sounded as though it came from many miles distant. It was like the cry of some big, scary animal."

"Well, I think I'll continue to keep my window closed, but if you hear it again, come and knock on my door and I'll have a listen."

That night, Jenny did just that.

I rubbed my eyes free of sleep, got out of bed, and opened the door a crack. "What's wrong?" I asked, surprised, forgetting for a moment what I'd said earlier.

"You told me to knock if I heard that strange cry again. Well, I just heard it—it's louder tonight. Open your window and listen. There's something big out there, and it sounds really angry."

"Go back to bed," I told her. "I'll listen now, and then we'll talk in the morning."

When she'd gone, I lifted the sash window slightly and got back into bed. I could hear the wind whistling through the trees, but that was all. Eventually I drifted back to sleep, only to awake a couple of hours later to a freezing bedroom. Annoyed, I reached across, slammed down the window sash, and went back to sleep.

At breakfast the following morning I was a bit short-tempered with Jenny. "A spook needs his sleep!" I told her. "And so does an apprentice. Tonight I suggest that you shut your window and sleep. Understood?"

"So you heard nothing?" she asked, buttering a thick slice of bread. She certainly had a healthy appetite.

"Nothing at all. The bedroom got cold, and this morning I have a headache. So don't bother me again with your strange noises."

That should have been the end of it.

But it wasn't.

The following night I awoke suddenly with a strong sense that something was terribly wrong. Something dangerous was out there. And I knew roughly where it was.

Jenny wasn't the only one with gifts, but this one wasn't given me because I was a seventh son of a seventh son. This was something I'd inherited from Mam, courtesy of my lamia blood. It was a useful gift and had helped me in the past.

It was not a good feeling. I was sweating, my heart was racing, and I was filled with dread. I felt compelled to do something; to act in order to make those awful feelings go away. Moreover, it was my duty as a spook to investigate. I dressed quickly, pulled on my boots, and ran downstairs. At the back door I threw on my cloak and snatched up my staff. Then I paused for a moment to concentrate.

My gift didn't let me down. I was able to locate the danger precisely. Then, knowing where I was going, I paused for a moment to buckle on the belt that held the scabbard, and I slid the Starblade into it.

When I stepped outside into the garden, I saw to my surprise that Jenny was already standing there, bathed in the light of the gibbous moon.

"You heard it?" she asked, her eyes bright with excitement. "It's really loud tonight."

I'd still not heard anything, but I wasn't going to correct her—and then, the next moment, I *did* hear the sound she meant. Although not very loud, it was somewhere between a roar and an angry screech; it certainly wasn't the warning cry of the boggart. It came from miles away, just as Jenny had described.

I suddenly knew that it came from the big oak tree that the Kobalos mage had made his lair. That's where my gift told me the danger lay. I didn't know what it was, but I thought it might well have something to do with the dead mage. It might involve Kobalos magic; that's why I'd brought the Starblade.

For a moment I considered telling Jenny to wait in the safety of the house while I investigated. But danger came with this job—I'd warned her about that already. She needed to come with me and take her chances, whatever the risk. It was something that John Gregory had always expected of me.

"Right, follow me, but stay well back. Understand?"

She nodded, and we set off toward the source of the sound.

18
The Vartek

WE walked fast, and within three quarters of an hour we were approaching the lair of the dead mage. Every ten minutes or so, that unearthly screech echoed through the trees, each cry louder and more terrifying than its predecessor. My sense of danger was growing by the minute. What could we be walking toward? It was surely something big and fierce.

I wondered if Grimalkin was still in the vicinity, or if she had gone off without telling me.

Ahead, the moonlight illuminated the big oak, but when another screech split the heavens, I realized that the sound actually came from somewhere beyond it.

We strode past the oak, emerging from the trees into a wide meadow—to be greeted by an astonishing sight. Someone had scythed the grass very short and marked out a gigantic chalk circle, within which was a five-pointed star.

It was a magic pentacle of immense size.

Sometimes a mage would stand safe within such a pentacle and conjure something on the outside of it. Alternatively, he or she could stand beyond it while the entity was contained within it.

Was there a dark mage in the area? I wondered.

I noticed that at each of the five points of the star, a large candle made of black wax was burning. Although there was a breeze blowing from the west, the tall blue flames did not so much as flicker. Who else but a witch would use black wax candles? This had to be Grimalkin's work, but there was no sign of her. What was this pentacle for?

Moving out from under the trees, we approached the circle, and I began to walk around the edge in a clockwise direction, with Jenny following at my heels.

"Don't touch the circle!" I hissed at her. "Keep your boots well clear."

There could be something invisible trapped within it.

We were almost halfway around when the ground began to tremble. I sensed danger behind me, so I turned quickly and looked down. As I watched, something thrust its way up through the grass like a sapling growing at an insane speed. It was as thick as a human arm and flexed in a spiral as it grew.

When two more followed, I took three rapid paces back,

holding my staff across my chest in a defensive position. I now saw that they were tentacles, each tipped with a hard, sharp bone like a blade.

Jenny gasped in astonishment, and then we both stepped back rapidly as a huge head erupted from the earth. Next, thin legs emerged, got a purchase on the grass, and began to heave the rest of the monstrous black-scaled body out into the moonlight. It had legs beyond counting—a giant insect, something like a centipede.

Jenny opened her mouth wide, as if to scream, but no sound emerged. She just stared at the monster with wide eyes.

What was it? I racked my brains but could think of nothing similar that existed in the County.

It was about the height of a large breeding bull, but perhaps three or four times longer, with long jaws full of fearsome teeth. They moved strangely within its mouth and kept changing their angle and length, as if they were adjustable.

The bulging eyes regarded me carefully, and I could see myself reflected in each one. Then the beast breathed out, and foul acid breath washed over me, drawing tears from my own eyes. I started to cough and choke.

It scuttled forward to attack, and I heard Jenny give a moan of terror. I jabbed toward its left eye with the blade at the end of my staff, but the creature retreated out of range, then opened its jaws wide and gave that loud, screeching roar. At close quarters it was truly terrifying, and I was almost deafened by the sound, my teeth set on edge.

I realized that it was preparing to attack again, and I readied my staff, but just then I heard an eerie cry from somewhere near the trees. I risked glancing behind me and saw that it was the witch assassin. Grimalkin repeated the cry, and the creature turned, with great agility for its size, and scuttled toward her.

She turned and ran.

Somehow she had attracted its attention, perhaps by use of dark magic. She had been only too successful: she was running and had almost reached the trees—but it was catching up fast, getting closer and closer.

I ran after the creature, and Jenny followed behind me. Grimalkin was out of sight now, and the creature plunged into the wood, snapping branches and crushing saplings.

Under the branches, the light of the moon was obscured and it was suddenly dark. I slowed a little, fearful of blundering into the beast's murderous jaws. Then came a crashing, tearing sound, as if trees were falling to earth, and then a terrible shrill scream.

For one heart-stopping moment I thought it was Grimalkin, caught in the jaws of the beast, but as I reached a small clearing I saw her facing me, a blade in each hand.

At her feet lay a large pit. I stepped forward and looked down into it. The huge creature was thrashing and twisting in agony, impaled on dozens of sharpened stakes that had pierced its long body. Two protruded from the top of its head.

I knew then what had happened. Grimalkin had dug the pit, camouflaged it, and lured the beast after her so that it fell in as she'd planned.

"You chose a bad moment to arrive," she said brusquely. "You could have been killed. This beast can spit globules of acid. And beware of its legs—they are coated with a deadly poison. . . . But as you are here, you might as well be of use. Help me to finish it off."

She jumped down into the pit; I followed nervously and, under her direction, set to work. Jenny remained above, staring down in horror at the grisly sight. The creature was still twisting and thrashing in a desperate effort to tear itself free. As it did so, it roared out its agony.

It gave off a strong acrid stench, and its breath was foul. I took care to keep well clear of its jaws, but the stink alone was almost unbearable. Grimalkin pierced its eyes with her blades, lancing them like boils, while I stabbed it again and again with the retractable blade at the end of my staff. Although the scales on its back were like armour, I now saw that its underbelly was soft and vulnerable.

Eventually the creature's convulsions slowed, and then it lay still. The blood pooled beneath it, bubbling and hissing as it soaked into the soft earth.

Later Grimalkin walked back with us to the lair of the dead mage.

"I managed to contain that creature within the pentacle you saw, but it burrowed down to a great depth to escape. It's called a vartek," she told us. "That one was just a baby—imagine meeting one that's fully grown."

"How big do they grow?" Jenny blurted out, her eyes wide.

"One day I fear that we will find out," Grimalkin said with a grimace.

"This is Jenny, my apprentice," I told the witch assassin. "The girl who found the Kobalos mage."

Grimalkin stared hard at her and gave the briefest of nods.

Jenny nodded back. She was staring at the witch with wide eyes. She looked almost as scared as she had when we faced the vartek.

"You did well, child." Grimalkin's voice was more gentle now. "I wish you good fortune. If you prove to be half as good an apprentice as your master, you will have chosen the right trade. And as for you, Tom, I am pleased that you have chosen a female apprentice. That shows courage. Many will disapprove of your decision, I'm sure."

I was secretly pleased by Grimalkin's praise, but there were more important things on my mind. "Where did the creature come from?" I asked her.

"I grew it," she said simply. On seeing the shock in our faces, she explained, "From a sample in one of the jars I found in the mage's lair. We are lucky that he did not manage to do the same. Imagine what damage such creatures could do to the County."

At that moment I felt more uneasy than ever, and sweat formed on my brow. This was indeed a terrifying new threat. Then I suddenly sensed something else—another dark entity was out there still. I opened my mouth to speak, but before I could do so, there was an angry roar from somewhere far to the southeast of us. ·

I saw the look on Grimalkin's face, and it confirmed what my gift had told me.

Another vartek was on the loose!

19
The Pursuit

"It's heading southeast!" I cried. "Did you know there were two?" I asked, turning to Grimalkin.

"No," she admitted, her face grim. "They are burrowers, and while they were born on the surface, they immediately disappeared underground. Later, only one reemerged. The young eat each other—only the strongest should have survived. I truly thought this meant that there was only one remaining."

Then, without another word, the witch assassin turned and sprinted through the trees in pursuit of the vartek.

Jenny and I followed her, trying to keep up. It was dark in the wood, and there was a real danger of blundering into a tree, tripping over a log, or stumbling into a hole and breaking a leg. Somehow we reached the edge unscathed, and then had the light of the moon to guide our progress.

My gift was working well—it meant that I could sense

the creature directly ahead. It was moving fast.

We crossed a meadow before coming to a high, thick hawthorn hedge. This forced us into a detour; we had to clamber over a locked five-barred gate before continuing. A sequence of small fields further impeded our pursuit.

In the distance, farther to the east, I could see lights from a farmhouse. At some point the creature's route would take it past human habitation. We had to stop it before that happened.

We had reached an area of flat moss land with no obvious obstacles and were making better progress. Then, from somewhere ahead, the creature gave another roar.

To my dismay, it sounded even more distant. The vartek was much faster than we were—but why was there no sign of its passage, no trail of destruction?

Moments later, I discovered why. It had been moving underground. Directly ahead lay a large pile of freshly excavated earth; at its center, a dark hole gaped where the creature had emerged. We could see tracks leading away into the distance. This was where we'd heard its first roar. There was a smell of loam and dank earth, then something else—the acrid stench that I had smelled on the one that Grimalkin had lured into her pit. I remembered how she had warned me that it could spit globules of acid.

Grimalkin sprinted on beyond the hole. I was struggling

to keep up with her, and I glanced round. Jenny was falling behind. It couldn't be helped—I had to keep going. Perhaps it was for the best anyway. If we caught the creature, it would be an extremely dangerous confrontation. I didn't want her to get hurt.

Although we were now back among a patchwork of cultivated fields, our progress became much easier. When it had reached a hedge, or a stand of trees, the vartek had simply crashed straight through, flattening everything in its path, so our route was clear.

We continued running for an hour or so, still following its trail. I'd gotten my second wind now, and was running easily. However, I knew that I couldn't keep it up forever. I could still sense the creature moving ahead, but then at last it slowed and came to a halt.

I heard another roar, followed immediately by terrified shrill screams. Then, directly ahead, I spotted the lights of another farmhouse.

Five minutes later, we reached a scene of total carnage and devastation. The vartek hadn't attacked the farmhouse but had crashed straight through a large barn, slaying and devouring the animals within.

Judging by what remained, there had been cattle in there, and at least one horse. Now the stands were flattened and wet with blood. Grimalkin and I halted, staring at the grisly remains. I saw fragments of dead animals everywhere, and bile rose in my throat. I saw Jenny coming toward us. She too came to a halt, and immediately bent forward and vomited onto the grass.

The farmer had emerged from his house, and he came running toward the ruin of his barn, carrying a lantern and a big stick. It was fortunate for him that he hadn't gotten there in time to confront the creature.

We turned and raced off into the dark without waiting to speak to him. There was no time for explanations.

Soon afterward, the vartek went to ground again. We halted at the fresh mound of earth, struggling to regain our breath. I concentrated hard, trying to sense where the creature was. For a second or two the picture was vague, but then a light flared inside my head. Even before Jenny caught up with us, I had located the creature. It had come to rest less than fifty yards away from the entrance to its burrow, but it was deep underground.

"We'll have to follow it into the tunnel," I said.

Jenny tried to say something, but she was still fighting for breath and couldn't get the words out.

In reply, Grimalkin simply pointed down at the burrow.

I peered into the dark hole and, for the first time, saw that it was packed full of earth.

"It fills in the burrow behind it as it moves!" I realized.

Grimalkin nodded. "It eats the earth and rock, using its teeth and the acid in its saliva. They pass through its body after it has extracted the nutrients it needs, sealing the tunnel behind it."

"But it eats flesh too—those poor animals!" Jenny gasped.

"Yes, child, it has been created to require flesh also. It is a brutal creature, designed as a battle entity to devour the soldiers of an opposing army."

Without speaking, I set off after the vartek, and Grimalkin and Jenny followed behind me. Soon I halted and pointed down at the grass. "It's directly below us—about fifty feet down, I think."

"How can you know that?" Jenny asked, staring at me in astonishment.

"You've got your gifts, and I have mine," I replied. "It doesn't always work, but I can often locate a person or an object from a distance. Fortunately it's working well in this case. I know exactly where the vartek is."

Grimalkin already knew of my gift and made no comment. She appeared to be deep in thought.

"It is too far down for us to reach by digging," she observed at last. "And even if we could do so, it would be too dangerous."

I concentrated again. I was sure that the vartek was not moving.

"The creature's at rest," I said, "but it may not actually sleep. It may also be aware of our position. We could be ambushed."

"So that leaves us with just one option," Grimalkin decided. "We must slay it as it comes to the surface."

I nodded. "It'll either emerge here, or travel for some distance underground . . . in which case it will be much slower. We should be able to keep up or get ahead of it."

We settled down right there. There was no point in taking turns to sleep, because I was the only one who could detect movement by the vartek. So Grimalkin and Jenny dozed off while I kept watch.

About an hour before dawn, it began to move again. Quickly I roused the others, and we followed its underground progress. It was still heading in the same direction.

I looked up at the fading stars and took my bearings. I felt sick with dread.

This was the approximate route that I took when traveling from Chipenden to Jack's farm. If the beast continued in the same direction, my family lay ahead.

"Jack's farm is in its path," I told Grimalkin. "If it misses the farm, it will still pass through Topley. More than sixty people live there, and tomorrow is Friday, market day. People converge from all the nearby hamlets and outlying farms. There'll be hundreds of people in the streets and on the village green."

Had this vartek knowledge of what we had done to the haizda mage? I wondered. Was it heading for Jack's farm out of revenge? If so, why hadn't it made a beeline straight for me? It seemed preposterous, but whatever the truth, the danger was real.

Grimalkin remained silent. She was staring into the distance.

The vartek might pass right underneath the farm and the village, but if it sensed what was above it, the farm animals might draw it to the surface. And how could it not sense all those people at the market?

This creature, which Grimalkin had termed a battle entity, had been designed to kill and devour soldiers. Those villagers going about their business would probably be indistinguishable.

I began to grasp at straws. What could I do to stop this attack? Could I summon the boggart to my assistance?

I had no doubt that Kratch would be able to deal with the vartek, but I needed a ley line to allow the boggart to travel here. Picturing my master's maps, which had been destroyed in the fire, I vaguely remembered that there was one a few miles farther east. But how could I get the vartek to cross its path? I couldn't think of any way to achieve this.

The creature continued moving until about an hour after midday. Then it came to a halt again, and it still hadn't moved at nightfall.

By now I was desperate to find some way of halting the vartek. I spoke to Grimalkin, hoping that she might have some ideas.

"Couldn't you use your magic against it?" I asked. I glanced across at Jenny. She was fast asleep, exhausted by the chase.

The witch assassin shook her head. "I have already tried spells of binding and confusion," she replied. "They have no effect on it at all. I am dealing with an entity that seems resistant to human witch magic. Such defenses may have been built into it quite deliberately. Of course, in time I may learn ways to overcome such a creature. That is why it is vital that I obtain knowledge of Kobalos magical practices. But for now we can only be patient and make sure that we are there when the vartek emerges."

Her words were like a blow. It seemed that there was nothing we could do. I felt so helpless. Soon I sensed the vartek stir beneath us, and I quickly shook Jenny awake. It was moving much more slowly now, but still heading in the same direction.

As we followed, my anxiety grew.

Just before dawn it speeded up again, and our stroll became first a fast walk and eventually a jog. I was soon running, and Grimalkin and Jenny kept pace with me.

The sky was pink with the dawn light, and I could see trees ahead and a couple of low hills, which functioned as landmarks. I took my bearings again, and a wave of relief crashed through me as I realized that the creature would miss Jack's farm.

But the village of Topley was now directly in its path.

My relief gave way to shame. *What about those hundreds of innocent people at the market?* I thought.

Then I realized that my family was not safe after all. My brothers visited Topley market on Friday mornings. At least one of them would be there, I was sure of it.

By now I could see the familiar hill in the distance and felt a surge of hope.

"Is that Hangman's Hill?" Jenny gasped, struggling to keep up.

I nodded, saving my breath.

"Then it should miss your brother's farm."

"There's a chance that it might just miss the village too," I told her.

We would pass half a mile to the east of the hill. Beyond it lay Topley. Although the vartek would pass close by, it seemed likely that it would just miss the village. What was the creature planning? I wondered.

As we passed Hangman's Hill, leaving Jack's farm behind, the vartek paused for a moment, and I thought it was about to surface.

Then it set off again at an angle. My worst fears were realized. It must have sensed the presence of people.

It was now heading straight for the center of the village.

20
The Fanatical Gleam

YEARS earlier, when I'd visited the market with my dad, the early-rising farmers had done their business first: cattle, sheep, horses, and hens were penned and displayed before being bought and sold; farm implements were on display; bales of hay were neatly stacked. Only later, toward noon, did the streets become thronged with mothers and children browsing among the stands.

It was now nine o'clock, still early. The air was chilly, but the sun was high enough in the sky to bathe the village in light and radiate a pleasant warmth. As a result, there were more people on the streets than usual, and the stallholders, anticipating good business, had already set out their wares. Never had I seen it so busy this early.

As we raced down the main street, heading toward the village green, still following the line taken by the vartek, heads turned to watch us. Many stalls were set up in the streets that radiated like spokes from the large village green; others stood on the periphery. People turned to gaze at us in astonishment. Fear flickered on their faces at the sight of the witch assassin, and there were a few shouts of fear and anger. Ignoring the reactions of the shoppers, we ran on down the cobbled street.

Suddenly I knew where the vartek would emerge: right at the heart of the green, where the cattle were penned. I didn't know what senses it used to find its prey—perhaps it located its victims by scent, even when deep underground. Maybe it could see through rock or sense warm blood from a great distance. Whatever the reason, the closely penned cattle had attracted it in preference to the people.

Perhaps so much flesh and blood collected together was irresistible, compelling it to attack. After all, wouldn't that be the design of its Kobalos creators? They would require it to strike at the heart of an enemy army, erupting from the ground to take the soldiers by surprise, spreading panic through the ranks.

My gift was working perfectly now, and I sensed the vartek pass beneath the market stalls and move toward the cattle pens. I imagined its jaws working feverishly, its acidic saliva working on the earth and rock it ingested.

So far we had kept pace with the creature, no more than twenty or thirty yards behind it at any point. Now, suddenly, it took me by surprise and accelerated away from us; it was moving as fast as it had on the surface.

How was that possible?

Maybe the earth under the green was softer, I thought. Perhaps the creature was propelled by a frantic bloodlust as it neared its prey . . . but all that mattered was that we confront it before it had fully emerged from its burrow.

I sprinted after it, jostling an aproned man aside, dodging between the stalls and onto the grass. Suddenly there was a terrible scream from the center of the green. I saw three black tentacles coiling and swaying high in the air above a herd of cattle. Meanwhile, a farmer was running toward the pen, no doubt fearing for his stock.

Seconds later, the terrified cows broke through the hurdles that enclosed them, scattering them like matchwood, and stampeded toward us. The farmer turned on his heel and ran for his life.

Grimalkin and I stood shoulder to shoulder, while Jenny stayed close behind. The witch assassin had drawn two of her blades and I raised my staff, pointing the blade toward the approaching animals. They were big long-horned cattle and could easily trample us into the ground. When I was young, at least two local farmers had been charged by their own cattle; one had died, and the other had never walked again without the aid of a stick.

However, we stood firm, and at the very last moment, just as I thought we were going to be impaled by their horns, the beasts parted like two curtains being drawn aside. They passed on either side of us, splattering us with clods of mud.

But as they thundered away, another scream rent the air.

The vartek was about thirty yards ahead of us, and I saw that it had taken a cow in its huge mouth; it was shaking it as a dog shakes a rat. It had grown since we last saw it aboveground, and its three tentacles, with their sharp bone tips, now reached at least twenty feet into the air.

I saw that another cow had been injured. It was bellowing with pain and trying to rise, but it was missing a leg, and the stump was spurting blood.

As we ran forward, the first animal gave another cry, and we heard the crunching of bone as the vartek closed its jaws, cutting it clean in two. As the bloodied halves fell onto the grass, the monstrous creature seized the other injured cow.

This was what saved our lives as we prepared to attack. With its mouth full, the vartek couldn't spit globules of acid at us.

Grimalkin reached it first and thrust a blade into the bulbous right eye, twisting the weapon as she did so in order to do maximum damage. Meanwhile I went for the other eye, stabbing deep into it with the blade of my staff.

The vartek was blinded, but it was far from finished. Its response was to spit out the remains of the second cow, splattering us with blood as it surged up onto the grass, its many legs scrabbling for purchase.

My staff, still embedded in its eye, was snatched out of my hand, and I fell backward. I rolled over, came to my feet, and drew the Starblade. I studied the vartek's many thin legs. They had a slimy yellow coating, and I remembered Grimalkin's warning—they oozed a deadly poison, so I had to keep away from them.

The witch assassin had already renewed her attack, hurling three blades in quick succession into the beast's throat and soft underbelly as it attempted to climb out of its burrow. Now she was rushing toward it again, a long blade in her left hand.

To my surprise, I suddenly realized that Jenny was running past me, heading straight for the vartek. She stopped a little to the left of the massive jaws. The retractable blade at the end of her staff glinted in the sunlight as she buried it deep into the side of its neck.

"Watch out for its legs!" I warned, running toward her.

But the immediate threat came from another direction. Although blinded, the vartek clearly had other senses to guide it. One of the tentacles scythed toward Jenny, the sharp tip heading straight for her head.

Just in time, I managed to bring my sword around in a circle, cutting the tentacle off just above the bone, so that it flicked backward, spraying us with blood. Then I went for the throat, swinging wildly into the soft flesh, each deep cut bringing forth spouts of fresh blood to soak the grass.

At last the vartek was weakening; its tentacles lay inert and useless. It shuddered and gasped, opening its mouth wide to reveal the rows of movable teeth. And then it let out a deep sigh, its foul breath washing over us. With that dying breath, its legs buckled. It had not managed to climb out of its burrow, and now its body slid slowly back in until only its head was visible.

"It's a pity it didn't emerge fully," Grimalkin said, wiping her blades on the grass as she tugged each one from the creature's throat. "I would have liked to see its full length. My fear is that this creature is still far from fully grown. Imagine what a score of these could do to a human army!"

There was much to discuss, but this was not the place to do it, and so we left the village almost immediately.

Once the cattle had been rounded up, and the farmers and villagers had finally summoned up the courage to approach the green, they would be asking plenty of questions. The presence of a witch would further complicate matters, so it was best to get away as quickly as possible.

As we walked, I saw cattle milling around in the distance, and people staring at us from outside the nearest cottages. Perhaps my brothers were among them, but it made no difference. There was no sense in staying to offer explanations.

Nobody had died. Apart from the two dead animals and the broken fence, little harm had been done. The vartek was dead. Topley had gotten off lightly.

We headed back toward Chipenden, saying little. Jenny was unusually silent. I could tell that she was angry—her jaw was firmly set—but I didn't question her. There'd be time for that later.

I'd hoped to get away without being questioned, but that wasn't to be. Soon we were being followed by a crowd of agitated villagers, about a dozen of them. At one point Grimalkin turned and glared at them. They paused for a moment, but when we set off again, they continued to keep pace with us.

As we left the last of the cottages behind us, Grimalkin suddenly turned to face them again. This time they came closer and halted less than twenty strides away. They were muttering angrily; some of them were brandishing sticks. They would have no chance against Grimalkin and would flee at the first serious threat from her blades, but I didn't want any of them to get hurt.

"What do you want?" I demanded, coming to stand at Grimalkin's side.

"What are you doing with a witch, boy?" asked their leader, a big brawny man with a shaved head and an angry, jutting chin.

I searched desperately from face to face, hoping to see someone I knew from my childhood visits to Topley with my dad, someone I could appeal to. But these were strangers, people from outlying farms to the south.

"She has helped me to save *your* village!" I retorted.

"Save it from what—her own dark magic? She conjured a hell beast, and you did nothing."

"I'm Tom Ward, the Chipenden Spook. She fought by my side to save you from a monster that would have devoured you all. If you don't believe me, go back to the green. There you'll find the body of the creature we killed to save you."

"You're lying, boy. All three of you are coming back with us. We'll send to Priestown for the quisitor—he's due to visit there this month. Then we'll have ourselves a burning. At the end of it there'll be three cinders . . . a witch and her two accomplices."

Quisitors hunted and burned witches; they had no liking for spooks, either. The man's threat was real: if they managed to capture us, the future was bleak. But I couldn't let Grimalkin kill these angry and frightened people. Once they returned to the village, they'd soon realize the truth of what I'd said. But their leader was a hothead and would have to be dealt with.

"Go back and see what we killed," I said softly. "Then think again. What was done was for your own good. Now let us be on our way."

Their leader took a couple more paces toward us. "You first, boy. Surrender your weapons, and it'll go easier with you. Come with us peacefully, and you'll get a fair trial," he said, stepping closer to me.

"Do you want me to kill him for you?" Grimalkin hissed into my ear.

I shook my head and strode toward the man. He was carrying a wooden club about the length of his forearm; it was thick and heavy at the business end, stout enough to split my skull. He swung it at my head with surprising speed, but I stepped to the side and danced away. He swung and missed again, and came after me, brandishing the weapon wildly.

A second later, I rapped him hard on the wrist with my staff; he groaned but wasn't deterred. He attacked again, cursing, his face red with rage. I hit him twice more, once on the knee and once on the shoulder. It hardly checked his advance. He looked ready to tear me apart with his bare hands.

Suddenly my own anger flared. I thought of my job as a spook—how I tried to keep the County safe, always putting duty first despite the danger. I thought of my own master, who had given his life to save men like this from the dark. I remembered how people used to cross to the other side of the road as we approached. They needed spooks, but they were afraid of what we did. Most of them didn't like us one bit.

So I attacked with renewed energy, in a fury now. My first blow caught the man hard across the mouth, and he staggered backward. Then I rammed the base of my staff deep into his belly, and he fell to his knees, fighting for breath. He looked up at me, his face twisted with pain, and spat two bloodied teeth out onto the grass.

I strode past him and approached the others. "Who's next?" I demanded.

They backed away warily, so I turned and strode away. Grimalkin and Jenny followed hard on my heels. I was still seething with anger, and nobody spoke for a long time.

"What if they do talk to a quisitor?" Jenny finally asked, breaking the silence. "You told them you were the Chipenden Spook. They know where we live. He could come after us."

I shrugged. "Once they see what we killed on the green, they'll forget all about that," I told her. "That was just anger and bluster talking."

To my surprise, Grimalkin took her leave of us just before dark, with no explanation of where she was going.

"I will visit you early next week," she said. "I have concluded my experiments and will then tell you something of what I have learned."

Later, as we sat around a fire cooking a chicken I'd bought from a farmer on the way home, Jenny finally exploded.

"Hundreds of people could have died in that village!" she said. "Had the witch no sense of the terrible risk she was taking?"

"You mean her experiments?" I asked. "I suppose she thought she could contain the creatures. Grimalkin's magic is extremely powerful. She would not have expected the varteks to escape."

"But she was dealing with something completely unknown to her. It was foolish to take such risks. Surely you can see that. . . ."

I nodded. "Yes, with hindsight I can see it. No doubt that's why she said she'd finished her experiments. But you have to see what happened through her eyes—"

"The eyes of a witch! The eyes of a fool! You can see the fanatical gleam in her eyes."

"I wouldn't say that to her face," I warned. "Look, she was proved wrong to take such risks, and now she certainly knows it. But she took them because she believes she must grasp every opportunity to learn about an enemy with whom we may one day be at war. At least we now know what we're up against."

"She was certainly wrong to take such risks!" Jenny said vehemently, her voice raised in anger. "She could have gotten a lot of innocent people killed. *We* could have died attempting to sort out the mess she'd made. That witch is dangerous to be around. Life is cheap to her!"

I sighed but didn't defend Grimalkin any further, and eventually Jenny calmed down. I could see her point, but reckless or not, the witch assassin had demonstrated something more important—the enormity of the threat we faced.

21
Grimalkin's Notes

However great that threat, it was now back to routine spook's business.

As I began Jenny's practical lesson the next afternoon, I got out the measuring rod and checked the dimensions of the boggart pit she had dug previously.

"Well done! It's perfect," I told her. "If you were doing this for real, by now the stonemason and the riggers would have gotten to work." I had managed to calm Jenny's anger, and she beamed at me. "The stone lid would be in position over the pit, leaving you just three things to do. What are they?"

Jenny remembered what I'd told her earlier. "First I line the pit with salt and iron to stop the boggart from escaping. Second, I use a bait dish to lure it in. Third, I wait for nightfall, when the boggart will sniff the blood and go down into the pit, but I must have the riggers standing by to lower the lid."

"Well done again!" I said, keen to give her praise when she remembered my lessons. "Now for this afternoon's practical. Your job is to line the pit."

I tugged the lid off the big bucket we'd carried with us into the southern garden. Instantly the strong smell of the glue made Jenny frown and hold her nose. It was boiled up out of the bones of dead animals, and it stank to high heaven.

There were also two sacks on the grass: one contained iron filings, the other salt.

"Use half a bag of each," I instructed.

I was pleased with the way the practical lesson was going. John Gregory had taught me well, and I realized that I had a lot of information to pass on to my new apprentice.

Jenny tipped half a bag of each into the glue and then began to stir the thick mixture with a big stick. I made her persevere for a good ten minutes, until the salt and iron were properly mixed in. Then I helped her, using a rope to lower the heavy bucket into the pit. Jenny jumped down beside it and, using an ordinary paintbrush, began to coat the walls.

"You have to cover every inch," I told her, "or the boggart will make itself really small and escape. If it was a ripper boggart, then you'd be the next person on the menu. It would drain your blood in less than a minute. If it was a stone-chucker, then it would probably come back with a small boulder and drop it on your head, cracking it open like an egg. Boggarts are dangerous, so you've got to do the binding correctly. Make one mistake, and you're dead."

After Jenny had finished the walls to my satisfaction, I took her hand and helped her climb out. Then I hauled up the bucket. Next I showed her how to tie the brush to a long stick, and she used this to reach down and paint the bottom of the pit with the mixture.

She'd almost finished when I heard a shout from the edge of the western garden. It was Grimalkin. I went and called out to the boggart, letting it know that she was not to be touched, and then escorted her back to the pit.

"I see you work your apprentices hard!" she exclaimed, watching Jenny. Then she turned to me. "Here." She held out a sheaf of paper bound with string. "These are my findings and speculations concerning the haizda mage and the Kobalos creatures I studied. It is the sum of what I have learned so far. Study it well. I will return within the week, and we will talk again."

"Are you heading north now?" I asked.

"Northeast," she replied. "I have a few things to organize."

When she had left, Jenny and I got cleaned up and went into the library. She spent the first half hour writing down what she'd learned about binding boggarts, while I began to read Grimalkin's notes.

The Contents of the Glass Containers: These are all biological, and in most cases held within some preserving material, usually a gel. Some are seeds; others animal (mammalian or reptilian samples plus hybrids).

Many are still alive, held in a state of suspended animation. I believe that, if planted, the seeds would grow. The same is probably also true of the animal samples. (I tested only three, which confirmed this.) They are all capable of development and growth, but into what I cannot say without further dangerous experimentation.

However, we know that the Kobalos have used dark magic to create many special creatures, such as builders (the whoskor, which maintain and extend the walls of Valkarky) and fighting entities (such as the haggenbrood). They may well use similar creatures in war. It could be that the dead haizda mage was preparing to create such entities locally and hide them within our borders, ready for a preemptive strike.

The First Animal Sample: I removed this sample (labeled ZANTI on the jar) from its gel preservative and introduced it to a growth medium (two parts human blood, three parts ground bone of sow, two parts sugar, three parts human spittle).

The sample was placed within the most powerful containment environment that I could generate—a large pentacle whose inner circle was fifty feet in diameter—in a meadow at least two hundred yards from the nearest tree. I also protected the pentacle from prying eyes and intrusion with spells of cloaking and menace.

I was impressed by Grimalkin's methodical approach and attention to detail, but a chill ran down my spine as I read on. The witch assassin, for all her knowledge, intelligence, and courage, had been dealing with unknown forces, and as Jenny had pointed out the day before, she'd greatly underestimated the danger posed by the varteks—a mistake that might have resulted in many deaths in the County.

The first sample had been activated on the night of the full moon. There were lots of the small insect-like creatures. Just before dawn, they had burrowed into the soil, only to emerge again after dark the following day. At this point they were fewer in number, but the remaining creatures had grown to the size of a human finger, and Grimalkin believed that while underground they had been hunting and eating each other.

They carried on doing this until only two remained.

She described them as very thin, but roughly human in shape, with long claws on their fingers and toes. Finally she entered the pentacle and killed them with her blades. Grimalkin was brave, but I thought that sometimes she had too much self-belief for her own good. She'd been dealing with entities with unknown fighting capabilities.

Not content with that, she repeated her experiments using a second sample from the jars. These new creatures chased and ate each other on the surface all day and night. These had long, cylindrical bodies in three segments like insects, although they eventually grew as big as a sheep, and much longer. They had a sharp protrusion on their foreheads, which they used to sting and paralyze their prey. Grimalkin nicknamed them stingers.

These stingers had the power to summon their prey, and this worked even though Grimalkin had fortified the pentacle with a spell of menace to keep animals and humans away. They summoned and killed crows, wood pigeons, seagulls, geese, ducks, magpies, rabbits, hare, and even a deer before finally focusing their attention on the witch assassin.

She'd felt their power as they tried to lure her into the pentacle. This time she had been wiser, slaying them from a distance with her throwing knives. After dissecting the dead creatures, she found that each of their body segments contained a heart, stomach, and brain tissue. A subsequent experiment showed that if one segment was destroyed, the creature could regenerate it. This made them fearsome entities indeed.

Her final experiment was with the varteks. It went wrong because, after the young had burrowed underground, only one apparently emerged alive; she didn't realize that a second one had also survived. When she learned that the creature was capable of eating rock and soil, she resorted to scrying. The future she saw was of a lone vartek burrowing under the pentacle to escape. So she prepared a pit and intended to lure it to its destruction there. But Grimalkin hadn't foreseen my arrival with Jenny at the moment it escaped. Nor had her scrying told her of the second vartek. Despite the terrifying nature of all that I was reading, I smiled toward the conclusion of Grimalkin's account: she had completely failed to mention our part in slaying the creature. No doubt our untimely appearance was an annoyance that she preferred to forget. She hadn't described the pursuit and killing of the second vartek, either.

I didn't smile for long. I soon remembered that she had so nearly caused the deaths of many innocent men, women, and children. What was the future threat to the County from such creatures? Commanded by the Kobalos, they would cut swathes of death through any enemy that confronted them.

Suddenly I knew what book I could contribute to the Spook's rebuilt library. Combining the information from Nicholas Browne's glossary, Grimalkin's notes, and whatever we learned in the future, I would write a Bestiary of the Kobalos. It would be something worthwhile to bequeath to those who followed in my footsteps.

I looked across at Jenny. She was staring into space, having lost concentration.

"That's enough writing for today," I told her. "Go back to the garden and practice lowering the bait dish into the pit!"

This was a tricky task that required a lot of skill. The dish contained blood, which was used to lure a ripper into a pit so that it could be bound there. This would keep her busy.

She obeyed, but she didn't look happy. She'd probably have preferred to carry on daydreaming.

Once she'd left, I continued with my own studies.

22
Times Are Changing

SHAKING my head, I read the final lines of Grimalkin's report on the Kobalos for the third time:

I believe that this third creature, the vartek (plural form: varteki), is the most formidable of the three samples I investigated. There could also be something far worse within the jars that I did not study.

In view of our approaching conflict with the Kobalos, this does not bode well.

What the witch assassin had learned was terrifying. These savage entities would no doubt be used by the Kobalos against us. How could we defend ourselves against creatures that had been crafted to kill?

Previously I had looked upon the threat from the Kobalos as distant, both in terms of geography and time. I had managed to convince myself that they dwelled far from the County; it would be many years before they could fight their way to the eastern shore of the Northern Sea. Even then, they'd have to cross that stormy expanse of water to reach us.

My opinion had now changed completely. That haizda mage had reached us already; moreover, it had the means to give life to creatures that could cause havoc in the County. There might be others of his kind, as yet undetected, already living here and growing fearsome creatures.

I needed to clear my head, so I left Grimalkin's report in the library and went out to see how Jenny was doing.

As I'd instructed, she was practicing lowering a bait dish into the pit. I watched her as she frowned in concentration.

The metal dish was attached to a chain by three small hooks, each located in one of three holes on its outer edge. Usually, especially when dealing with a ripper boggart, the dish was filled with blood. For practice sessions, we used milk. The first task was to lower the dish to the floor of the pit without spilling a drop.

I smiled with satisfaction as Jenny completed this stage perfectly. Of course, it was far more difficult on a real job. Nerves could be a problem; your hands might shake and your palms sweat.

Jenny was still holding the chain and concentrating. You had to relax the hooks a little, then give a flick. If you got it right, they came free, leaving the dish at the bottom of the pit.

She gave a cry of frustration. She was close, but she hadn't yet gotten the knack. Two of the chains had come free; the other hadn't. It tipped the dish over onto its side, spilling all the milk.

"Don't worry about it," I told her. "Have five minutes' rest and then try again. It took me weeks of practice to get it right. Better still, why don't you go down into the village and collect this week's groceries?"

Jenny did just that, and on her return successfully set the dish down on the floor of the pit and released the hooks. Not one drop of milk was spilled.

I was pleased. Her training was going well, and I liked working with her. My loneliness was fading by the day.

Our recent encounter with Bibby Longtooth had been traumatic—especially when we found the bones of the children in her cottage afterward, some still wet with blood. It had resembled a butcher's shop. For a few days I had wondered if Jenny would ever get over the experience, but now she seemed much more cheerful.

John Gregory had trained so many boys who didn't make the grade; lots ran away and didn't complete their training. I really wanted my first apprentice to become a spook. I wanted it to work out. It was still very early days, but I had high hopes for Jenny.

As she had promised, Grimalkin returned within the week. "You have read the notes I made on the investigations into the Kobalos war beasts?" she demanded.

I nodded.

"And you saw varteki in action—young ones, at that. So you see how dangerous the threat is . . . ?"

"It's very much worse than I imagined," I agreed. So it was that when she asked me once more to accompany her on her journey north, I found it difficult to refuse. It now seemed the right thing to do.

"We would be away for two months—three at the most," she told me. "Surely you can spare that much time?"

"What about Jenny? It hardly seems fair to drag her off into such danger so early in her apprenticeship. She's enjoying her training and making real progress," I replied.

"Bring her with you. We will all learn together. Learn we must if we are to have any chance at all of defeating this terrible and powerful enemy. Or, if you prefer, give her the choice of staying here. You can continue her training on your return."

❁ ❁ ❁

As she'd once done before, when preparing for the Battle of the Wardstone, Grimalkin set up camp in the garden. Up in the library, I broke the news to Jenny.

"We're going on a long journey with Grimalkin," I told her. "We need to study the Kobalos so that we can discover how to defeat them. So we're going to cross the Northern Sea and travel to the edge of their territory."

"How long will we be away?" she said, looking far from happy.

"We'll be back before winter really bites."

She nodded but didn't seem convinced.

"Can you ride?" I asked.

She looked puzzled. "I've ridden a horse at one of the farms where my foster dad works, but not recently. It was when I was little."

"If it makes you feel better, I'm not much of a rider myself. Spooks prefer to journey on foot, but we're traveling a long way, so we'll be on horseback."

Jenny was silent.

"I'll tell you the truth," I said eventually. "It will be dangerous. I feel that I must go, but you *could* stay here. You'd be safe enough, with the boggart to guard you. You could continue to develop your practical skills and work your way through the library, making notes. I might also be able to find someone else to train you for a while."

Jenny didn't appear too happy at the prospect.

"I'll take you to meet another spook north of Caster, and then you can decide. I'm going to ask him to keep an eye on Chipenden while we're away. It would mean extra work for him, but I'm sure he could deal with the most important spook's business in both areas. Once you've met him, you might agree to him training you."

Jenny's face fell further at this.

"What's the matter?" I asked.

"Nothing . . . well, it's just the thought of leaving Chipenden to travel to the far north. I like to travel—I've seen most of the County on my wanderings—but to sail overseas and see foreign lands is something I've only dreamed about. I'm not sure what to think, but I reckon I'd rather stay here. And I don't want to be trained by anyone but you."

"I'd rather stay here too, Jenny!" I told her. "I feel exactly the same, but I don't really have much choice."

So I spent another ten minutes spelling out the threat from the Kobalos and what their intention was: to kill all human males, boys and men, and then enslave all females. Then I reminded her about the varteki we'd faced and how those would be used against us.

"So you see, Jenny, I have to go. Anyway, keep an open mind until after you've met Judd."

Jenny frowned again, but now that I'd made up my mind to help Grimalkin, I had no time to dawdle.

We traveled north over the fells, passing east of Caster and then continuing along the bank of the canal, which ran northward. I set a fast pace, for there was a real nip in the air now. Long before we reached Kendal, I headed west, leading Jenny along a path by a stream until we came to the edge of the shallow moat that surrounded the water mill.

It had once been a working mill, and then home to Spook Bill Arkwright. My master had sent me to work with him for a while; he wanted me to learn about water witches and other creatures of the dark that dwelled in that region. But Bill's main task had been to toughen me up and give me combat training. He had certainly done that. I'd grown to like him, though, and still mourned his passing.

Judd Brinscall, another ex-apprentice of John Gregory, was the Spook in residence now. He had not impressed me on our first encounter: he had been threatened, his family in fear for their lives; under such duress, he'd betrayed my master. But later he had helped us, and my master had forgiven him. I'd not found his actions so easy to forget, but he had been useful since, and besides, he was the only other Spook I knew of nearby, the only one qualified to give me further training, something he'd promised to do.

Looking down at the moat, I turned to Jenny. "This is designed to keep water witches at bay," I told her.

"If they're water witches, why are they deterred by water?" Jenny asked, her face creased in puzzlement. "That doesn't make sense."

"In common with most types of witches, they don't like salt," I explained. "Every few days, Judd tips a few barrels into the moat. That keeps them out."

"Are there a lot of water witches around here?" Jenny wondered.

"Yes, they're drawn to the marsh," I said, pointing toward it. The sun was setting, and a mist was coming in from the distant sea. "It's an important place for water witches. It's sacred to them in some way. So despite the presence of a spook and his dogs, they come here from time to time. Then Judd hunts them across the marsh. He covers a big area, ranging north of Morecambe Bay as far as the lakes, right to the northern County border."

As I waded through the salted moat, I heard dogs barking, which meant that Judd was at home.

As the two animals bounded toward us, I felt Jenny flinch behind me. I didn't blame her. They were big, fearsome wolfhounds.

They reached me before I came to the door, and I paused to pat them and to be licked in return. I was happy to see them, but sad as well. There were only two of them now, Blood and Bone. Their mother, Claw, had been killed at the Battle of the Wardstone, where my master had also died.

"Come inside!" a voice shouted. "It's like the middle of winter out here!"

Judd was waiting at the door, and he greeted me warmly. However, I noticed that as we approached, he gave Jenny a strange look.

"This is my apprentice, Jenny," I told him.

I watched his jaw drop in astonishment. I supposed I would have to get used to this sort of reaction.

Soon we were at his table, tucking into a supper of delicious cod. This close to the sea, there was always plenty of fresh fish available.

I'd recently communicated with Judd by letter, but it was the first time we'd met face-to-face since the battle, and I had a lot to tell him. I decided to delay that until after we'd eaten.

"How's the hand, Judd?" I asked him. He'd lost two of his fingers at the Wardstone; they'd been bitten off by an enemy witch.

He held up his right hand and grimaced. "The soreness is gone, though the hand is still a little stiff. But we adapt, don't we? I can't do anything about it, so I just carry on as best I can. The truth is, I'd have given twice as many fingers if I could have Claw back. I hadn't had her long, but I'd grown really attached to her."

After that, we talked little as we ate, but Judd kept glancing at me and Jenny curiously; as soon as I'd cleared my plate and eased my chair away from the table, he pointed to the stairs.

"Your room is on the first floor, the second on the left, young lady," he told Jenny. "There are fresh sheets and pillowcases in the cupboard on the landing. You look tired, so you'd best get up to bed."

Jenny didn't argue, as I expected her to, and with a nod to us both, she left the table and set off up the stairs. She'd been unusually quiet since we arrived at the mill; she hadn't spoken at all during the meal. I wondered if she was sickening for something.

"So, Tom . . . ," Judd began. "How are you coping with work as the Chipenden Spook? Have you come to ask for help? If so, I'd only be too glad. I've neither the skill nor the knowledge of poor John Gregory, but I'm sure I've plenty to contribute to your training."

It annoyed me that Judd used the word "poor" about my master. He wasn't to be pitied: he'd died fighting the dark and had been a champion of the light all his life. It was the way he'd have chosen to leave this life. But I realized that

Judd didn't really intend anything by the comment, so I let it pass.

"It's been very quiet at Chipenden," I told him. "The dark seems almost dormant."

"It's been the same here, too," Judd said. "I've seen neither hide nor hair of a water witch for over a month. And the recent plague of skelts is well and truly over."

At this, I remembered the night I'd faced a dangerous skelt outside this very mill; it had thrust its long bone tube into my neck and tried to drink my blood. I'd been lucky to escape with my life.

I concentrated on what Judd said next.

"It's been almost too quiet . . . it feels as if the dark is gathering its strength."

"That could well be the case," I told him.

"So has anything else strange happened since you wrote—apart from the fact that you've taken on a girl apprentice, that is?"

I ignored his jibe and began my account. "When I wrote, I told you what I'd learned about the threat from the Kobalos, but it seems that they might launch their attack on the County a lot sooner than I expected. One of the Kobalos, a haizda mage, was here. It had built a lair in a tree less than an hour's journey from Chipenden. It killed three girls before I realized what I was dealing with. The beast's dead now, but there could well be others."

I went into more detail, describing exactly what had happened and Jenny's part in it all. At the first mention of her name, Judd raised his eyebrows. But I finished my story, concluding with Grimalkin's investigation of the lair of the dead mage. I told him about her experiments and the varteki we'd encountered. After that, Judd was silent for a long time.

"Without that sword, it would have been the end of you," he said at last. "Perhaps you could ask the witch assassin to make one for me too. If I ever come up against one of those Kobalos mages, my staff wouldn't be much use."

"I can't tell how effective a staff might be. I'd left mine with the girl, so I never got a chance to use it. But you're correct: such a mage uses powerful dark magic. Though it wouldn't be easy for Grimalkin to craft another sword like mine. It's not just infused with her magic—she forged it from a piece of ore that fell from the sky."

"From a meteorite?"

"Yes, and a very rare one, too. We need to find other ways to deal with such a mage. Hopefully Grimalkin will come up with something."

"I'm surprised you took that girl on as an apprentice," Judd said suddenly, changing the subject. "She hung around here for days awhile back, begging that I do the same. Eventually I had to set the dogs on her. It was the only way to be rid of her. You should have seen her run! One of the dogs tore off a piece of her skirt!"

No wonder she had been reluctant to come here. I was learning that Jenny kept things to herself and told you little unless you asked outright. It was cruel of Judd to have set the wolfhounds on her—Jenny hadn't deserved that. I remember how scared I'd been of such big, fierce hunting dogs when I'd first met them. But what was done was done, and I saw no point in antagonizing Judd by bringing him to task for it.

I shrugged. "I suppose I felt guilty about underestimating that mage. Because of that, I almost got her killed."

"Well, you'd be better off without her. For one thing, you've still a lot to learn yourself without the added responsibility of an apprentice. Even if she really *is* the seventh daughter of a seventh daughter, there's no precedent for a woman becoming a spook."

"There has to be a first time for everything," I said, starting to feel angry again. "And I stand by my decision. She had the guts to face up to the ghasts on Hangman's Hill. I'm sure she'll make a go of things."

"It won't work, Tom. I never dreamed you'd be daft enough to take on a girl. What would John Gregory have said?"

I shrugged. "Times are changing, Judd, and we have to change with them. Let me come to the main reason for my visit. I'm going north with Grimalkin to visit the kingdoms that border the Kobalos lands. We're going to try and learn what we can about our new enemies—I'll be away for two months or so. Would you be prepared to visit Chipenden and deal with the worst manifestations of the dark there? I know it's asking a lot for you to manage two large areas, but I've nobody else I can turn to."

"You're not leaving the girl behind for me to look after, are you?"

I shook my head. "No, she's traveling with me," I told him. After what Judd had just said, I didn't want Jenny to have to stay with him. Whether she wanted to leave the County or not, she'd surely rather be out of his way.

"Well, in that case, as things are relatively quiet for the time being, I'd be only too happy to help out, Tom," he said with a smile. "A girl apprentice . . . I never thought I'd see the day!"

23
The Scream of the Boggart

On our journey back to Chipenden, I spoke to Jenny about Judd. After his treatment of her, she was understandably reluctant to stay at home if he was to be there.

"I assume that you don't want to stay behind with Judd when I travel north?"

"I certainly don't!" Jenny replied with some force.

"I gathered as much. He told me about setting the dogs on you. Judd was wrong to do that, and I understand your anger. And he won't stay at the mill. He'll be visiting Chipenden to keep an eye on things. So even there you'd sometimes be in his company. So are you happy to travel north with us?"

"I'm not happy at all!" she replied. "The thought of it makes me nervous, but it's for the best. I'll just have to get used to the idea."

There was no sign of Grimalkin when we crossed the

western garden. No doubt she had gone off to make preparations for our journey.

The first night back, I was awakened in the early hours by a terrible scream. It was so loud that it rattled the lower window sash. It was a scream of rage that I knew well, and it came from nearby.

The boggart was challenging an intruder.

I climbed out of bed and dressed quickly. While I was pulling on my socks, the boggart screamed out its challenge for the second time. I knew that it would give three warnings before attacking. It always kept to the rules we had agreed.

It gave its third warning while I was hastily lacing up my boots.

What could have entered the garden? I wondered. Normally I'd have been confident that Kratch could deal with it. But with all that was going on at the moment, we could well be facing the Kobalos. After my encounter with the varteki and the haizda mage, nothing was certain.

Jenny was already waiting for me at the foot of the stairs. She had her staff in her hand and was ready to fight, having already released the blade at its tip.

"Stay just inside the back door!" I told her. "If anything approaches the house, shout loud enough to awake the dead!"

"I want to go with you!" she insisted, grabbing my arm.

"Do as you're told!" I snapped, reaching for my staff. "You'd be in danger from the boggart."

I buckled on the scabbard and sheathed the Starblade before racing across the lawn and into the trees of the western garden. There was some truth in what I'd just told Jenny. The boggart had been instructed not to harm her, but it would now be filled with bloodlust; in the heat of the moment, she could well be at risk. But my main reason for leaving her behind was to keep her at a safe distance from this unknown intruder.

Suddenly I heard other screams. These did not come from the thirsty throat of the boggart; they were cries of agony, probably the dying shrieks of the creature it had attacked. I began to sense the position of the intruder in my mind, though I didn't really need that gift—the cries drew me to the spot.

All at once there was silence, and I slowed down, approaching more cautiously. In the moonlight, a scene of carnage greeted me, and I turned and retched. I stood there for a moment, taking a few deep breaths and swallowing to bring my stomach under control.

The grass was slick with blood. There was a lot of it—too much, I realized, for just one intruder. Then I saw the first of the heads. It had been impaled on a sapling, and its staring eyes were on a level with my own.

It was a Kobalos mage—there was no doubt about it. I studied the elongated jaw, which hung open, showing sharp teeth. Unlike the mage I'd fought in the tree, the face of this creature was not shaven, and it looked even more bestial. Its long hair was pulled into a single pigtail behind its head.

All at once I heard the lapping of a rasping tongue. Kratch wasn't about to let any blood go to waste. After a while, the sound stopped and a purring began; moments later, something furry and cold rubbed against my left leg. It was the boggart in its cat form, and immediately it spoke inside my head.

They were tasty but strange, it hissed. *It was blood of a flavor I've never sampled before. I could grow to like it. I want more.*

"How many were there, Kratch?" I demanded.

There were three. Will more come this way?

"They might. They are Kobalos mages, and they are my enemies. Soon I must journey across the sea to learn more about them. While I am away, the Spook called Judd Brinscall will come here to work. Allow him entry to the garden and house, and touch not a hair of his head. Is it agreed?"

Yes, it is agreed. If you need me while you are away, just call my name and I will stand by your side. We will hunt together.

"If danger threatens, I'll do so, but I will be far away across the sea. Would it be possible for you to travel such a distance?"

It would be difficult but not impossible, Kratch replied. *Some lines extend across the beds of deep seas. They were there before the land sank and was flooded.*

The boggart was referring to ley lines, which it used to travel rapidly from place to place. It rubbed against my leg again, and then the purring gradually faded away.

I went back to the house, deciding to leave the gruesome work of collecting up the bloody remains until the morning.

Once the sun was up the following day, I gave Jenny the task of digging a burial pit while I collected what remained of the three Kobalos.

"You get all the fun and I get all the digging!" Jenny complained as I returned to her side.

"Fun, you call it? Collecting fragments of flesh and bone is hardly fun, is it?"

"Don't be daft—I didn't mean that. I mean last night. I wanted to go with you; I wanted to share the danger."

I felt annoyed. I couldn't imagine any situation in which I'd have called my own master daft. But I took a deep breath and spoke to her calmly.

"If your apprenticeship turns out to be even half as eventful as mine, you'll have had your fill of danger long before the first year is done and dusted," I told her. "In this job, you don't go running toward danger—it comes searching for you!"

Jenny fell silent at that, but she didn't look happy in her work.

I had already used a mirror to tell Grimalkin what had happened. She arrived as I was adding the final pieces to the bloody pile of remains.

In addition to the body parts, there were pieces of armor, three sabers, and a number of long blades. I had laid these out in a row on the grass.

"They were assassins." Grimalkin held up one of the heads and inspected it closely. "The single pigtail denotes that. The most powerful brotherhood of Kobalos assassins is called the Shaiksa—they have three pigtails—but they would no doubt have suffered the same fate at the hands of your boggart. Of course, the Shaiksa have great skill with weapons. You would not wish to meet three of them away from the protection of the boggart."

"Do you think they were sent to kill me?" I asked.

"Not necessarily. I suspect they were sent to reinforce the haizda mage for some other common purpose. No doubt they found its grave and noted that its lair had been entered and searched. It would have been an easy matter to track you back to this house. I would like two of those sabers," Grimalkin said. "I may have a use for them."

"Take what you like," I told her. I wondered what she wanted them for, but she didn't volunteer the information and I didn't ask. Despite our alliance, the witch assassin did not share everything with me. There was much about her that would forever remain a mystery.

I walked across to inspect the pit Jenny had dug, and then sent her back to the house to study in the library so that she wouldn't be part of the grisly task I now had to perform.

Grimalkin helped me to bury what was left of the Kobalos assassins. Apart from the two sabers, I stored the rest of their weaponry in the small room where I kept the spare staffs.

The entry into the garden by these assassins only made me more certain that I was doing the right thing in traveling north with Grimalkin.

The Kobalos threat was indeed imminent.

24
The Journey Begins

THE following day, we started to prepare for our journey.

We bought provisions, and Grimalkin carried a tent into the western garden, setting it up to show us the quarters we would share on the journey. It wasn't like the ridge tents that I'd seen the County military use; it was a tall, conical structure—a covering of skins was supported by five long poles that bent over to meet at the top. Each pole was formed of three short sections that could be slotted together when erecting the tent. It made them easier to carry.

One thing caught my eye. Stitched onto the skins were a number of circular pieces of what appeared to be silk; each was embellished with the image of a red County rose. The tent was functional, no doubt well suited to its purpose, but the roses made it look somewhat grand.

Grimalkin told me that we would need such a tent in the far north, where it was difficult to keep warm at night, but she didn't mention the roses. I wondered where she had gotten the tent.

I bought long sheepskin jackets for me and Jenny; we could wear them under our cloaks. At the moment, the County weather was chilly enough to make them welcome. Winter would come early this year.

By the end of the week, our preparations were complete. Grimalkin already had her own horse and had procured three more—one each for Jenny and me, and one to carry most of our supplies. My final act was to leave a note for Judd Brinscall, telling him of the assassins and their fate at the hands of the boggart. I wanted him to be aware that there could be further intrusions into the garden.

With that, we set off, heading eastward. At the end of that first day, we rode through a valley in single file, high hills on either side. Grimalkin was in the lead, while I brought up the rear. The sun had already sunk, and darkness was not far away. I'd already had enough. I was far from comfortable in the saddle, and the prospect of weeks of riding filled me with dismay.

Ahead I saw a small lake, and Grimalkin signaled that we should set up camp beside it.

She left Jenny and me to put up the tent while she lit a fire and caught some fish for our supper. We struggled a bit—erecting the tent required some skill; no doubt we'd get plenty of practice as we went.

After we'd eaten, we sat around the fire for a while.

"How has the first day's riding been?" Grimalkin asked.

"Not comfortable," I replied.

"My bum's sore and the insides of my legs are rubbed almost raw," Jenny complained, "but no doubt I'll get used to it."

"You'll get used to it, all right," said the witch assassin. "Today we have begun slowly to allow you to adjust. Tomorrow we will go a little faster. After we reach the coast and sail across the Northern Sea, we will get up to full speed. We have a long way to go."

Soon after that, we turned in for the night. The ground was hard, but the tent proved surprisingly warm. Wrapped in my blanket, I fell asleep within minutes.

At last we reached Scarborough, a small coastal port with a high castle. There we booked our passage and boarded a large three-masted ship.

We left our horses behind at a livery stable; the owner halved his exorbitant price after one threatening glare from Grimalkin. We stowed our baggage in the hold, intending to buy or hire new mounts on the other side of the Northern Sea. Grimalkin had traveled this way many times before and knew what she was about.

And so we sailed slowly away from our own land, across an expanse of water that was quite calm. I'd been warned that, more often than not, the crossing here could be extremely rough.

"What's bothering you?" asked Grimalkin, looking at me closely as we leaned over the starboard rail, staring down at the calm water. The lack of wind meant that our vessel was making little progress. "You seem deep in thought."

The witch assassin wore a thick gown with a hood and gloves. Had there been a rough sea with spray, she would doubtless have retreated to her quarters belowdecks; even Grimalkin was vulnerable to salt, although she had a far greater tolerance than others from the Pendle witch clans.

"You've convinced me of the need to make this journey," I told her. "But I don't like to be away from the County for too long. I feel I'm letting the people down—not doing my duty as John Gregory would have expected."

"By traveling with me, you are doing more to help the County than you can imagine. Together we can gather knowledge about our enemies that might make the survival of the County possible. Soon the Kobalos will attack the northern kingdoms. If they fall, they will then press on southward to the coast. Our own lands lie just across this sea. We face a new darkness; one even worse than that threatened by the Fiend. The Kobalos intend to destroy and enslave humanity, make no mistake about it."

"But we really *will* be back in the County within a couple of months? You will keep your promise?"

"I will do my very best to bring you back well within that time. We are heading for the kingdoms that border the Kobalos lands. Once we disembark, we will head for the northern regions, where there is ice and snow all the year round. It is only September now, but in another couple of months, winter will be nigh and the cold will come south. We need to return before that happens. We shouldn't have to go far to learn what we need. If it comes to it, we will race the snows south."

The weather changed quickly, and soon we were being battered by a cold wind from the north. The sea grew choppy, then mountainous. Jenny was sick first, and less than an hour later, I too brought up my breakfast. Whether Grimalkin felt the effects of the stormy sea I never knew; long before the first salt spray stung my eyes, she'd retreated belowdecks.

At the end of our sea crossing lay a port called Amstelredamme. Here Grimalkin hired a fisherman to take us farther up the river to a small town where the proprietor of a large stable greeted Grimalkin with a low bow and called her ma'am. It was clear that Grimalkin was well known to him and that they had traded together previously. We were furnished with four excellent mounts. Grimalkin handed over the payment. She seemed to have an endless supply of money—most of it in the form of gold coins. It was what she referred to as her war chest.

Some of our provisions were carried in panniers attached to each side of our mounts. Once again the fourth horse was used for baggage, carrying the tent and the bulk of our food and equipment.

As we set off, Jenny patted her horse's head and whispered into its ear. It was a beautiful creature with a friendly disposition, and despite her earlier doubts and discomfort, she was clearly delighted to be riding it. But Grimalkin noted this and shook her head in warning.

"Don't get too attached to that mare, child. This is the first of several you'll be riding. We need to keep up a fast pace and will be changing our mounts every few days as they tire."

I wondered how *we'd* cope with the pace, never mind the horses.

We were now in a foreign land, but in truth, it looked very similar to certain parts of the County back home. This was a flat moss land with a huge sky; gangs of men were busy cutting peat and heaping it onto carts. However, we had a long journey ahead of us, and no doubt the scenery would change.

Grimalkin proved as good as her word. We rode hard from dawn until dusk each day, only pausing to rest, water, and feed the horses. We had our midday meal in the saddle, eating our one hot meal after dark. After two more days, we changed our mounts for fresh ones in another small town.

For the moment, we slept in our blankets without using the tent. We were traveling northeast, and at first the weather was considerably warmer and drier than that of the County we had left behind. We had a southerly breeze at our backs, and our horses' hooves raised clouds of dust so that we were forced to wrap scarves about our noses and mouths.

But after the first week, the wind changed and blew hard from the north, making the nights much colder. By dawn the grass was usually white with frost. We started to use the tent; erecting it each night and dismantling it each morning became part of our routine, accomplished without thought.

The plain we traveled across was vast and sparsely populated. We skirted the rare towns and changed our mounts at hamlets or roadside inns where Grimalkin seemed to be known to the landlord. She had clearly taken this route more than once.

One night, during the second week of our journey over-land, we were sitting around the campfire, listening to the howling of wolves in the distance, when Grimalkin started to tell us more about the purpose of our journey.

"We have crossed three countries so far; nations that, once roused, may prove to be at least a temporary buffer against the Kobalos. But tomorrow we will reach one of the small principalities that border the lands of our enemies. When the war begins, they will be the first to fall. There we will encounter our first Kobalos."

"Just one?" I asked.

Grimalkin nodded, her eyes glittering like the stars that were clustered overhead. "The Kobalos have many orders of mage, and almost as many brotherhoods of assassins. As I told you back in Chipenden, the most formidable of these are known as the Shaiksa—they are referred to in Nicholas Browne's glossary. Just over a year ago, one came to the border of the principality of Polyznia. He issued a challenge, offering to fight human champions in single combat—at least, any who dared accept, because he quickly demonstrated his ability to dispatch most of his opponents within moments. His name is Kauspetnd. I suspect that he is the most formidable member of his brotherhood."

The behavior of this assassin seemed strange, but before I could remark upon it, Jenny spoke up.

"What's the point of that? What does the assassin hope to achieve, apart from the deaths of his opponents?" she asked.

"That's a good question, child," Grimalkin replied. "But we must remember that we are dealing with minds alien to our own. The Shaiksa assassins live to fight and kill; they love to demonstrate their formidable prowess. However, something else may be happening here. I believe the haizda mage that your new master slew was a spy—but also something more. As well as gathering information, he was testing our strengths and vulnerabilities before the coming war. And that is precisely what the Shaiksa assassin is doing, in a different way."

"So you think he is trying to prove his superiority?" I asked.

"Yes, I'm certain of it. His intention is to demoralize the human foe and spread the belief in Kobalos martial supremacy. By issuing his challenge and dispatching so many of his human opponents so easily, he has demonstrated just how formidable he is. And in so doing, he is filling human warriors with dismay, destroying their morale. For him, it is a great honor to be the single vanguard of the Kobalos army."

"Is it working?" I asked. "What about those who witness the defeats of their champions?"

"Representatives of the rulers of the northern principalities—and, in some cases, the princes themselves—have gathered on the south bank of a river that marks the border with the Kobalos territory. The lone Shaiksa assassin is camped on the far side, and each day he issues a challenge. If the challenge is not taken up, he returns the next day to mock and insult the humans."

"Don't any of the rulers fight for their honor?" asked Jenny.

"At first the challenges were answered by local warlords—men little better than bandits, who have sworn allegiance to a patron and, in return, are free to base themselves in forts on main highways or at river crossings and exact tribute from travelers. Most of the princes now appoint skilled champions to fight on their behalf. Every week the assassin faces some such champion—faces, fights, and kills him very quickly," answered Grimalkin. "When, finally, one prince screwed up his courage and faced Kauspetnd in person, he lasted less than a minute."

"Do you hope to learn about the Shaiksa by going there?" I asked. "Or is there something else that you've not told me?"

Grimalkin smiled, showing me her teeth. "All will be revealed in good time!" she said.

"I'd like to know now," I insisted, meeting her gaze.

"I want to study Kauspetnd's skills," she told me. "We will learn and then eventually put that knowledge to good use. The time will come when he must die."

Somewhere in the distance a wolf howled, and I shivered. I sensed danger ahead.

The following day, just before noon, Grimalkin rode off alone to scout ahead. She told us that she had to check that the situation at the riverbank was unchanged.

She was away for about two hours, which allowed me the opportunity to talk to Jenny and give her a short lesson. I was listing the various categories of boggart and the usual steps for dealing with them. It was a lesson that I remembered learning from my master; his face kept drifting into my mind's eye, making it difficult to concentrate. And as I spoke, I could hear John Gregory's voice in my ear.

"There are four main stages when dealing with boggarts," I explained, "and we use the acronym NIBS as an aid to memory. We *negotiate*, *intimidate*, *bind*, and *slay*, in that order, though the final one is used only as a last resort. Sometimes a boggart will listen to reason and move on from a spot where it's causing problems."

I watched Jenny jotting down what I'd said in her notebook. But suddenly she stopped writing and looked up at me.

"Do you trust Grimalkin?" she asked.

I nodded. "It's wise always to keep in mind that she's a witch assassin and has her own agenda. But she's been a good ally in the past, and we have a common cause in dealing with the threat of the Kobalos. So yes, I do."

"We may have a common cause, but where the Kobalos are concerned she seems fanatical. Have you seen the expression in her eyes when she talks of them?"

I nodded, feeding the fire with fresh wood to keep the cold at bay. "Grimalkin has crossed blades with them already. She even spent time in their city, Valkarky. She's seen firsthand how they keep women as slaves. A witch like her, a woman of power, feels a sense of duty toward those who suffer like that. They may not be witches, but she looks upon them as oppressed sisters. She's sworn to free them and overthrow the Kobalos."

"I can understand that," Jenny replied, "and I can't fault her for it. If I had her power, I would try to do the same. But I don't like that fanatical gleam. People like that are capable of anything to achieve their goals. They use people. If necessary, they sacrifice them."

I didn't reply. I'd already had some experience of that. Although she'd loved me, my own mam had been prepared to use me in any way that she deemed necessary to destroy the Fiend. I found some of what had happened hard to contemplate now. At the time, when she'd demanded certain things of me, such as the sacrifice of Alice, I'd been upset. Looking back now, I was appalled by what I'd been asked to do—and hated myself more for having even considered it. So I understood exactly what Jenny was warning me about.

My apprentice glanced at me warily. She must have read the expression on my face and realized that her words had troubled me. So she changed the subject.

"Wouldn't it be better if you taught me about witches rather than boggarts?" she asked. "I mean, we're traveling with a witch. It might be useful to know about County witch clans."

Jenny had questioned me about this already, and for a moment I was irritated. "My master always gave lessons on boggarts in the first year and witches in the second," I explained. "I suppose I've just gone along with his routine. I remember thinking the same way as you."

I remembered it only too well: in the first weeks of my apprenticeship I'd faced great danger from two powerful Pendle witches—Bony Lizzie and Mother Malkin—and wished I'd been studying witches, not boggarts.

Suddenly I decided to break with the past. I had to find my own ways of doing things.

"All right, we'll do things differently. Boggarts can wait until next year. Tomorrow I'll start teaching you about witches."

Jenny's face lit up with a smile, but then she frowned. "There's something I need to tell you," she said.

"Don't be afraid to say what's on your mind. I kept things from John Gregory, and now I regret not being more honest with him."

"Well, it's happened more than once, and each time in almost exactly the same way. When I was sitting alone on the bench in the western garden, writing things up in my notebook—it never happened when you were teaching me—I'd sense somebody watching me. I'd look up, and there in the shadow of the trees, a girl stood staring at me. She was always scowling angrily."

"What did she look like?" I asked, my heart starting to beat faster.

"She was probably about my height, and slim, with dark hair. She was pretty, but as soon as I looked directly at her, she'd vanish. The first time I thought I'd imagined it, but later I knew for sure that she was there. Was it a witch? Was she using magic to disappear? And how did she get into the garden? I thought the boggart was supposed to guard it."

"Alice!" I exclaimed before I could stop myself.

"Who's Alice?" Jenny asked. "And why is she so angry with me?"

25
The Shaiksa Assassin

I sighed and decided to tell Jenny the truth—or at least as much as she needed to know.

"For a time Alice lived with John Gregory and me at Chipenden. But although we fought the dark together, she'd received two years' training in witchcraft from her mother, Bony Lizzie—she's dead now, but she was a powerful Pendle witch who specialized in bone magic."

"Bony Lizzie once passed through Grimsargh," Jenny told me. "It was before I was even born, but people still talk about it. They locked their doors and drew their curtains and refused to answer when she knocked. But it did them no good. A child went missing and was never seen again. And there were five dead cats floating in the local pond, each with its neck broken. Later that year the crops failed—all of them."

I nodded. "That sounds like Lizzie's doing. Anyway,

my master never trusted Alice; at the time, that made me angry, because I thought she was my friend. But eventually he was proved right. Alice went to the dark. She shares her life with a dark mage called Lukrasta now."

"Were you close . . . really close friends?"

"We went through a lot together. She saved my life more than once. Yes, we were close," I admitted.

Jenny nodded and stared off into space for a while. Then she came back with another question.

"But how did she get past the boggart and into the garden to stare at me?"

"She has really powerful dark magic at her disposal," I replied. "The boggart's not strong enough to stop her."

"And why would she be watching me? Why scowl at me like that? What have I done to her?"

I shrugged. "Who knows what's going through the mind of someone who's gone to the dark? But however angry she was, I don't think she'd hurt an apprentice of mine. I don't think she'd hurt either of us."

"Perhaps she scowled at me because she's jealous—"

"Jealous!" I exclaimed.

"She could be jealous of me living in the house with you. In a way I've taken her place, haven't I?"

"I suppose you have," I replied doubtfully.

Could Alice really be jealous of Jenny? Did she miss

being with me? I wondered. Angrily, I dismissed the thought from my head. My mind kept snatching at straws, building impossible hopes. Alice was best forgotten.

"Look," I said, giving Jenny a smile, "I'll teach you about witches, but there's something else we can study together—the Kobalos."

I pulled Grimalkin's working document out of my bag and gave it to her.

"Read it carefully," I instructed. "You'll see that I've made a few additions and notes on existing entries. Eventually you might want to do the same. We'll build up our store of knowledge on these creatures together."

Within the hour, Grimalkin returned and leaped down from her horse. She strode toward us impatiently.

"A challenge has just been made and accepted," she declared. "They fight an hour before sunset. If we ride now, we might be in time to see it."

We mounted our horses and followed a river that meandered through a valley. It was bordered by dark conifers—there were few deciduous trees in this place. From the heights above it, we could see scores of campfires sending brown smoke spiraling up into the sky. As we descended, we had a good view of the gathering below on the southern bank. There were perhaps two thousand people there—at least five separate camps, each cluster of tents marked by a standard. There were also a large number of stalls, along with a neat line of cooking fires and larger tents set up on the periphery of the camp. Traders, artisans, and merchants had moved in to meet the needs of all the people. I could smell roasting pork on the wind and hear horses being shod.

"That's the Shanna River," said Grimalkin. "And beyond it, to the northeast, is the Plain of Eresteba, which is Kobalos territory. Until recently, there were Kobalos settlements on this southern bank too. They retreated several months ago, and soon afterward the Shaiksa assassin Kauspetnd arrived to issue his challenge. Why they pulled out, I don't know. But there is something ritualistic about the challenge. Perhaps it must be done across a river that divides our peoples? There is still much for us to learn."

As she spoke, I saw the intensity in her eyes—hints of the fanaticism Jenny had spoken of.

Grimalkin led us down the slope toward the river, which ran from east to west. As we rode between the lines of tents, many warriors turned to gaze at us. The expressions on their faces ranged from curious to hostile. She guided us to a quiet spot, far from the other tents, and we set up camp. While I quickly erected our tent with Jenny, Grimalkin lit a fire and then did something surprising.

She took three pieces of wood that had been lashed to her saddlebags (I had originally assumed that they formed part of the tent) and fitted them together to make a long pole. Next she fastened to the end a piece of cloth, and as Jenny and I looked on in astonishment, she thrust the other end deep into the ground.

Instantly the cloth atop the pole fluttered out in the wind. It was a flag—the standard of the County: a red rose on a white background.

"Why?" I asked Grimalkin. "Won't that draw attention to us?"

"We will draw attention whatever we do, because we are strangers to this place; there will be a pecking order here. No doubt someone will soon be along to apprise us of the fact. We will be at the bottom of the pile until we demonstrate otherwise. Leave your staff here, but wear the sword at all times. We may need to defend ourselves."

My mind was buzzing with questions, but before I could speak, there was a roar of voices from farther along the riverbank.

"Come!" Grimalkin gestured in the direction of the hubbub. "We are only just in time. Look to the needs of the horses and guard the camp, girl!" she ordered Jenny imperiously.

Jenny opened her mouth to protest. I knew that she'd

be as curious as I was to see this Shaiksa assassin. But the witch was in charge here, and moments later I was walking along the river at her heels, while Jenny was left behind.

The farther west we went, the more crowded the bank became, and Grimalkin had to push her way through the throng. They were a motley bunch, armed with blades, spears, or bows. Some wore partial metal armor, mostly stained and rusty, or jerkins of toughened leather. But all reacted in the same way to the forceful advance of Grimalkin.

They turned angrily, death in their eyes. But then they met the eyes of the witch assassin.

Her mouth was open, so maybe it was the sight of her pointed teeth, or perhaps some subtle magic. . . . Whatever it was, they instantly lowered their gaze and turned away, all thought of confrontation forgotten.

Eventually the press of bodies became too dense for us to make any further progress. However, by good fortune we found ourselves on a raised bank and could see over the heads of those who stood between us and the fast-flowing water. The river was shallow here; this was the ford, and the water rushed west, bubbling furiously over the stones.

The human champion waited on this side of the river. He was bareheaded but wore a gleaming metal breastplate and a diagonal sash of purple and gold silk. He carried a short sword and a small round shield.

"He is the champion of the Princeling of Shallotte," Grimalkin hissed into my ear. "A better class of opponent than Kauspetnd usually faces—although I fear it will make precious little difference to the outcome."

"You seem to know a lot about the situation here," I observed.

She nodded. "I've made it my business to learn as much as I can—not only about the Kobalos, but also about the human kingdoms that oppose them."

I looked across the river and got my first view of the assassin waiting on the far bank. His face had the same elongated jaw as the haizda mage back in Chipenden; there was something feral and wolflike about it, especially when he opened his mouth to reveal his sharp teeth. His head was bare, and his hair was braided into three long black pigtails. His arms were also bare, and extremely hairy, like the hide of a beast.

He carried two curved blades, the weapons known as sabers—similar to the one the haizda mage had used against me back in the County.

The pair waded into the river, coming together at the halfway point. There the water just covered their ankles. For a moment they halted and stared at each other as if weighing up the opposition.

Then Kauspetnd shouted something in a loud voice. I couldn't understand a word of it, but the tone seemed to be mocking. He finished with a braying laugh, which displayed his sharp white teeth.

His human opponent called back to him, and once again I didn't understand what was said, though anger and defiance were evident. I realized that they had both used Losta, the language shared by the Kobalos and these northern lands.

Then the human rushed forward, his boots splashing in the water, and struck out at the Kobalos warrior.

The assassin deflected the blow with his saber and spun away gracefully, raising it to meet the next attack. Again he parried the blow and spun away. For a moment they faced each other once more, and then the champion of Shallotte launched his third attack.

It was to be his last.

This time, instead of waiting in the same defensive position, Kauspetnd leaped forward to meet his human adversary halfway. One saber flashed, and blood spurted upward. Then the human gave a cry, which was echoed by a groan from those watching on the bank. He fell facedown into the water. Downstream, the turbulent water turned red as it washed his blood away.

26
The Sign

"I've seen enough for now," said Grimalkin. "But I'd like to be a little closer next time."

As the body of the human champion was dragged away, she led me back to our camp. The sky had been heavy with gray clouds, but now it was breaking up into tattered fragments scattered by the wind and lit to orange flame by the setting sun.

Jenny turned from tending the fire and looked up at me questioningly, but Grimalkin spoke first.

"Go to bed now and get sleep. We need to be up at midnight," Grimalkin said, looking directly at me. She clearly expected to be obeyed without question.

Anger flickered through me at her presumption. The land and people here were strange to me, and I was forced to defer to her greater knowledge. But she sometimes expected obedience without question, withholding information until she considered the time right to reveal it.

"Aren't we going to eat first?" asked Jenny.

I sympathized with her. I was hungry too and had been looking forward to supper.

Grimalkin didn't reply, so I broke the silence.

"Why must we sleep now?" I asked. "What are we going to do at midnight?"

"There's something you should see. It's important. After that, we can eat while we talk," she replied before turning to the girl and smiling. "There will be supper, but it will be a late one."

Grimalkin always had a good reason for everything she did, so I nodded, swallowed my annoyance, and crawled into the tent first. I was asleep the moment I rolled into my blankets.

When I opened my eyes again and emerged to stare up at the star-filled sky, I estimated that it was close to midnight.

Grimalkin was already waiting outside, Jenny standing beside her.

Without preamble, the witch assassin pointed south, away from the river, and set off at a brisk pace. I looked at the forest of tents on the riverbank and saw lights moving. They were torches; others were walking in the same direction. "Is it safe to leave our possessions unguarded?" I asked.

"I have protected our camp with a spell," Grimalkin replied, glancing back at me.

Jenny leaned close and whispered in my ear, "Let's hope the thieves don't dig under it, then!"

We were crossing flat meadowland, but I could see a hill directly ahead, a dark silhouette against the stars. It wasn't particularly high, but it stood out from the plain around it. It was almost conical, but flattened at the summit.

As we drew closer, other people pressed in on either side, and we became part of the silent procession. At last we were brought to a complete halt; all we could do was gaze at the hill.

The starlight was bright enough to illuminate the slope facing us. I could see that although the silent gathering had formed a half circle at its base, nobody had set foot on it.

We waited in silence for about five minutes; I knew that it was very close to midnight now. Then three figures began to climb the hill. When they reached the summit, they turned to face us. All three were slim and bearded; they stared out, chins held high, as if their gaze was fixed not upon us but on something higher. They wore gloves and identical robes, their collars trimmed with white animal fur.

The one in the middle cried out in a loud voice. It sounded like a command.

"He told us to kneel and pray," Grimalkin said.

The people around us began to kneel, and Grimalkin followed suit.

It was astonishing to see her on her knees like that. But if she was prepared to kneel, then so was I; Jenny followed my example. I stared at the hill, where the three figures extended their arms and pointed up to the sky.

"Are they priests?" I whispered into Grimalkin's ear.

"Not priests of any conventional church. They are holy men called magowie; they are the mages of this land, who claim to see the true reality beyond this world. What we see—the sky, grass, hills, and rocks—is to them just an illusion. They wear gloves because none but a prince or a king may touch their bare hands. Now look at the sky directly above them. What do you see?"

I stared upward. For a moment I could see nothing, but then I made out against the starry background a point of light—very bright . . . and falling toward us.

It grew steadily larger and brighter. At first it looked like a bird, a dove perhaps, something feathered and white. Then a cry of wonder went up from those around us. I couldn't understand what all the fuss was about. Why was everyone so excited?

Most birds, apart from corpse fowls, owls, and a few other species, roosted at night. But who knew what was normal in these northern climes? However, judging by the crowd's reaction, this was something strange and wonderful, something that was worth dragging yourself from your bed at midnight for.

And then a shiver ran the length of my spine. I saw that it was not a bird after all.

This flying creature had a human shape!

"It looks like an angel!" Jenny exclaimed.

Lower and lower it came, until the figure hovered not more than fifty feet above the heads of the three mystics. Completely covered in white feathers but for the head, it had two wings, each at least the length of its body. The face was that of a girl, and it was beautiful, glowing with a silvery light. The limbs were thin, and the enormous wings were rather out of proportion with the body. I had to agree with Jenny: it *did* look like an angel. It was an astonishing sight—I just didn't know what to make of it.

Three beams of light were projected from the mysterious flying creature, each of them lighting up one of the three figures below. All three magowie cried out; for what reason I could not tell, but their faces were twisted as if in torment. As one, they fell to their knees, and instantly the creature vanished.

A groan went up from the crowd, which soon became an excited babble. I searched the sky carefully but could detect no sign of movement against the stars. What manner of thing was it that it could vanish like that? Powerful magic was at work here—but who was wielding it?

The central magowie rose unsteadily to his feet, while his companions remained on their knees. He held up his hand until everyone fell silent, then began to speak.

I turned to Grimalkin, who started to translate for my benefit. A burly warrior turned to look at us, but she gave him a withering glare and continued.

"The magowie says that a brave man died today, the champion of Shallotte. He did his duty, but he was not the chosen one. Now the angel has spoken. The one who will prevail against the Shaiksa walks among us! Soon he will declare himself—the moment is almost upon us. Then he will kill Kauspetnd, and before the moon is full he will lead us over the river to victory. Now the magowie bids us return to our beds and gather our strength for the coming battle."

The three magowie descended from the hill and merged with the crowd. We were forced backward, so we went with the flow and soon found ourselves approaching the camp again.

"How did you know this would happen tonight?" Jenny

demanded as she put more wood on the fire and set two rabbits to cook over it.

Grimalkin shrugged. "This has been going on for months. Every week a human champion is defeated and slain. I witnessed it myself on my previous visit here."

"I've seen flying lamias before, but what was that?" I asked.

"It was an angel, as your apprentice suggested. Weren't you listening to my translation?" Grimalkin asked with a smile.

"Angels are just things out of fables," I said, shaking my head. Did Grimalkin really believe this? If so, she was going too far. I just couldn't accept it.

"It flew down from heaven, cast beams of light, filled the three magowie with holy bliss, and then disappeared. Presumably it spoke to those three wise men in some mysterious fashion—perhaps giving them more of a message than they told us. It seemed very much like an angel to me," Grimalkin said, a hint of mockery in her voice.

I suddenly felt foolish. She was just being facetious. She didn't believe it was an angel at all.

"Maybe some form of dark magic was being used," Jenny suggested, turning the rabbits on the spit so that the juices dribbled into the fire and sizzled. The smell made my mouth water. "Perhaps it was an illusion?"

"What does it matter what *we* believe?" asked Grimalkin. "The important thing is that all gathered around that hill were believers. When someone defeats Kauspetnd, they will accept that victor as their leader and follow him across the river to attack our enemies. It's exactly what we want. This is why I brought you here, Tom. I need you to fight and kill that assassin!"

27
Prince Stanislaw

"But how could I?" I asked, looking at her in astonishment. "I've never seen anybody with so much skill with blades—except you."

Grimalkin was adamant. "He has two weaknesses that I have detected already. I will study him to find more. Then I will train you until your victory is assured."

"Why don't *you* kill him?" I asked. "You could use the Starblade to deflect any magical powers."

"You need to listen more carefully to what I tell you," Grimalkin said. She sounded annoyed. "The Starblade works only for *you*. It will only repel magic directed at *you*. Not that I need that type of defense to fight that Shaiksa assassin; it is a point of honor with them not to use magic. I could kill him with my own blades, but *you* must do it. You will use the Starblade in any case because its balance is perfect for you."

"Why won't you kill him?"

"My victory would achieve nothing because I am a woman—and a witch to boot. These petty princelings and warlords of the northern border would never follow me. But you are male, and soon we will state your lineage."

"What do you mean by my lineage?"

"Princelings will never deign to follow a commoner such as you," Grimalkin said. "Therefore we will have to exaggerate your status. Have no fear—these border kingdoms are far from our homeland. They know nothing of the County here. They will accept you as their leader, even if they do so reluctantly. Then we can use this army to probe the Kobalos defenses, and in the process learn what we can about them."

"This isn't what you told me before we traveled north," I said accusingly. "This was supposed to be a fact-finding mission, not a full-scale military offensive."

"It would be nothing more than a raid. Later I will explain my objectives," she replied.

"I still think it would be far easier and more certain for you to fight Kauspetnd. You're a skilled shape-shifter."

Grimalkin shook her head. "I do not truly shift my shape, as a lamia witch does. I merely use dark magic to create an illusion of being somebody else."

"But that illusion would stand up to scrutiny, wouldn't

it . . . ?" Before she could answer, I continued, "I could slip away, and you could assume my shape and fight the assassin."

"No, we both need to be here. Once you've dispatched the assassin, that motley assortment of warlords will challenge you. At the moment they regard the Shaiksa with awe, but once he's dead, they'll quickly convince themselves that you've been lucky. But you won't need to fight them too, because I will then be your champion. Their rules permit that, and they will be forced to fight me. I will kill as many as is necessary until they accept you as their leader."

"Rabbit!" Jenny called out, and began to hand it out.

I took my portion gratefully, wanting for the moment to put Grimalkin's dangerous plan out of my mind.

Out of sight of Grimalkin, Jenny rolled her eyes at me. She evidently did not like what had been outlined by the witch assassin either.

Once my stomach was full, I became drowsy and could hardly keep my eyes open. We were all fast asleep in our tent within the hour.

But I had a rude awakening.

Grimalkin was shaking my shoulder violently and hissing into my ear, "Wake yourself and dress in these clothes. Make yourself as presentable as possible." She thrust a pile of folded garments into my hands. "Take five minutes and step outside with your head high. Then look our visitors in the eye and follow my lead. If they bow to you, merely nod in return. If you do well, nobody will get hurt."

As soon as she'd gone, I examined the clothes by the light of a candle. The upper garment, an ornate tunic, was made of satin and looked very expensive; the trousers were more suited to the outdoors, but were expertly tailored. Finally there was a thick, warm cloak with a red clasp shaped like a rose. Grimalkin must have had these made in the County and hidden them among her own possessions.

I was still half asleep; the last thing I wanted was to dress up in these strange clothes and pretend to be what I wasn't. And I was becoming angry too.

Grimalkin had planned for me to fight Kauspetnd all along; she'd arranged everything in detail. She'd had a clear design, and I was a central part of it. I was being used.

After dressing, I tugged on my socks and pushed my feet into my boots. Next I rubbed the sleep from my eyes and dashed some water in my face. Jenny was still lying wrapped in her blankets, sleeping deeply. I envied her.

Finally I took a deep breath and stepped outside.

There were five armed men facing Grimalkin; four were on horseback, one had dismounted. The latter was dressed in expensive armor, with a chain-mail coat that came down to his knees and a metal breastplate in which I could see my own reflection. He was very tall and had a dark moustache that obscured his mouth. His dark eyebrows met in the middle, reminding me of my brother Jack.

Grimalkin spoke to the soldier in Losta. Then she turned, bowed to me, and translated.

"I've told him that you are Prince Thomas, the youngest son of the King of Caster." She gave me a smile. "I thought that was better than admitting you were a farmer's lad!"

It was only with great difficulty that I prevented my mouth from falling open. The man stared at me hard for a moment, as if measuring me for a coffin, and then he too gave a bow. Remembering Grimalkin's warning, I responded with the merest nod of my head.

The soldier spoke very quickly, directing his words at me. I couldn't understand what he said, but I could read his tone and attitude by the flickering of his eyes and the way his heavy brows contorted as he spoke. He began with an air of haughty arrogance, but as his conversation with Grimalkin went on, I detected a note of surprise in his voice.

"He says that his name is Majcher, and he is high steward to Prince Stanislaw of Polyznia. All who gather here, on this southern riverbank, must apparently pay tax for the privilege. That's why we have the honor of his visit. But now that he knows who you are, that is forgotten: all royals and their retinue are exempt." Grimalkin lowered her voice a little. "Now we come to our first problem—he is surprised that you travel with such a small escort. I suspect he doubts you are who you claim to be."

I opened my mouth, but Grimalkin was already speaking, so I closed it again. She had a lot to say.

Once again she turned to give me a translation of what she'd said to Majcher.

"I told him that you are the seventh and youngest son of your father; a favorite who is well loved and held on a short leash lest he come to harm. I said that this has made you impatient, as you have a natural love of adventure. Thus, when you heard of the events on the bank of the Shanna River, you rode off in the night to come here and challenge the Shaiksa assassin. I said that your father, the king, was concerned by your departure; he dispatched me and one servant girl to ride after you and keep you safe. Your retinue follows and should arrive any day."

"But we know that's not going to happen," I replied. "What about when they don't appear?"

"We'll worry about that later," she said. "Now I am going to ask him about the protocol for challenging Kauspetnd."

She turned to the steward again, and they continued to talk in Losta; this time the discussion went on for some time. At last Grimalkin turned and gave me the gist of what had been said.

"Now it is my turn to come under scrutiny," she observed, her eyes flickering with amusement. "He wonders why your father should send a woman to protect you. I confirmed what I believe he suspected already, that I am a witch. Each of these princelings has a pet mage, a magowie they consult, so I informed him that in our part of the world, witches perform a similar role. I also told him that not only am I skilled in the arts of combat, I am your father's champion. Who else was better fitted to follow and act as your protector?"

"Does he believe all that you told him?" I asked.

Grimalkin shrugged. "I do not think that he is totally persuaded, but it is his master, the prince, called the Wolf of Polyznia by his subjects, whom we must convince. Now Majcher is leaving to report back to him. When we finally meet the prince, I will use a little magic to ease the process."

The warrior nodded to me, climbed onto his horse, and led his men away.

"So far, so good," Grimalkin said with a smile.

The five men returned on foot before noon, and after a brief conversation, Grimalkin translated for me.

"We are to be given an audience with Prince Stanislaw, but must leave our weapons behind. The high steward gives his assurance that he will escort us there and back and, if necessary, protect us with his life."

"Do you believe him?" I asked.

"I think Majcher is speaking the truth. But to achieve what we need here, there must be risk, and we are in no position to refuse."

I nodded and handed the Starblade to Jenny. Grimalkin disarmed herself too, removing each blade from its sheath and finally handing Jenny her scissors. I never thought I'd see her willingly give up her weapons like this, and the look on Jenny's face showed that she was thinking the same thing.

"Stay behind and guard our possessions, girl!" Grimalkin commanded as we set off.

I could tell by her expression that Jenny was far from happy at being left behind. I had told her about what had happened during the night; she was worried about Grimalkin's plan, and keen to accompany us. "Can't you use a spell again?" I asked.

Grimalkin shook her head. "I don't wish to risk arousing people's suspicions. What's more, the girl is supposed to be the servant of a prince; she would not accompany you to visit another of royal blood—whereas I am your champion."

With no spell of protection to guard them, someone

did need to stay behind, or we might return to find our horses, provisions, and weapons gone. I didn't expect Jenny to fight off a band of determined robbers, but her presence would be a deterrent to opportunistic thieves.

The high steward walked ahead, our escort behind. We wound our way through the huge camp, passing tents of all sizes, until at last we came to a big circle of fires surrounded by vigilant guards armed with spears. Within this stood the largest tent I had ever seen. It was as big as three County cottages combined. Instead of the usual cone covered in animal skins, it was a giant oblong made from a heavy brown material.

I was uneasy and a little scared. Even if we could somehow persuade this prince to allow me to fight the Shaiksa, I saw nothing ahead but failure and death. I did not share Grimalkin's optimism. How could I hope to defeat such a formidable foe in single combat?

Majcher scowled at us, then went inside, leaving us surrounded by guards. A few moments later he reappeared, spoke briefly to Grimalkin, and then held up the tent flap so that we could enter without bowing our heads.

I gasped in astonishment at the inside of the tent. I could have been entering a palace. The walls were hidden by silken tapestries; most of the floor was covered with the same brown fabric as the tent walls, but there was a raised central dais constructed of polished wood and adorned with a variety of expensive woven carpets. Upon this stood a huge gleaming throne, fashioned from some alloy that contained silver. Upon it reclined Prince Stanislaw, a big man with close-cropped gray hair, a large nose, and close-set eyes. He was not young, probably the wrong side of fifty.

I'd always thought of a prince as a young man preparing to replace his aging father on the throne. But this wasn't a kingdom; it was a principality, and this was its ruler.

Behind the throne stood a huge barrel-chested warrior, his arms folded, a stern expression on his face. His breast-plate was engraved with the arms of the prince: a wolf howling at the moon. He seemed far from happy to see us.

Grimalkin would certainly need her magic to bend this prince to her will.

She bowed low and then addressed the prince, gesturing toward me. We were supposedly equal in rank, so I gave him the briefest of bows; more of a nod, really. In return, he gazed at me in silence, studying me like a predator judging the distance to its prey. Then he gave me a condescending smile and spoke to Grimalkin again.

"He says that he thinks it best that you return to your father," she translated. "I don't think he's impressed by your youthful appearance. He has a new champion who he believes will have a real chance against Kauspetnd—that's the fat warrior standing behind the throne who has yet to smile."

I almost let out a sigh of relief. Perhaps this strong-minded prince could not be manipulated. This might put an end to Grimalkin's scheme.

"Despite the prophecies of the three magowie, the princelings here have their own take on events," Grimalkin continued. "If his champion wins, then Prince Stanislaw will lead the attack on the Kobalos, and the glory and prestige will fall to him. But I will tell him that you are prepared to fight his champion for the right to fight the Shaiksa assassin. Neither prince nor champion are likely to refuse, as there are precedents; already there has been much jostling for power here. As your champion, I could fight him on your behalf, but it's best if you show your bravery and fighting prowess."

I opened my mouth to protest, but met the fierce glare of the witch assassin, willing me to silence. Then her face softened, and she smiled.

"Things are going well!" she told me.

28
A Premonition of Death

It was useless to object, so I watched nervously as Grimalkin offered my challenge to the prince's champion. As she spoke, the man behind the throne glared at me angrily; I could see the veins in his neck standing out. He probably felt insulted to receive a challenge from someone who looked to be barely more than a boy.

We were escorted back to our camp by Majcher and his soldiers, who still seemed none too friendly. Indeed, when the high steward left, two of the soldiers stayed behind.

"What do they want?" I asked Grimalkin. "Are we under guard?"

She shook her head. "No, they are here to protect us and guard our camp."

As I thought over what had just happened, my anger at Grimalkin grew. Now I was facing two fights against formidable opponents. I failed to see how I could win either.

I slumped down in front of the fire and stared into the flames.

"What's wrong?" Jenny asked, warming her hands.

I shrugged but made no reply.

"I know you aren't happy," she persisted. "Why don't you talk about it? Getting it off your chest will make you feel better."

"It's just that my death has now been arranged twice over," I said. "Before I face the Kobalos assassin, I have to fight the prince's champion."

"It is scheduled to take place in three days, but you won't have to fight that warrior. This I guarantee," said Grimalkin, sitting down cross-legged beside me.

"How can you be so sure? Have you scryed it?" I asked.

She didn't answer me directly. "All will be well. Focus your mind on the Shaiksa—he and he alone will you fight. It could not have worked out better. This Prince Stanislaw is the most powerful by far of the rulers gathered here. We will win his respect; eventually we'll control him, and the rest will fall into line."

Grimalkin proved to be correct. Less than twenty-four hours later, the news arrived that the prince's champion had suffered an injury while training and would be incapacitated for at least a month. I was to be permitted to take his place and face Kauspetnd; I had almost two weeks to prepare.

"*Did* you scry that he'd suffer an injury?" I asked as we walked toward the river to watch the fight between the Shaiksa and his next challenger. With the prince's men now guarding our camp, Jenny had been able to join us and was following close behind.

Grimalkin nodded. "Yes, it was almost certain to happen, but if it hadn't, I would have arranged something to make it so," she said with a smile.

The fight didn't last long. The human challenger was young and scared, and the whole thing was over in less than a minute. I noticed Jenny cover her eyes when he ended up on his knees, shrieking in agony, trying to prevent his guts from spilling out into the water.

A second later there was silence. With one blow, the Shaiksa struck his opponent's head from his body and put an end to the screams.

I felt sick to my stomach. The assassin was too good. What chance did I have against such a warrior?

Jenny kept shaking her head, her face pale. "It was awful," she said, her voice quavering with emotion. "At the end, just before he fell into darkness, he was so afraid."

I put my hand on her shoulder in sympathy. It was a terrible thing to have such empathy. But I was proud of her.

She had faced up to it. Back in the County, at the haunted house, she had run away, but not this time.

Grimalkin seemed unmoved by the death we'd just witnessed. The watching crowd was subdued after seeing Kauspetnd triumph yet again. With each victory he demonstrated the superior powers of the Kobalos. No human challenger could match him.

"Well, what have you learned today?" Grimalkin asked as we walked back toward our camp across the frozen ground.

I thought carefully about what I had seen.

"He fights with two blades but has more skill with his left. I should press him on his right side."

"No," said Grimalkin. "Press him on his stronger side for the first fifteen minutes. He will think that you have failed to spot his slight weakness. Make no mistake, he knows each facet of his combat abilities and has worked hard to improve them. But then you should switch suddenly and press him on his right. In this way, you might just win an early victory."

"Wait for *fifteen minutes*?" cried Jenny, aghast. "I doubt whether any challenger has ever lasted even five against him."

Grimalkin glared at her angrily. "Your master will last the course, but it may be a long fight," she insisted, turning her gaze back to me. "If things go badly, it might take you more than an hour to kill him. Tomorrow I will begin your training. Soon you will start to feel more confident. Listen well, for I will speak truly now. You are already an excellent swordsman. I think you have the potential to become great—perhaps peerless. To achieve that, you will need just two things: practice and self-belief."

I had fought successfully against opponents before, but I still felt that Kauspetnd was more than a match for me. Grimalkin was simply trying to bolster my confidence. That was why she'd looked so angry when Jenny challenged her.

The witch assassin was as good as her word. Each morning we went in among the dark trees and fought for hours. Grimalkin had trained me before—I still had the scars to prove it—but here she pressed me so hard that at times I feared for my life. Jenny looked on and winced from the sidelines.

On the first day of training, while I was resting between bouts, trying to get my breath back, Grimalkin turned to stare at Jenny. "One day, girl, you too may have to fight for your life. Have you any skill with blades?"

Jenny shook her head.

Grimalkin drew a throwing blade from its scabbard.

"Catch!" she commanded, throwing it slightly to Jenny's left.

I watched it turn over and over in the air, but Jenny reached out and caught it as if it was the most natural thing in the world.

Grimalkin smiled. "You have good reactions, child. I will train you too."

"Just so long as you don't expect *me* to fight the Shaiksa!" Jenny retorted.

And so, in the intervals between our own bouts, the witch assassin began training her. She took it slowly, showing her how to position her feet and achieve the grace and balance necessary in combat. She also instructed her in the art of throwing blades.

It gave me a brief respite, but all too soon, it was my turn to fight again.

When we fought, the witch assassin used the two sabers she had demanded of me back in Chipenden. Had she been planning this even then? Had her intention been for me to fight Kauspetnd all along? It seemed very likely.

Now she used those sabers just as the assassin had, assuming both his strengths and weaknesses; thus the practice could not have been better matched to what I'd eventually face.

She also taught me what she called her dance of

death—the whirling, spinning sequence of attacks that were hard to defend against.

Each time the Kobalos fought a new human challenger, we were there, watching, and each time Grimalkin learned something new to pass on to me. I tried to detect any weaknesses myself, but could find none. The Shaiksa seemed flawless, and none of the challengers lasted more than a minute or two. The contests were very one-sided, but one thing had changed.

It hadn't rained for some time, and I wondered whether up in the mountains, as winter approached, the source of the river was now frozen. Whatever the reason, the river was far lower than it had been when we first arrived. The contests no longer took place in swirling water; they were now mostly fought on dry stones, accompanied by the crunch of boots on gravel.

Somehow I still found time each day to teach my apprentice her trade. It helped to keep my nerves at bay. We were both missing the County; this chilly camp on a riverbank was very different from our life in Chipenden— the life she'd expected to lead as a spook's apprentice.

"I wish we could go home," she said. It was a sentiment she expressed at least three times each day.

"What do you miss most?" I asked, wondering if I could make things here more bearable for her.

"The trees—ash, oak, and sycamore. The ones here are all conifers, and they all look the same. And I miss people talking in words I can understand. I really do need to make an effort to learn the language."

"Grimalkin did promise that we'd return before the onset of winter, before the journey becomes impossible. She'll keep her word," I replied.

"A lot has to happen before then," she said sadly. "You have to defeat that creature. Can you do it? And don't put on a show of confidence for me; I can sense your fear and doubt."

"Of course I'm afraid," I told her, annoyed to find her using her gift of empathy to discover how I was feeling. "But bravery is about overcoming fear. We are all afraid at times. What matters is rising above it."

"But do you *really* think you can win? Some of those slain here are the champions of princes, warriors who've spent their lives training in combat. A few lessons from the witch are hardly going to help you defeat him. You're a spook—your staff is your main weapon."

"I defeated that beast in the tree," I pointed out.

"That beast was young and still learning to be a mage—that's what Grimalkin said, didn't she? This opponent is different. He is an assassin, a trained killer, an expert with his chosen weapons. The haizda mage mostly relied on his magic, not his blades. The Starblade defended you against that, and you proved to be better in combat. But this is different. I don't see how you can win this time."

"You'd be surprised," I replied. "I've been taught by Grimalkin before. Not only has she exceptional skill with weapons, she also has a gift for passing on those skills to others. She's been analyzing the way the Shaiksa fights and finding weaknesses that I should be able to exploit."

But my words sounded hollow, even to my own ears. Somehow Jenny's doubts were more than canceling out Grimalkin's confidence. I felt very uneasy.

"Even if you somehow manage to win," Jenny went on, "we'll have to head north with this ragtag army, deep into a territory controlled by thousands upon thousands of the beasts. I find it hard to believe that we'll survive. It seems to be getting colder by the day; even if we do somehow escape being massacred, winter will have set in, and we'll be forced to spend long dark months in this inhospitable northern land."

"My, aren't you the eternal pessimist!" I tried to joke. "Trust me to take on a gloomy apprentice who spends most of her time anticipating the worst."

"I'm sorry to sound so despondent, but I just want to go home."

"So do I." I patted her shoulder in reassurance. "Trust

me, please—everything will turn out for the best. We need the information that Grimalkin hopes to gather; she seeks knowledge of the tactics of the Kobalos in battle, and of the dark magic they may use. Once she knows more about it, she may be able to create effective countermeasures. If she doesn't succeed, the Kobalos will simply fight their way to the sea. That won't stop them; they'll sail across, and in a few years the County will be overrun and enslaved. We have to do this now."

I was determined to go through with it, and I tried to think positively and achieve that "self-belief" that Grimalkin said was necessary . . . but as the days passed, I experienced something new: a type of fear I'd never felt before.

I had often been afraid when dealing with the dark. There had been moments of extreme terror—when I'd confronted the Old God Golgoth under the Round Loaf up on Anglezarke Moor, for example. He'd had the power to snuff out not only my life, but my soul. Then there was the fight with Siscoi, the Romanian vampire god: I'd faced a terrible death at his hands. And there had been many other moments of dread; as the Battle of the Wardstone approached, I'd feared that I might die there.

But what I felt now was different . . . less intense in a way, but it crept into my very being. I had a strong sense that I would not survive the fight with Kauspetnd. I had always been someone who looked to the future. As a boy, I'd dreamed of completing my apprenticeship and becoming a spook, with my own territory to protect. Now there seemed to be no future. I could not see beyond the approaching fight.

It is the night before I face the Shaiksa. I can't sleep. So I am writing in my notebook, trying to describe my thoughts and feelings. Ice-cold fingers of fear clutch at my throat and squeeze my heart. I have tried to put on a brave face in front of Jenny, but I know that she can see the truth.

In my imagination I keep reviewing, over and over again, each death that I have witnessed at the river. I watch the heads fall; I see the blood swirl away in the current.

Will that be my fate tomorrow?

Jenny Calder

29
The Worst Day of My Life

I am writing this in Tom Ward's notebook. It seems the most appropriate place to record what has happened.

I don't think he would mind. All spooks keep careful notes—they believe in recording the past so that they can better prepare for the future. So I will carry on doing so just as long as I am able.

Yesterday was the worst day of my life.

I had seen the Shaiksa assassin fight on only one occasion, but it scared me. He had displayed such effortless skill and ferocity that I feared for Tom. How could he possibly win against such an adversary?

Because we were supposedly Tom's servants, and the only people from his own land, Grimalkin and I were given a good view of the contest. We were seated in straight-backed wooden chairs to the left of Prince Stanislaw, looking directly down upon the river.

Above, the sky was blue, with just a few clouds on the horizon, tinged with red by the setting sun. The air was chilly but full of scents, some of which I could not identify. Some were spices, others aromas of food, and then there was the bitter leaf that was chewed by the men of the region, which made their breath smell foul.

An hour before sunset, a figure came into view on the far bank and strode to the edge of the ford. It was Kauspetnd, with his fearsome lupine face, hair braided into three pigtails. He carried two gleaming sabers and glared across the river toward us.

A great silence fell. Nobody spoke. Nobody moved.

Then a lone figure left our side of the river and began to cross the ford, his boots splashing through the shallow channel, heading for the bank of stones in the center. He had only one weapon clutched in his right hand—the Starblade given to him by Grimalkin. Unlike the blades of the Shaiksa, his blade did not gleam in the sunlight; it was a dull, rusty brown.

Now his boots crunched on the stones as he approached the center of the ford.

It was Tom Ward, and even from this distance my gift of empathy told me how he was feeling. He was scared, desperately trying to control his fear and still the shaking of his limbs. He felt a terrible sense of doom—the inevitability of his own death. And he was angry that he had been manipulated into this situation. He wished that he had stayed in Chipenden and continued his life as a spook.

My heart went out to him. I did not like the way Grimalkin had used him. She could only see the threat from the Kobalos and seemed determined to employ everyone and everything to counter it. It was so unfair. No human had stood a chance against this dangerous, bestial warrior. For all the training he had received from Grimalkin, what could Tom hope to do?

By now Kauspetnd was also making his way across the dry stones of the ford.

I could get very little sense of this creature's mind. I was aware of determination, aggression, and total confidence, but his thoughts were beyond me. In the past I had experimented with my gift of empathy. Some people were easier to read than others. I had tried animals too, sensing the feral willfulness of cats and the simple joy of dogs, but little more. Their minds were mostly closed to me; the thoughts of another species seemed unknowable. And now, with this Kobalos warrior, it was the same. I could not reach him; neither could I influence his behavior.

The combatants came to a halt. They were now facing each other, just a few feet apart. It seemed a long time before either of them moved, and when they did, they were tentative.

Tom thrust his sword toward the mage, who blocked it with one of his sabers—the one in his left hand, I think, though it all happened very fast. They circled widdershins, their boots crunching on the stones; the only other noise was the rush of the narrow river channel chuckling over its rocky bed.

Then the Shaiksa aimed a couple of blows at Tom's head. He blocked them easily, and they continued to circle each other. I could sense that Tom's fear was gone now. He was concentrating, focusing on the fight, his confidence slowly growing.

Then it began in earnest. Kauspetnd launched a furious attack, both blades flashing in the light of the setting sun. My heart was in my mouth as Tom was forced backward, desperately parrying each blow, the Starblade held in both hands.

But he survived, and began to hold his ground; then the assassin yielded a few steps before renewing his onslaught.

How could Tom hope to survive such a ferocious attack for long? No wonder most of the fights had been over in a matter of minutes.

But survive he did, matching the Shaiksa blow for blow. Soon time became meaningless. I felt as if we were trapped in eternity, where all clocks ceased to tick. All that existed, all that had ever existed, and all that would ever exist, was this furious struggle. It would go on and on forever.

Grimalkin told me afterward that it lasted just over an hour. That must be correct because finally, when the end came, the sun had set and the light was beginning to fail.

After a while, Tom was clearly gaining the ascendancy. He attacked with speed and precision. He kept passing the Starblade from hand to hand, each time throwing Kauspetnd onto the back foot.

The human audience was no longer silent. Now they were shouting out in excitement and anticipating a long-awaited victory.

Tom drew first blood. He found a gap in his enemy's defenses and caught him on the shoulder. The Kobalos warrior staggered back, red streaming down his front, while those around me gave a great roar of triumph.

Then Tom pressed the Shaiksa hard. He spun, whirling in Grimalkin's dance of death. Almost too fast for the eye to see, he dealt a succession of rapid horizontal blows until one found its mark.

He struck the head from the Shaiksa assassin.

He had won!

The head rolled across the stones and into the shallow water, the current swirling away a ribbon of red blood. As the body collapsed, more blood gushed from the neck.

But the great roar of victory gradually died away to a subdued murmur. All eyes were on Tom, who staggered and then dropped the Starblade. He was looking down at his stomach.

My focus had been on Tom's offensive and the blow that had slain his opponent. I had not noticed what Kauspetnd had done. But now a lump came into my throat and my heart lurched as I saw what had happened.

One of the assassin's sabers had pierced him. Only the hilt was visible. He staggered again and turned, attempting to keep his balance. I could see his back. The curved, bloodstained blade protruded by at least a foot. Tom reached behind, feeling the steel of the blade, then turned toward us again, his eyes wide with disbelief.

Finally he pitched forward onto his face.

Yesterday was the worst day of my life.

It was the day Tom Ward died.

30
The Grief of Grimalkin

As long as I live, I will never forget the look of horror on Tom's face when he understood what had happened. I knew exactly what he was feeling. I empathized with him. My gift was a curse, because it meant that I shared his experience.

He was in extreme pain, but even more terrible was the realization that he was dying.

I could not bear it.

I remember Tom falling facedown onto the stones, the saber blade protruding from his back. Only one person moved; everyone else was stunned into silence.

It was Grimalkin who splashed through the water and ran to where Tom lay. She lifted him carefully and carried him up the bank toward us. She passed quite close to where I was standing. I saw that his face was ashen. He didn't seem to be breathing, and blood dripped from his wound, leaving a red trail on the grass.

He was dead—I was sure of it. I could sense nothing from him. But Grimalkin was a powerful witch. Could she use her magic to save him?

As I stared at Tom, Grimalkin met my eyes.

"The sword! The sword! Get the Starblade, child!" she shouted at me. "Keep it safe!"

I hurried away in the opposite direction from everybody else. I splashed through the water, averting my eyes from the severed head of the Shaiksa assassin, and across the stones to retrieve the Starblade.

It had been made for Tom, but he wouldn't be able to use it now. Why did Grimalkin want it? I wondered.

I followed the crowd, carrying the rusty sword in my hand. A throng of people had gathered outside the prince's huge tent.

That must be where Grimalkin had taken Tom.

Desperate to help, I tried to squeeze through to the front, but it was impossible. A double row of blue-jacketed Polyznian guards were holding everybody back; they started to advance, their spears at the ready.

It was hopeless, and the situation was starting to turn ugly. Most of the crowd retreated, but some of the soldiers of the other princes stood firm. The guards had provoked a hostile reaction, and swords were being drawn.

I could do nothing, so I made my way back to our camp and crawled inside the tent. I laid the sword on the ground beside my blanket, then curled up into a ball and tried to forget what had happened.

I couldn't sleep. Each time I closed my eyes, I saw the fight over and over again. I felt Tom's terror and anguish—I couldn't stop it. I began to sob.

How long I lay there, I don't know. But after a while I heard someone come into the tent. A candle was lit, and I opened my eyes and saw Grimalkin sitting cross-legged on her blanket. Her eyes were closed, and she was rocking backward and forward, her arms clasped across her chest. There was blood all down her front, and on her bare hands and arms.

I shivered with cold and misery. I knew that it was Tom's blood.

I sat up and faced her. "Is he dead?" I asked.

The witch assassin opened her eyes and glared at me. She looked angry, and I didn't think she was going to reply.

Her answer was merely a nod, and I began to cry.

Grimalkin immediately rebuked me. "Foolish girl, your tears won't bring him back. Be quiet while I think!"

I fell silent. I had always found the witch intimidating, but now her fury was such that I almost fled the tent. I began to tremble.

I had never been able to get inside Grimalkin's head; there were barriers there. I could sense a little of her emotions—mostly anger—but that was all.

Then she began to speak. At first her words were not addressed to me. She seemed to be thinking aloud. "This should never have happened. This I did not foresee . . . I did not think to send him to his death. I tried to save him. . . ."

She turned and fixed me with her fierce eyes. "I have brought others back from the edge of death before, child. At first I thought I would succeed here too. I used magic and herbs to staunch the bleeding; I breathed my energy into him. He began to breathe again, and as his lungs filled with air, I started to hope. . . ."

She shook her head, muttering words that I couldn't hear.

"What happened?" I asked, my voice hardly more than a whisper.

"There was no choice but to remove the blade. It was something that I feared to do—a moment of crisis. When I did so, the internal damage proved too severe. All my magic, all my knowledge of herbs, could not stop the bleeding. I was so close, so very close to succeeding. And if I had, I could have healed him from within. Such things can be done. . . ."

She shook her head and fell silent again, closing her eyes. "He died. I failed. It is over. Tomorrow he will be buried. You can do one last thing for him. You must help me. The body must be washed and cleaned—will you do that?"

I nodded, the "Yes" choking in my throat.

"Then tomorrow at dawn, we will go to the tent and prepare him for burial. Now try to sleep."

I couldn't sleep, and morning took a long time to arrive. Grimalkin did not sleep either. All night she sat cross-legged, rocking to and fro. At times she seemed to be talking to herself; I think she even uttered a short sob—but it was too faint for me to be sure.

But of one thing I was certain: although the witch assassin was cruel and dangerous, she felt Tom Ward's loss keenly. They had been allies against the Fiend for some time; Tom had told me so. There was much in their past that I did not know, but there had definitely been a strong bond between them.

In her own way, Grimalkin was grieving.

31
Washing the Body

Soon after dawn, an escort of soldiers led by the high steward arrived to take us to the camp of Prince Stanislaw. As usual, two remained behind to guard our tent. They seemed much friendlier: Majcher even gave Grimalkin a stiff bow, and I could see the respect in his eyes. Tom's achievement in defeating the assassin had changed their attitude toward us.

Tom's body had been removed from the prince's tent to a smaller one, slightly closer to the water. Guards surrounded it, and people sat about on the grass staring at it.

What did they want? Had they been there all night? I wondered.

I followed Grimalkin into the tent. Lanterns had been lit to dispel the gloom. Tom's body, wrapped in a blanket, was lying on a low trestle table. His eyes were wide open, as if staring at the ceiling, but when I touched his face with the back of my hand, it felt ice cold.

I was not proud of the thoughts that drifted into my head. They came unbidden, but I couldn't easily get rid of them. I wondered what would happen to me now. Here I was, alone in the far north, with no hope of returning soon. Would Grimalkin even take me back to the County? I had only been tolerated because I was Tom's apprentice. She might well abandon me to my fate.

If I did manage to return home, I would have to live with my false mother and father in Grimsargh. I'd little hope of continuing my apprenticeship unless I could find some as yet unknown spook to train me. The others I'd met—Judd and Johnson—wouldn't take me on; nor did I wish to be trained by them. So unless I could find some other way of making a living, I'd end up married off to some man who just wanted me to cook, clean, and look after our children until I was old and bitter like my foster parents.

I thrust those dark thoughts from my head and forced myself to concentrate on the task before me. Water was brought, and rags. But first we had to strip Tom's clothes from him. It wasn't easy, and Grimalkin used her knife to cut away his breeches. When the shirt was peeled off and the wound in his belly was revealed, Grimalkin gave a gasp of surprise.

"Bring the lantern nearer!" she commanded.

I hastened to obey, and when I returned to the table, she was tracing around the wound with her forefinger. There was something strange about it. It had almost closed up, but it appeared ridged, and what looked like scales had formed.

"If only I could have staunched the bleeding a little longer," she said. "Perhaps I pulled the blade out too soon. . . . He would have healed himself, I'm sure of it. Do you see those scales? The process had started, but death ended it."

"Yes, but why scales and not skin?"

"He has lamia blood in him, from his mother."

"Lamia?" I said in puzzlement. "Isn't a lamia a type of witch? Don't they have wings?"

"The ones with wings are rare; mostly they crawl or walk. His mother raised him on a farm, and assumed human shape while he was young. Only later did she reveal the truth to him. She is dead now, and sadly he has not outlasted her by long."

I looked at Grimalkin in astonishment. There was much that I'd been in ignorance of . . . things that, had he lived, Tom might have told me.

"Wash the body," the witch commanded. "I will hold the lantern."

I soaked the rag in water and used it to wash his body, slowly removing the bloodstains and grime. At one point

Grimalkin helped to turn him over. When I'd finished, we dressed him in the trousers and satin shirt that had been brought from the County to make him look like a prince.

"Should I put his boots and socks back on?" I asked.

Grimalkin nodded, and with some difficulty I tugged on the socks and then pushed his feet into the boots and laced them up.

As we prepared to leave the tent, I took one last look at Tom. The witch assassin had closed his eyes, and he could almost have been asleep.

Outside the tent, Majcher was waiting. He and Grimalkin exchanged a few words in Losta.

"The burial will take place tomorrow at noon," she told me as we walked back toward our tent. "Prince Stanislaw will attend to honor Tom. He was impressed by his courage and fighting prowess. The funeral procession will leave from here tomorrow morning. They are preparing a headstone for his grave, and asked me what I wanted to be carved upon it. I left it to the prince to decide. After all, whatever they write, it won't be true. I wish he could be buried next to his master in the garden at Chipenden, but that is impossible."

I awoke soon after dawn, after barely an hour's sleep. Instantly, the memory of Tom's death was like a needle piercing my heart. My eyes began to brim with tears.

Grimalkin was awake; she was sharpening her blades. I watched her in silence.

It had rained hard during the night. The noise as it drummed on the ground and the roof of our tent had repeatedly awakened me—that, and the memory of the terrible thing that had happened. Now I could smell the rich aroma of earth and grass.

"Later today, after he is buried, I will take you home, girl."

"I have no home," I responded bitterly, but I was secretly relieved to discover that she didn't intend to abandon me here. Yes, I did very much want to return to the County.

"Your home now is Chipenden, and no doubt Judd Brinscall will move in and become the new Chipenden Spook. You will become his apprentice."

"He won't take me on. He has already refused at least five times. He doesn't like me. He set his dogs on me and just laughed when one of them ripped my skirt."

"He will do as I say!" Grimalkin exclaimed fiercely. "You have earned your right to be trained, and it *will* happen."

I was stunned by the vehemence of her response. I suddenly realized that she truly could coerce Spook Brinscall into taking me on. But did I want it that much? Could I bear to be trained by him?

The witch picked up the Starblade and balanced it on her knees, looking thoughtful.

"What will you do now?" I asked.

"I will spend the winter back in the County. Tom is dead, and I am truly sorry that it happened. But although my first plan has been thwarted, it cannot be the end of my endeavors. I will travel north again next spring and continue to learn what I can about our enemies. If we are to have any chance of survival, it must be done. The threat grows by the day. The Kobalos may even attack the northern principalities this winter."

32
A Terrible Mistake

Tom Ward was dead. On the day of his burial Grimalkin and I left our tent about an hour before noon. I looked up at the sky. It had stopped raining for now, but to the south, clouds threatened another deluge.

When we arrived at the tent of Prince Stanislaw, Tom's coffin was resting on the grass in the open. The prince was standing next to it, a sword at his hip, flanked by two of his guards. He looked angry—more ready for battle than for a burial. But he nodded to us, then beckoned four of his men forward, and they hefted the coffin up onto their shoulders.

Without further ado, we set off north. The prince and his escort led the way. I was surprised to see how many warriors lined the route, with many others joining the procession behind us. I suppose they must have been impressed by the fact that, although he had been fatally wounded,

Tom had first put an end to the assassin who had been killing their own champions for so long.

I remember thinking that the burial site must be on high ground, because we were trudging upward. It made sense. No doubt the river flooded the plain in spring as the snow and ice melted.

At last we reached an open grave with a large headstone. The bottom of it was full of water. There were other graves too—perhaps a couple of dozen in all—but they had been filled in. Some were recent, the earth freshly mounded; others had become shallow depressions, and others still were already covered with grass. Just two or three had headstones; most had a rough wooden cross, while a few lacked any marker at all. The challenge of the Shaiksa assassin had lasted for months. No doubt these were the graves of those who had died at his hands.

We took up positions close to the open grave, facing the headstone. Grimalkin stood on my left; the high steward, Majcher, on my right; and Prince Stanislaw beyond him. The guards waited behind us.

Standing behind the stone was one of the bearded and gloved magowie, no doubt the one who advised Prince Stanislaw. He held his arms wide and began to chant in a singsong voice. I was glad that I couldn't understand a word that he was saying—it was just so much false nonsense. All that was required to show respect to the dead was a few quiet words.

So I said them, silently, inside my head.

Thank you for taking me on as your apprentice, Tom Ward, and for giving me a second chance when I ran from the ghasts. I'll miss you. You didn't deserve to die like this. And you would have become a really good spook, one of the best ever—your master would have been proud of you. Thank you for having faith in me. . . .

Suddenly my doubts fled, and I made up my mind. Tom had believed in me and had wanted to train me to the best of his ability. So I would go on, despite my hatred of Judd Brinscall.

I'll do my best to be a good spook too. Thank you for setting me on the right path. Thank you for everything.

I glanced at Tom's coffin, which had been set down next to the grave, beside the mound of earth from the excavation. It was hard to believe that his body was lying inside it, cold and still, and would soon be interred in the damp earth. I would go back to Chipenden with Grimalkin while he stayed here, and soon winter would be upon us; snow would cover his grave.

I tried to put the depressing thought from my mind, telling myself that the contents of the coffin were just Tom's remains. By now his soul would have passed through limbo and gone to the light. But he was so young. He hadn't had time to live his life fully. That was what made me sad; that, and the loss of the master who would have trained me, guided me, and eventually become a colleague—and maybe, if I was really lucky, a close friend.

I glanced at the headstone and read what had been carved upon it.

HERE LIETH PRINCE THOMAS OF CASTER,

A BRAVE WARRIOR

WHO FELL IN COMBAT

BUT TRIUMPHED WHERE OTHERS FAILED

The final two lines were a warped assessment of what had happened. It seemed no triumph to me. This was all a terrible mistake, and now the lie was inscribed forever upon his gravestone. Tom was a young spook who had fought the dark . . . this should have been mentioned.

I heard a deep growl of thunder and looked up. Dark clouds were above us; the storm was almost here. Moments later, it began to rain hard, and there was a flash of lightning almost directly overhead, along with a boom of thunder that seemed to shake the ground beneath our feet.

The magowie was still chanting, but his voice could not compete with the storm. The pounding rain drenched my hair and clothes. I wondered if the prayers would be cut short—the priest would have neither the nerve nor the sense to curtail the service, but a nod from the prince should be enough.

I glanced at him, but in the gathering gloom his face was impassive. He seemed content to stand there, getting soaked to the skin. It was growing really dark—we'd need lanterns soon.

But then, at last, the prince raised his hand and gestured toward the grave. In response, the magowie came to a stuttering halt, and the four warriors who'd acted as pallbearers stepped forward, two on each side of Tom's coffin. There were two ropes beneath it, and using these, they took up positions near the grave and began to lower it down. They were having difficulty holding on to the rope, which kept slipping through their fingers.

The coffin wasn't going into the grave evenly. At one point they almost lost it, but at last it splashed into the water at the bottom of the pit, and they pulled the ropes free. I saw that the coffin was almost covered by the rainwater that had accumulated.

I was surprised when the four men then picked up spades and began to fill in the grave. The custom back in the County was for each mourner to throw a handful of soil over the coffin and then leave; the gravediggers only began their work when everybody else had left.

So, with lightning flashing and thunder crashing overhead, we all watched the men working: rain ran down their faces and dripped from the ends of their noses as they hastily threw sodden earth onto their wooden target.

Then I heard another sound—an eerie screech from almost directly overhead. I looked up, and the flash of lightning blinded me for a few seconds. When I could see again, I noticed that everyone else around the grave was looking upward, shielding their eyes against the driving rain. Even the four men had stopped work.

There was a figure up there, high above us. I could make out wings—huge wings, compared to the slender body. It was the being we had watched hovering over us while the three magowie foretold the coming of a champion to defeat the Shaiksa assassin and lead humans across the river to victory.

It hovered there, but suddenly folded its white wings and dropped down toward us like a stone. When it came to a halt, it was less than thirty feet above our heads—near enough for me to make out the beautiful face shining with silver light.

But then I was distracted by another noise, which drew my eyes downward.

I thought my eyes were playing tricks on me, but I wasn't the only person now staring down into the grave. The casket was slightly tilted, and the sodden earth that covered it was sliding away to reveal the wet wooden surface.

Grimalkin hissed in anger and stared up at the winged being . . . but I was filled with new hope.

The coffin was moving.

Could it be that Tom was alive?

Grimalkin's Notes
The Contents of the Glass Containers

THESE are all biological, and in most cases held within some preserving material, usually a gel. Some are seeds; others animal (mammalian or reptilian samples plus hybrids).

Many are still alive, held in a state of suspended animation. I believe that, if planted, the seeds would grow. The same is probably also true of the animal samples. (I tested only three, which confirmed this.) They are all capable of development and growth, but into what I cannot say without further dangerous experimentation.

However, we know that the Kobalos have used dark magic to create many special creatures, such as builders (the whoskor, which maintain and extend the walls of Valkarky) and fighting entities (such as the haggenbrood). They may well use similar creatures in war. It could be that the dead haizda mage was preparing to create such entities locally and hide them within our borders, ready for a preemptive strike.

The First Animal Sample

I removed this sample (labeled ZANTI on the jar) from its gel preservative and introduced it to a growth medium (two parts human blood, three parts ground bone of sow, two parts sugar, three parts human spittle).

The sample was placed within the most powerful containment environment that I could generate—a large pentacle whose inner circle was fifty feet in diameter—in a meadow at least two hundred yards from the nearest tree. I also protected the pentacle from prying eyes and intrusion with spells of cloaking and menace.

As I had predicted, the sample began to grow on the night of the full moon. At first the entities resembled small insects; they scuttled about on the grass. However, just before dawn, they burrowed into the soil; it was possible that they could not function in sunlight.

Soon after dusk the following day, they emerged again. After a while I noticed two things. They were fewer in number, and those that remained were somewhat larger, about the length and thickness of my index finger. It seemed likely that they were devouring each other in a process whereby only the fittest might survive.

This process continued for seven nights before I intervened. By then, just two of the creatures remained. Approximately human in shape, they were very thin, with spindly scaled arms and legs. The head of each was hairless but covered with black scales, and the small eyes were wide-set like those of a bird, allowing 360-degree vision. In height they came up to my shoulder, but the final victor might well have reached a height of at least eight feet.

I stepped into the pentacle and despatched both of them with my blades. Unlike the haggenbrood, which I fought in Valkarky, the zanti did not share a single mind and seemed unable to fight as a unit. Additionally, although their hands and feet were clawed, they had no weapons. No doubt their Kobalos masters will have crafted specialized weapons for them.

I think a lone armed and full-sized zanti would be a much more formidable opponent.

The Second Animal Sample

Experiment One

I placed the second sample (labeled ZINGI on the jar) into a growth medium identical to the first, and again used a pentacle for containment, along with spells of cloaking and menace.

The sample started growing immediately, even though the sun had not gone down. This suggested to me that they could function in daylight, which made them more formidable than those in the first experiment. My assumption proved to be correct: they were active throughout the whole twenty-four-hour cycle and never slept.

The creatures were small at first, but their original shape did not alter despite many subsequent growth spurts—again the result of devouring one another.

They were covered in brown hair, and each had six three-jointed, muscular legs. Their bodies were cylindrical and formed of three segments. From the first protruded what appeared to be a long, thin tusk; beneath this was a wide mouth. They did not have eyes or noses, and must have used other senses to locate their prey.

The first stage (devouring one another) continued until only five remained. At this point, each was about the height of a sheep, but perhaps three times as long.

Now they began to look elsewhere for sustenance.

The spell of menace should have driven off any creature that attempted to approach the outer rim of the pentacle. However, the creatures (which I have nicknamed stingers) somehow managed to summon their victims with an even more powerful force . The first of these were birds.

A large black crow landed on the pentacle where the stingers were confined. The first of the creatures darted forward and stabbed its tusk into the breast of the bird, which immediately collapsed, its legs twitching and its whole body suffering violent convulsions. Within seconds, the other four fierce entities had devoured it. Their wide mouths had double rows of needlelike teeth, which they used to tear the bird into small pieces.

Crows, wood pigeons, seagulls, geese, ducks, and magpies suffered a similar fate. They did not summon smaller birds. After that, it was the turn of rabbits, hares, and even a deer. All ignored the spell of menace and were drawn into the pentacle to their deaths.

Then, toward nightfall, the stingers became aware of me. They gathered on the edge of the pentacle, sharp tusks pointing toward me. I was filled with the urge to enter the pentacle. They were attempting to summon me to my death.

I was their new prey.

They did not get their wish. Only a fool enters a bear's den when it can be killed from a distance. I countered their summoning spell, then used my throwing blades to slay all five of the creatures. They did not die easily.

My subsequent dissection of their bodies revealed the

reason. Each segment had its own heart, lungs, stomach, and brain tissue.

Experiment Two

My findings prompted me to repeat the experiment. This time I caught one of the stingers early, when it was no bigger than a domestic cat. I removed and burned the foremost of its segments and waited for the result.

It was as I had predicted: the wound quickly ceased to bleed, and within forty-eight hours, the creature had regenerated its missing segment.

Once more I terminated the experiment.

The Third Animal Sample

I placed the third sample (labeled VARTEKI on the mage's jar) in the same growth medium, and again used a pentacle for containment and spells of cloaking and menace to deter intrusion. But the containment was insufficient. From the very beginning, things did not go well.

The sample started moving immediately, so fast that I saw only a blur of motion. The entities went underground, too fast for me to count them.

I expected them to emerge, like the creatures in the

other experiments. But only one returned to the surface, and it was still quite small—no bigger than a hare. I wondered if it had reached its maximum size. After all, it had no others of its kind to devour.

The vartek had a long tubular body, the top covered with black scales, a short thin neck, and a round head with elongated jaws, a wide mouth, and two bulging eyes. It resembled a monstrous millipede, with a multitude of long, sticklike legs.

Three days passed, and each night the creature went underground, tripling in size each time it emerged. I was puzzled. What could it be eating that made it grow so rapidly? I felt very uneasy and decided to resort to scrying. It is fortunate that I did so; otherwise, the County would have suffered many violent deaths.

I had less than twenty-four hours to prepare for what I had foreseen. I had only just taken up position close to the trees when the vartek erupted from the ground outside the pentacle. It was a deep burrower, evidently capable of tunneling through rock.

The creature was now about the size of a bull, but perhaps five times longer; however, I believe that it had not yet attained its full size. At rest, its long belly touched the ground. As it moved, it extended its legs, which tripled its height. When it opened its mouth, I saw that its teeth were very unusual. There were three rows in both top and bottom jaws, and they seemed to be able to move; the creature could change the angle of its bite and lengthen and shorten the teeth.

As it chased me into the wood, it projected a globule of thick brown liquid. I dodged to one side, and when the liquid splattered on the ground, it boiled and steamed, giving off clouds of noxious fumes and eating into the vegetation and the earth beneath. It was now clear to me that the combination of the acidic liquid and the moving teeth helped the creature to burrow, and that they could also be used as weapons.

But these were not its only weapons: three long tentacles sprouted from its back and whipped through the air toward me. Each had a sharp piece of bone at its tip.

I ran deeper into trees, luring the vartek toward the trap that I had hastily constructed. The previous Malkin witch assassin, Kernolde, had often used hidden pits filled with sharp spikes to kill her enemies; I did the same here. I leaped across the long pit I had prepared, and the creature fell in. Its head and part of its body were impaled upon the spikes.

Next I had to climb down into the pit and end its life. It was not easy, but I managed to kill it before it could struggle free. The scales on its upper body were hard and difficult to penetrate, but its underbelly was soft. Its bulbous eyes were particularly vulnerable to my blades.

On dissecting it, I learned that its food is earth and rock. I can only wonder at the final size it would have attained.

I believe that this third type of creature, the vartek (plural form: varteki), is the most formidable of the three samples I investigated. There could also be something far worse within the jars that I did not study.

In view of our approaching conflict with the Kobalos, this does not bode well.

Glossary of the Kobalos World
Original written by Nicholas Browne
Notes added by Tom Ward and Grimalkin

Anchiette: A burrowing mammal found in northern forests on the edge of the snow line. The Kobalos consider them a delicacy eaten raw. There is little meat on the creature, but the leg bones are chewed with relish.

Note: I tried eating the creatures (which are hardly bigger than mice), and I definitely prefer rabbit. However, they are numerous and easy to catch, best eaten in a stew. With the addition of the correct herbs, the meal is tolerable.—Grimalkin

Askana: The dwelling place of the Kobalos gods. Probably just another term for the dark.

Note: This is intriguing. Nicholas Browne might be right, but could it be that the Kobalos gods exist outside what we term the dark? Cuchulain dwelled within the Hollow Hills, accessed from Ireland. That too was not directly within the dark.—Tom Ward

Baelic: The ordinary low tongue of the Kobalos people,

used only in informal situations between family members or to show friendship. The true language of the Kobalos is Losta, which is also spoken by humans who border their territory. For a stranger to speak to another Kobalos in Baelic implies warmth, but it is sometimes used before a "trade" is made.

Balkai: The first and most powerful of the three Kobalos high mages who formed the triumvirate after the slaying of the king, and now rule Valkarky.

Berserkers: These are Kobalos warriors sworn to die in battle.

Bindos: Bindos is the Kobalos law that demands each citizen sell at least one purra in the slave markets every forty years. Failure to do so makes the perpetrator of the crime an outcast, shunned by his fellows.

Boska: This is the breath of a Kobalos mage, which can be used to induce sudden unconsciousness, paralysis, or terror in a human victim. The mage varies the effects of boska by altering the chemical composition of his breath. It is also sometimes used to change the mood of animals.

Note: This was used on me; it leached the strength from my body. But I was taken by surprise. It is wise to be on our guard against such a threat and not allow a haizda mage to get close. Perhaps a scarf worn across the mouth and nose would provide an effective defense. Or perhaps plugs of wax could be fitted into the nostrils.—Tom Ward

Bychon: This is the Kobalos name for the spirit known in the County as a boggart.

Note: It will be interesting to discover whether these boggarts fall into the same categories we have in the County or whether there are new types there.—Tom Ward

Chaal: A substance used by a haizda mage to control the responses of his human victim.

Cumular Mountains: A high mountain range that marks the northwestern boundary of the Southern Peninsula.

Dendar Mountains: The high mountain range about seventy leagues southwest of Valkarky. In the foothills is the large kulad known as Karpotha. More slaves are bought and sold here than in all the other fortresses put together.

Dexturai: Kobalos changelings that are born of human females. Such creatures, although totally human in appearance, are susceptible to the will of any Kobalos. They are extremely strong and hardy and have the ability to become great warriors.

Eblis: This is the foremost of the Shaiksa, the Kobalos brotherhood of assassins. He slew the last king of Valkarky using a magical lance called the Kangadon. It is believed that he is more than two thousand years old, and it is certain that he has never been bested in combat. Members of the brotherhood refer to him by two other designations:

He Who Cannot Be Defeated and He Who Can Never Die.

Erestaba: The Plain of Erestaba lies just north of the Shanna River, within the territory of the Kobalos.

Fitzanda Fissure: This is also known as the Great Fissure. It is an area of earthquakes and instability that marks the southern boundary of the Kobalos territories.

Note: The fissure is north of the Shanna River, but both have been described by Browne as boundaries between Kobalos and human lands. It is likely that the borders have changed many times over the long years of conflict.—Grimalkin

Galena Sea: The sea southeast of Combesarke. It lies between that kingdom and Pennade.

Gannar Glacier: The great ice floe whose source is the Cumular Mountains.

Ghanbalsam: A resinous material bled from a ghanbala tree by a haizda mage and used as a base for ointments such as chaal.

Ghanbala: The deciduous gum tree most favored as a dwelling by a Kobalos haizda mage.

Haggenbrood: A warrior entity bred from the flesh of a human female. Its function is ritual combat. It has three selves, which share a common mind; they are, to all intents and purposes, one creature.

Haizda: This is the territory of a haizda mage; here he hunts and farms the human beings he owns. He takes blood from them, and occasionally their souls.

Haizda mage: A rare type of Kobalos mage who dwells in his own territory far from Valkarky and gathers wisdom from territory he has marked as his own.

Homunculus: A small creature bred from the purrai in the skleech pens. They often have several selves, which, like the haggenbrood, are controlled by a single mind. However, rather than being identical, each self has a specialized function, and only one of them is capable of speaking Losta.

Note: In Valkarky, I encountered the homunculus that was a servant to Slither. The one that could speak was like a small man, and it reported directly to the mage; another took the form of a rat and was used for espionage. I found it easy to control and subvert to my will. There was a third type, which was able to fly, but I did not see it. Such a creature could be used to gather information about us at long range. The three selves of the homunculus share one mind (as did the haggenbrood); thus, whatever it sees is instantly known back in Valkarky.—Grimalkin

Hubris: The sin of pride against the gods. The full wrath of the gods is likely to be directed against one who persists in this sin in the face of repeated warnings. The very act of becoming a mage is in itself an act of hubris, and few live to progress beyond the period of novitiate.

Hybuski: Hybuski (commonly known as hyb) are a special type of warrior created and employed in battle by the Kobalos. They are a hybrid of Kobalos and horse, but possess other attributes designed for combat. Their upper body is hairy and muscular, combining exceptional strength with speed. They are capable of ripping an opponent to pieces. Their hands are also specially adapted for fighting.

Kangadon: This is the Lance That Cannot Be Broken, also known as the King Slayer, a lance of power crafted by the Kobalos high mages—although some believe that it was forged by their blacksmith god, Olkie.

Note: Grimalkin told me that this lance was finally broken by Slither, the haizda mage with whom she formed a temporary alliance. He used one of the skelt blades, Bone Cutter, to do so.—Tom Ward

Karpotha: The kulad in the foothills of the Dendar Mountains that holds the largest purrai slave markets. Most are held early in the spring.

Kartuna: This kulad lies beyond the Shanna River. I believe it to be the tower once visited by the haizda mage called Slither; he escaped after slaying the incumbent high mage, Nunc. I believe that the second most powerful mage in the present triumvirate has now taken up residency there, in preference to Valkarky. Many of his magical artifacts will be stored in that tower.

Kashilowa: The gatekeeper of Valkarky, responsible for either allowing or refusing admittance to the city. It is a huge creature with one thousand legs and was created by mage magic to carry out its function.

Kastarand: This is the word for the Kobalos holy war. They will wage it to rid the land of humans, who they believe to be the descendants of escaped slaves. The war cannot begin until Talkus, the god of the Kobalos, is born.

Kirrhos: This is the "tawny death" that comes to victims of the haggenbrood.

Kobalos anatomy: A Kobalos has two hearts. The larger one is in the same approximate position as a human one. However, the second one is smaller, perhaps a quarter of the size, and lies near the base of the throat. If decapitation is not possible, both hearts must be pierced; otherwise, a dying Kobalos warrior will still be dangerous.

Kulad: A defensive tower built by the Kobalos that marks strategic positions on the border of their territories. Others deeper within their territory are used as slave markets.

Note: A number of kulads are also controlled by high mages. They use these as dwellings; they are also used to store their magic and magical artifacts.—Grimalkin

League: The distance a galloping horse can cover in five minutes.

Lenklewth: The second of the three Kobalos high mages who form the triumvirate.

Losta: This is the language spoken by all who inhabit the southern peninsula. This includes the Kobalos, who claim that the language was stolen and degraded by mankind. The Kobalos version of Losta contains a lexis almost one third larger than that used by humans, and perhaps gives some credence to their claims. It is certainly a linguistic anomaly that two distinct species should share a common language.

Note: The mage that I killed near Chipenden spoke the language of our own land, rather than Losta. Grimalkin says that the Kobalos mages have great linguistic skill and have made it their business to learn the languages of more distant lands in preparation for invading them. —Tom Ward

Mages: There are many types of human mage; the same is also true of the Kobalos. But for an outsider, they are difficult to describe and categorize. However, the highest rank is nominally that of a high mage. There is also one type, the haizda mage, that does not fit within that hierarchy, for these are outsiders who dwell in their own individual territories far from Valkarky. Their powers are hard to quantify.

Mandrake: Sometimes called mandragora, this is a root that resembles the human form and is sometimes used by a Kobalos mage to give focus to the power that dwells within his mind.

Meljann: The third of three Kobalos high mages who form the triumvirate.

Note: During my visit to Valkarky, I fought and slew Meljann in the plunder room when attempting to regain my property. I do not know who replaced him.—Grimalkin

Northern kingdoms: This is the collective name sometimes given to the small kingdoms, such as Pwodente and Wayaland, which lie south of the Great Fissure. More usually it refers to all the kingdoms north of Shallotte and Serwentia.

Note: I am surprised that Nicholas Browne does not mention Polyznia, the largest and most powerful of those principalities.—Grimalkin

Novitiate: This is the first stage of the learning process undertaken by a haizda mage, which lasts approximately thirty years. The candidate studies under one of the older and most powerful mages. If the novitiate is completed satisfactorily, the mage must then go off alone to study and develop his craft.

Note: I believe that the haizda mage slain near Chipenden by Thomas Ward had only just completed his novitiate, which was fortunate indeed. A haizda such as Slither, the one I encountered in Valkarky, would have proved a much more deadly opponent.—Grimalkin

Oscher: A substance that can be used as emergency food for horses; made from oats, it has special additives that can sustain a beast of burden for the duration of a long journey. Unfortunately, it results in a severe shortening of the animal's life.

Olkie: This is the god of Kobalos blacksmiths. He has four arms and teeth made of brass. It is believed that he crafted the Kangadon, the magical lance that cannot be deflected from its target.

Oussa: The elite guard that serves and defends the triumvirate; also used to guard parties of slaves taken from Valkarky to the kulads to be bought and sold.

Plunder room: This is the vault where members of the triumvirate store the items they have confiscated, by the power of magic, force of arms, or legal process. It is the most secure place in Valkarky.

Note: In order to retrieve the property that had been stolen from me, I successfully breached the defenses of this place, which Nicholas Browne describes above as "the most secure place in Valkarky." I did not find it difficult—but this may be accounted for by the fact that my abilities, both magical and martial, were unknown to the Kobalos. I will no doubt find their defenses much stronger the next time I venture into that city. Additionally, the birth of their god Talkus will at least triple the magical strength of the Kobalos mages.—Grimalkin

Polyznia: This is the largest and most prosperous of the northern principalities that border the Kobalos lands. Their army is small but well disciplined, and their archers and cavalry are first-class. They are ruled by a brave prince called Stanislaw.

Purra (plural purrai): The term used to denote one of the female purebred stock of humans bred into slavery by the Kobalos. The term is also applicable to those females who dwell within a haizda.

Salamander: A fire dragon tulpa.

Shaiksa: This is the highest order of Kobalos assassins. If one is slain, the remainder of the brotherhood are honor bound to hunt down his killer.

Note: Grimalkin told me that at the moment of death, a Shaiksa assassin has the ability to send a thought message to his brethren, telling them of the manner of his death and who is responsible. Members of the order will then hunt down his killer.—Tom Ward

Shakamure: The magecraft of haizda mages, which draws

its power from the taking of human blood and the borrowing of souls.

Shanna River: The Shanna marks the old border between the northern human kingdoms and the territory of the Kobalos. Now Kobalos are often to be found south of this line. The treaty that agreed on this border has long been disregarded by both sides.

Note: Before the ritualistic challenge by the Shaiksa assassin, all bands of Kobalos warriors retreated to their own side of the river. We have yet to learn the reason for this. Much of Kobalos behavior still remains a mystery.—Grimalkin

Shatek (also known as a djinn): This is a warrior entity with three selves and a single controlling mind. It differs from the haggenbroood in that it was created to be deployed in battle. A number of them have rebelled and are no longer subject to Kobalos authority. They dwell far from Valkarky, bringing death and terror to the lands surrounding their lairs.

Shudru: The Kobalos term for the harsh winter of the northern kingdoms.

Skaiium: The time when a haizda mage faces a dangerous softening of his predatory nature.

Skapien: A small secret group of Kobalos within Valkarky, who are opposed to the trade in purrai.

Shelt: This is a creature that lives near water and kills its victims by inserting its long snout into their bodies and draining their blood. The Kobalos believe it is the shape that their god Talkus will assume at his birth.

Shleech pens: Pens within Valkarky where the Kobalos keep human female slaves, using them for food or to breed other new species and hybrid forms to do their bidding.

Shlutch: This is a type of creature employed by the Kobalos as servants. Its speciality is cleaning the rapidly growing fungus from the walls and ceilings of the dwellings within Valkarky.

Shoya: The material of which Valkary is constructed. It is formed within the bodies of whoskor.

Shulka: A poisonous water snake whose bite induces instant paralysis. It is much favored by Kobalos assassins, who use it to render their victims helpless before slaying them. After death, its toxins are impossible to detect in the victim's blood.

Slarinda: These are the females of the Kobalos. They have been extinct for more than three thousand years. They were murdered—slain by a cult of Kobalos males who hated women. Now Kobalos males are born of purrai, human females held prisoner in the skleech pens.

Talkus: The god of the Kobalos, who is not yet born. In

form he will resemble the creature known as a skelt. Talkus means the God Who Is Yet to Be. He is sometimes also referred to as the Unborn.

Therskold: A threshold upon which a word of interdiction or harming has been laid. This is a potent area of haizda strength, and it is dangerous—even for a human mage— to cross such a portal.

Note: When I examined the lair of the haizda mage near Chipenden, there was no barrier in place. This was no doubt because Tom Ward had already killed the mage. So I have yet to test the strength of such a defense. Whether or not the barriers that protected the plunder room were examples of therskold or something similar, I do not know. However, they provided little hindrance.—Grimalkin

Trade: Although the unit of currency is the valcon, many Kobalos, particularly haizda mages, rely on what they call trade. This implies an exchange of goods or services, but it is much more than that. It is a question of honor, and each party must keep its word, even if to do so means death.

Triumvirate: The ruling body of Valkarky, composed of the three most powerful high mages in the city. It was first formed after the King of Valkarky was slain by Eblis, the Shaiksa assassin. It is essentially a dictatorship that uses ruthless means to hold on to power. Others are always waiting in the wings to replace the three mages.

Tulpa: A creature created within the mind of a mage and occasionally given form in the outer world.

Note: I have traveled extensively and probed into the esoteric arts of witches and mages, but this is a magical skill that I have never encountered before. Are Kobalos mages capable of this? If so, their creatures may be limited only by the extent of their imaginations.—Grimalkin

Ulska: A deadly but rare Kobalos poison that burns its victim from within. It is also excreted from glands at the base of the claws of the haggenbrood. It results in kirrhos, which is known as the tawny death.

Unktus: A minor Kobalos deity worshipped only by the lowest menials of the city. He is depicted with very small horns curving backward from the crown of his head.

Valcon: A small coin, usually referred to as a valc, accepted throughout the southern peninsula. Made of an alloy that is one-tenth silver, a valcon is the wage paid daily to a Kobalos foot soldier.

Valkarky: The chief city of the Kobalos, which lies just within the Arctic Circle. Valkarky means the City of the Petrified Tree.

Vartek (plural varteki): The vartek was the most powerful of the three types of entity that I grew from the material found within the lair of the haizda mage. The fact that it can burrow through solid rock means that it could burst up out of the ground right in the midst of a human army, so that they scatter them in terror. It has three bone-tipped tentacles, the ability to spit globules of acid that could burn flesh from bone, and fearsome teeth. It also has many legs and is capable of great speed. Although it is protected by black scales, its eyes and underbelly are vulnerable to blades. It is impossible to know what size a vartek would achieve once fully grown. It could be the most daunting of the battle entities that the Kobalos may deploy against us.—Grimalkin

Whalakai: Known as a vision of what is, this is an instant of perception that comes to either a high mage or a haizda mage. It is an epiphany, a moment of revelation, when the totality of a situation, with all the complexities that have led to it, are known to him in a flash of insight. The Kobalos believe this is a vision given to the mage by Talkus, their God Who Is Yet to Be, its purpose being to facilitate the path to his birth.

Whoskor: This is the collective name for the creatures subservient to the Kobalos who are engaged in the never-ending task of extending the city of Valkarky. They have sixteen legs, eight of which also function as arms and are used to shape the skoya, the soft stone that they exude from their mouths.

Widdershins: A movement that is counterclockwise or against the sun. Seen as counter to the natural order of things, it is sometimes employed by a Kobalos mage to assert his will upon the cosmos. Filled with hubris, it holds within it great risk.